FAREWELL, DRESDEN

A NOVEL

by

Henri Coulonges

TRANSLATED FROM THE FRENCH

BY LOWELL BAIR

SUMMIT BOOKS

NEW YORK   LONDON   TORONTO   SYDNEY   TOKYO

SUMMIT BOOKS
SIMON & SCHUSTER BUILDING
ROCKEFELLER CENTER
1230 AVENUE OF THE AMERICAS
NEW YORK, NEW YORK 10020

PUBLISHED BY SUMMIT BOOKS
ORIGINALLY PUBLISHED IN FRANCE AS *L'Adieu à la Femme Sauvage*
SUMMIT BOOKS AND COLOPHON ARE TRADEMARKS
OF SIMON & SCHUSTER INC.

DESIGNED BY LEVAVI & LEVAVI
MANUFACTURED IN THE UNITED STATES OF AMERICA

1   3   5   7   9   10   8   6   4   2

LIBRARY OF CONGRESS CATALOGING IN PUBLICATION DATA
COULONGES, HENRI, 1936–

[ADIEU À LA FEMME SAUVAGE. ENGLISH]
FAREWELL, DRESDEN / BY HENRI COULONGES; TRANSLATED FROM THE
FRENCH BY LOWELL BAIR.
P.   CM.
TRANSLATION OF: L'ADIEU À LA FEMME SAUVAGE.
1. WORLD WAR, 1939–1945—FICTION.   I. TITLE.
PQ2663.08114A6513   1989   88-29452
843'.914—DC19   CIP

ISBN 0-671-61779-6

FAREWELL,

DRESDEN

I

YET IT WAS ALMOST ENOUGH TO BE

GROWING UP IN THAT CITY.

—John Ashbery

O N E

he had been so disappointed when the horses came into the ring that later, after everything had changed irrevocably, her disappointment was what she remembered best.

The circus program had promised a "tournament in the spirit of the Middle Ages" as the closing act. Johanna, thinking of the glorious engravings in her history book, was expecting a troop of knights on massive, prancing steeds, bursting into the ring with upraised lances, flying banners, and waving plumes, all in a whirlwind of colors. Instead, emaciated, riderless horses ambled onto the sand while the band struck up a lively polka. The horses' tails were braided with spangled ribbons, and when they formed a circle and began dancing mechanically in place they reminded her of a bunch of silly old women wearing too much makeup.

She was even more disgusted when a troop of clowns rode into the ring on donkeys.

"Isn't this dumb?" she whispered in Hella's ear.

Hella was dressed as a Spanish princess. Her earrings sparkled in the darkness when she moved.

"They must have changed the last act because it's carnival time. Don't you think it's funny? I do."

Johanna shrugged. "You're not hard to please," she said sullenly.

She was suddenly irritated with Hella. For one thing, she had worn that outfit to the circus without telling her beforehand. Johanna's sister, Grete, had warned her that Hella might wear a costume, but Johanna had answered, "No, she would have told me. And anyway, I'm too old for that kind of thing." So when Hella had shown up in her embroidered blouse and long skirt, Johanna couldn't help saying spitefully, "Grete's going to laugh when she sees you like that. Won't you ever grow up?" Leni had overheard her, and understood. As the two girls were leaving, she had said to Johanna, "Take this, darling, you know how cold it is in the streetcars." It was the Bavarian scarf that Johanna had gotten for her twelfth birthday, a few months earlier. No one could call it a costume, of course, but with its embroidery and bright colors it had a festive air. "Oh, Mutti," she had muttered, impatiently tossing the scarf over her shoulders.

With blasting trumpets and clanging cymbals, the band was now bringing the polka to a triumphant conclusion. Johanna squeezed Hella's hand, as though to apologize for being annoyed with her. And, as if the band had sensed her mood, the polka was followed by a nostalgic Viennese waltz. Here, at last, was music suited for daydreaming. . . . She saw herself in a spacious ballroom lighted by chandeliers, inside a palace on the Danube. It was a snowy winter evening, with darkness falling. Standing at the ballroom window, she watched heavy sleighs silently gliding past. Inside, the dancers seemed to float over a floor so highly polished that it reflected the soft, flickering light of the chandeliers. An officer invited her to dance. He was not a modern officer, but an Austrian from the last days of the Hapsburgs, with epaulets and gold braid on his uniform. When their dance was over, he accompanied her back to her place and bowed gravely. Only then was she able to see his face. . . .

She sighed so deeply that the man sitting to her right looked at her strangely. Feeling vaguely anxious, she turned to Hella and saw that she too seemed lost in reverie, a faraway expression on her delicate face. *What can she be thinking about, to be so pretty?* Johanna wondered, and at that moment she realized that she loved Hella (in spite of her embroidered dress) almost as much as Leni. Dear Mutti . . .

It was strange that Leni had let them travel across the city by streetcar alone on that carnival evening. "You're both twelve now," she had said. "There are some things you can do without me. I'm tired, and Grete has to study her Latin." She really had seemed tired, but not at all worried. As for Grete, Johanna was glad she wasn't coming. She hadn't said a single nice thing to Johanna for weeks and weeks. And she didn't really have to study her Latin: she was only using that as an excuse for being alone with Leni and telling her stupid secrets. "I'm fourteen now," she had said to Johanna. "I have things to talk about that you couldn't understand."

Irritated by the memory of those words, Johanna turned her head to look over the audience.

"Stop moving all the time," a child's voice protested behind her.

She would always remember that voice, because it was just then that everything changed. At first, absorbed in her thoughts, she didn't notice a harsh, strident sound that rose above the sound of the band. But then murmurs of annoyance came from all over the room and she felt the nervous pressure of Hella's hand on hers.

The band stopped and the horses began milling randomly around the ring, tossing their heads. Then, alone this time, without the competition of the band, the relentless, hostile wail of the air-raid siren filled the circus.

Johanna sat with her mouth open. Around her, everyone stood and began moving into the aisles. Hella was standing in the center aisle, gesturing for her to hurry. Why did this have to happen on her first night away from Leni and Grete? Air-raid sirens had sounded dozens of times in the last few months, but usually when she was at home. Often

Hella was there too, holding her hand as they calmly went down to the basement with Leni and Grete. There they had books and games to help them stave off boredom until the alert was over. Leni reassured them, too, telling them that Dresden would never be bombed. It was outside the war zone, it contained priceless art treasures, and it had no munitions factories. When the siren sounded again—more briefly, almost joyfully—to signal the end of the alert, Leni would smile brightly, as if to say, "I told you so!" They would go back upstairs, and learn the next day that Cologne, Hamburg, or Leipzig had been heavily bombed. A radio announcer would read off a long list of casualties while Leni listened anxiously for a familiar name.

"It's a good thing they waited till the last act," Hella said, shouting in Johanna's ear to make herself heard over the siren.

Then the siren stopped. Johanna looked at her watch: twenty to ten. A man standing in the ring made an announcement she couldn't hear, but the clowns slapped their knees and laughed in response. The trainers had already taken the horses away.

"He said the basement is so big they can finish the last act in it if we want them to," a boy in front of Johanna reported.

"Very funny," Hella responded.

Ahead of them, people crowded together in front of the entrance to the basement.

"What are they waiting for? Why don't they go down?" Hella said, pinching her skirt nervously.

"They *would* have to do this on a holiday," Johanna muttered.

As they moved down the aisle, she noticed something she hadn't earlier when they came in late and took their seats in the dark: Hella wasn't the only one wearing a costume. Other children were disguised as pirates or shepherds, milkmaids and queens. A chimney sweep passed them, his top hat not much higher than the backs of the deserted seats. The crowd was now moving steadily, in gloomy silence.

Soon they reached the level of the ring, where the musicians were wearily putting away their instruments. With people pressing in on all sides, Johanna and Hella started down the stairs to the basement.

"Do you think we'll sleep in our beds tonight?" Johanna asked.

Hella crossed her fingers, as she did in class when she wanted to ward off bad luck, like a question from the teacher.

The basement was already crowded. Bare bulbs hung between rows of steel pillars, giving off a feeble yellow light that made everyone's face look drawn and pale. People sat on the cement floor in silent groups. Johanna and Hella found space against the wall and sat down, tightly pressed together. A ventilation fan hummed overhead.

Nearby, parents called out to their children each time they began to stray.

"Your coat, Dieter!" a woman cried shrilly. "What have you done with your coat?"

The boy was wearing tinfoil armor.

"Don't you know I didn't bring a coat tonight?" he said with a puzzled expression.

"Do you think our families are worried about us?" Hella asked Johanna.

"I'm sure Mutti is worried about me, but not Grete."

"What makes you say that?"

"Grete always turns on the charm when you're there, so you don't know what she's really like. But I do. She treats me like a child, when she's only two years older than me, and she tries to act like a grownup when she talks to Mutti and tells her all kinds of silly secrets."

Hella smiled. Johanna put her arm around her and felt her barrette against her cheek. A few feet away, the little chimney sweep lay next to his mother with his top hat beside him on the floor.

Suddenly the bulbs hanging from the ceiling went out and the hum of the ventilation fan stopped. In the darkness, Johanna took the long scarf Leni had given her, tied it first around her waist and then Hella's, and pulled on it to see if the knots would hold.

"If this comes untied and you don't see me, call me as loud as you can."

"Don't worry, we can still see."

Hella was right: Johanna could still see her in the faint glow coming from a small window high up in the basement wall. A boy had already climbed onto his mother's shoulders to see what was happening.

"Balls of fire are falling," he announced, his voice becoming shrill and excited. "I can see the whole city! The Japanese Palace! The Hofkirche! The Sophienkirche! The Opera . . . It's like the Führer's birthday!"

His mother abruptly put him back down on the floor.

"Johanna," Hella said solemnly.

"Yes?"

"This time it's us."

"But Mutti always says . . ."

Hella shook her head.

"This time we're going to get it. I can feel it."

"But they know it's carnival time, and the streets are full of children," Johanna argued.

Hella had taken off her velvet hat and was toying with it as she stared at the floor a few feet in front of her. Her blond braids, pinned to the top of her head, were shaped like a squirrel's tail. Nearby, an old couple were telling an endless story to a little girl who sat between them, seemingly spellbound. When one of them stopped, the other took over.

"Hear that?" Hella asked suddenly.

"The story?" Johanna nodded toward the old couple.

Hella shook her head and pointed upward. Johanna listened. Everyone had stopped talking and she could hear a distant drone gradually growing louder.

"I told you," Hella whispered.

As they instinctively pressed closer together, Johanna could feel Hella trembling. She wanted to calm her, but suddenly she felt so empty that she couldn't think of anything to say.

The drone became a heavy, implacable rumble, punctuated by a series of distant explosions. A little boy began crying uncontrollably. Other children followed suit, as their parents tried desperately to quiet them. More explosions, louder this time, made the walls tremble. An old lady near Johanna prayed aloud as the light in the basement became still brighter. A man climbed onto a table and looked out the narrow window, standing on tiptoe. Then he came back down, without a word.

"It's as bright as daylight outside," he finally said. "They're dropping flares."

"My daughter was in Hamburg and she told me it always began like that," a woman said.

"Hamburg," the old lady repeated. "Dear God, please . . ."

She was interrupted by an explosion nearby, then there were some less loud. It seemed that the bombs were falling farther away.

"Those must have hit the Grosse Garten," someone said.

"Or the station."

"It's getting closer to our house," said Johanna.

She and Hella began crying softly, still pressed closely together. Johanna thought about her room: the bed with the covers turned down, the opal glass lamp that Leni had given her for her tenth birthday. "The wallpaper, the Würtemberg landscape, my pink nightgown spread out on the quilt . . ." she said aloud.

"What are you talking about?" asked Hella.

Just then they were jolted by an explosion so close that the walls trembled violently.

Johanna began sobbing uncontrollably. Her teeth chattered. Hella put her hand on her arm.

"Please stop," she begged, "you have to stay calm. You're older than I am."

"By two months," Johanna wept. "That doesn't count."

"At times like this it does!"

Again the explosions moved farther away. Hella began to breathe more easily. The man had climbed back onto the table and was trying to take stock of the situation.

"The Opera is hidden by a column of smoke," he said. "No bombs seem to have fallen on this side of the river."

"And I hope none fell in our neighborhood, either!" said Johanna.

The explosions had stopped but everyone was still afraid to move. Soon the light coming in through the basement window faded to a faint glow.

"Now at least we'll know what happened," Hella said.

"Do you remember that day when we got lost at the Glashütte and there was a big thunderstorm?"

"What does that have to do with anything?"

"You're as pale now as you were then," Johanna said with satisfaction.

"You can't even see me!" Hella exclaimed. "You're making that up! Besides, *my* teeth aren't chattering the way *yours* were a little while ago!"

"I was cold. I'm not wearing a heavy skirt like yours."

They both laughed. *A huge thunderstorm, and now it's over,* Johanna thought. She would go to bed a little later than usual, that was all. She closed her eyes and fervently imagined how Leni would hug and kiss her when she came home. Even Grete might treat her a little less unpleasantly from now on. Leni wouldn't have to tell her ten times a day, "Be nicer to your little sister."

The lights were still off and the siren hadn't yet signaled the end of the raid.

"The power plant must have been hit," said the man who had looked out the window.

Several people stood up. Others told them to sit down. Someone opened the door at the end of the basement. Cold air flowed in, and immediately there was a rush for the door. Johanna grabbed Hella.

"Don't go yet," she said in an anguished tone. "We might get separated."

"You're forgetting we have the scarf," said Hella, clutching it as if it were a talisman.

Someone struck a match and Hella's fresh, reassuring face came out of the shadows.

"When I think that I might not have had you with me," Johanna said passionately, "that I might have been alone with all these people I don't know . . ."

"You would never have gone to the circus by yourself."

Suddenly there was a little more light: a circus employee

had brought down some lanterns. The children stared at each other curiously, amazed by their costumes, as if they had never seen them before.

"I don't want to be Queen Idelfonsa any more," a little girl said, taking off her paper crown.

Hella began to giggle, hiding her mouth with her hand. Then she took Johanna firmly by the arm and led her toward the stairs, where the crowd was slowly flowing out of the basement. Johanna turned her head to take one last look at the place where she had just spent what seemed like the longest hour of her life.

The two girls started up the stairs, holding hands. Soon they saw a patch of dirty yellow sky through the doorway at the top of the steps. When they were finally outside, the acrid smell of smoke stuck in Johanna's throat and she felt light rain on her face.

She could make out the familiar clock of the Dreikönigs-kirche, but not the time. She looked at her watch. It was twenty past eleven.

Around her, people stood in dazed silence, broken now and then by the protests of children eager to go home. But the circus staff, led by the clowns with lanterns, were asking everyone to stay near the building and not try to cross the river. People were still coming up from the basement and the crowd in front of the building was steadily becoming denser. Johanna and Hella, still tied together by the scarf, climbed to the top of a little wall and stared at the curtain of flame and the immense pall of smoke that hung over the Old City. At the foot of the wall sat a woman holding a boy who had fallen asleep with his head on her shoulder.

"Let's go," Johanna said to Hella, pulling on the scarf.

The woman stood up. They could hardly see her face.

"You can't get out," she said. "My mother and my older daughter went to see and they said that no one can leave."

"Why not?" asked Hella. "Who's going to stop us? The clowns?"

The woman pointed. Johanna looked, but it was hard to see

anything. She jumped down from the wall. Followed by Hella, she made her way past a group of circus performers and then understood what the woman had meant. All exits from the square were blocked by members of the air-raid police. Their arms linked against the crowd, they kept repeating that no one was allowed to go any further.

Johanna was surprised that people didn't try to break through. Their homes and families were all on the other side of the river, yet they stood in silence, looking at the massive buildings of the Marktplatz.

"I know one thing," she said, "we're not going to stay here all night!"

She felt an overwhelming need to get home. Taking advantage of a shuffle in the crowd, she led Hella toward the cordon of policemen. A few feet away, a boy of about fifteen was talking with them. He wore the uniform of the Deutscher Jungvolk.

"I'm a messenger and I have to go to the Civil Defense Office," he said, taking a card from his pocket.

The human chain opened.

"Go ahead. But I warn you, there's fire everywhere. Even the bridges are burning."

"I know," the boy said curtly.

He walked off into the night. For a moment, the policeman who had examined his card stood watching him, leaving a gap in the chain. Johanna pulled Hella forward, pointed to the messenger and said, "He's our brother, we'll be right back." The policeman let them through, but she heard him shout when she and Hella began running. She looked back: the cordon had already closed. As she ran, she was relieved to be free of the stifling crowd. But Hella was hampered by her long, full skirt, and had a hard time keeping up with her.

They finally reached the Marktplatz and stopped to catch their breath at the foot of the equestrian statue. Reflections danced on the enormous rump of Augustus II's horse. The refugee tents recently set up at the base of the monument were silent. A gust of warm, damp wind brought the acrid odor they had smelled before, along with a powder that stuck to their faces. Johanna passed her hand over her cheek.

"It's ash," she said quietly.

They walked along the edge of the deserted square, toward the bridge, then into the arcade of the Blockhaus, through which they could see a long line of abandoned streetcars. Sheltered by a massive wall, they approached the bridge. On the other side of the river, a fiery glow filled the sky. As soon as they left the arcade and started toward the river, a blast of hot air struck them full in the face. They ran back into the arcade and leaned against one of the pillars, panting and bewildered.

As they waited, wondering what to do, they heard footsteps coming toward them from the Marktplatz. Two men came into the arcade and caught them in the beams of their flash-lights.

"Not that way, girls!" one of the men shouted, pointing toward the bridge. "You'd have to be crazy to go over there! Stay on this side of the river!"

Johanna and Hella froze. After observing them a few moments, the men heard someone calling them from the center of the square and began running toward the statue. The girls watched the two circles of light move away from them and disappear. There was silence again, except for the muffled roar coming from the other side of the river. Johanna felt Hella's hand tighten on her forearm.

"It can't be," Hella whispered. "I'm dreaming. Tell me I'm going to wake up."

"You're going to wake up in the circus," Johanna replied, trying to be funny. "Aren't you lucky?"

"Do you think we should go back?"

Johanna hesitated.

"I don't know what else to do," she said softly.

She stepped onto the sidewalk. The light rain had stopped and the night seemed a little less dark. She could see the bell tower of the Rathaus rising above the New City.

"There are even a few stars in the sky over the railroad station," she said, feeling slightly reassured.

"Our families must think we're dead," Hella said.

Johanna imagined Leni seeing the fiery glow above the Old City, not knowing that the right bank hadn't been hit.

"You're right," she said. "We have to let them know we're safe. There's a phone booth near here, at the corner of the Rathaus."

"They must still be in the basement. They won't hear the phone ring."

"It's worth a try," said Johanna.

Soon they found the telephone sheltered in its booth.

Johanna picked up the receiver and waited. There was no dial tone. Even so, she put a coin in the slot. It fell with a clatter and the receiver remained silent. She stood looking at it with her teeth clenched.

"We should have known," Hella said. "With all those phone lines that pass through the Old City . . ."

They went back to the arcade. In the distance they could see the Augustusbrücke and the Hofkirche lighted by flames. Johanna moved cautiously along the sidewalk, her hand on the railing. At the end of the loggia, where a triple street lamp stood near the beginning of the bridge, she stopped. Three hundred yards to her right, on the other side of the Elbe, the Opera was sinking into the Theaterplatz, as if into a pool of incandescent lava. She turned around and looked for Hella behind her.

"You see!" Hella cried.

"It's only the Opera. The bridge and the church aren't on fire."

"Don't you feel the heat?" asked Hella. "It won't be long before the fire crosses the river. Look at the bridge: there's no one on it! No one is doing what you want us to do! I'm going back."

Johanna took her by the shoulders.

"We have to let our mothers know we're alive. Imagine how they must feel."

"You think they'll feel better if we're burned to death?"

"Do what you want, Hella. I'm going."

Johanna stepped onto the ramp, and was assaulted again by the heat coming from the left bank. She walked a few feet and turned around. Hella hadn't moved. Johanna went back to her.

"Please don't make me go," Hella moaned. "Stay here."

"We'll be fine," Johanna said impatiently. "It will be hot on the bridge, but that's all. When we come to the Hofkirche we'll turn left and avoid the fire. Then we'll go to the station, and in a little while we'll be home and in bed."

"If you think it's that easy, you're out of your mind! Didn't you hear what those men said?"

"I want to be in *my* basement, sitting on *my* folding chair, with Mutti and you and Grete and your mother. We can be there in twenty minutes if we start right now, instead of standing here arguing. Once we're there, I don't care what happens. If there's another bombing, I want us all to be together."

"Don't even talk about *another* bombing!"

Hella anxiously looked up at the sky. In the direction of Bernhardistrasse and the railroad station, it was clear and calm, as if nothing had happened.

As she followed Johanna across the long, deserted bridge, she held her handkerchief tightly against her face to protect her nose and mouth from the blasts of hot air and the pieces of hot ash that burned the backs of her hands. Suddenly the roar of the flames devouring the Theaterplatz, to her right, seemed so close that she panicked. She couldn't move. She saw Johanna walking away but couldn't call out to her. Just when she was about to turn back there was a brief lull in the roar of the fire, and she was calmed by the familiar sound of water splashing against the supports of the bridge. She caught up and Johanna gave her an encouraging look over her handkerchief.

To their left, the dome of a church, the Frauenkirche, gradually emerged from the darkness. Without saying a word, the moment they left the bridge they began running toward the church with their backs to the fire, and didn't stop until they were sheltered by its high stone wall.

"I don't think we'll be able to stay here long," said Hella.

Beyond the wall, the roar of the fire seemed to have diminished, but now they could hear its hissing and crackling, punctuated by terrifying explosions.

"At least we didn't hear all that on the other side of the river," Hella said during a brief moment of quiet, and she added softly, "I was right."

"Yes, you may have been right," Johanna said. "We can go back across the bridge if you want to. It's probably not too late."

Hella shook her head.

"No, we can't go back now. It would be stupid."

"If you hadn't come with me, I wouldn't have dared to cross the bridge by myself. I thought, 'If she doesn't follow me, I'll go back.' I could tell you were trying to make up your mind."

"Really?" Hella said, surprised. "Do you know what I was thinking about? I was remembering how we got lost in that storm last year, and how Fräulein Bodendorf was crying when we came back, because she was afraid we were dead and it was her fault."

"I can't wait to see the look on Grete's face!" said Johanna. "From now on you'll be able to shut her up whenever you—"

Hella stopped short. The roar of the fire had suddenly grown louder, and it was now accompanied by a shrill, piercing sound. The two girls leapt to their feet. A group of people hurried across the square, then veered off toward the botanical gardens. Johanna and Hella ran after them, too frightened to pay attention to where they were going. They followed them along Rampischestrasse, a narrow little street where the night seemed to regain its usual coolness and calm.

As they approached the Zeughausplatz they realized that they had gone in a completely different direction than the one they meant to take, and that the people they had been following must have turned off somewhere, because they were no longer just ahead of them.

"We'd better go back toward the Neumarkt," Hella said.

They turned right, into Landhausstrasse. Near the square

ahead, people suddenly became silhouettes against a background of bright light, and Johanna and Hella again felt a wave of heat strike them in the face. The whole left part of the Neumarkt, toward the Johanneum, was on fire.

Johanna hadn't expected to find fire here, around the Statue of Peace. Her legs weakened. Hella tugged at her sleeve and pointed to a dark side street, down which the crowd was disappearing. They turned toward it, and as they moved away from the Neumarkt the roar subsided until finally they could hear people around them calling out to each other. But it seemed to Johanna that the fire might break through the high walls on either side of the street at any moment. Luckily, Hella was holding her hand and seemed to know where she was going.

"Where are we?" asked Johanna.

"Moritzstrasse."

"Stop. I have to rest a minute."

They sat down on the sidewalk and, bending forward, tried to catch their breath.

"You *were* right," Johanna said. "We shouldn't have crossed the bridge. And I dragged you into it."

"You couldn't know the Neumarkt would be burning."

"It may be because the wind has changed."

They began walking again, holding hands, listening. The street now seemed calm and deserted. *Where did everyone go?* Johanna wondered. Hella stopped in front of a three-storied house.

"This is Charlotte Müngerer's house," she said.

"That's why you knew this street!"

"Charlotte and I don't get along very well anymore. But I can still knock on her door if you want me to."

"No, don't," Johanna said. "I don't want to go and bury myself in the Müngerers' basement when we're already halfway home."

"All right," Hella said, "but I think it's getting warmer again."

"You're imagining things!"

A few moments later it began raining again, a light, warm rain that brought a smell of wet ashes. Johanna happily let it

moisten her face. When she licked her parched lips, she
found that the rain tasted bitter, like charcoal.

"Look," said Hella, pointing toward the end of the street.

Since the raindrops reflected the fire in the Old City, the
sky seemed filled with fireflies. The twin spires of the Sophienkirche stood out in black, like two arms raised in anxious
prayer.

"At least we have the fire behind us," Hella remarked.

"Don't count on it. We thought that before. . . ."

Johanna examined the sky. In the direction of the train
station, the rain was dark.

"It's strange they didn't bomb the tracks," she said. "I've
heard that's always the first thing they try to hit."

"Sh! You'll bring our neighborhood bad luck."

They came to a little square with a church on one side,
and then to another square with a broad avenue running
past it.

"The Zwinger!" said Hella. "I don't understand . . . We
must have gone in a circle."

"No. I know where we are. That was the Reformed church.
Now we're on Friedrichstrasse. The station is ahead of us."

They climbed the steps that led up to the raised square.
The rain and wind had stopped.

"I can't go on," said Johanna, sinking onto a bench.

Hella sat down beside her and tried to pull her tattered
velvet skirt over her legs.

"I'll help you sew it back together."

Hella nodded sadly. Suddenly she put her hand to her
waist.

"The scarf," she exclaimed.

"We still had it at the Neumarkt," said Johanna. "I'm
sure."

They began examining the ground around the bench.

"It had such pretty colors," Hella said disconsolately.

"I'm glad we had it in the basement of the circus, but now
I'm sure we won't be separated."

Hella looked up.

"If we can find it," she said, "years from now we'll show it to people and say, 'This piece of cloth is what kept us together that night.' "

Hella suddenly gripped her hand.

"Listen," she said, almost in a whisper. "Do you hear it?"

Johanna listened so intently that her whole face tensed. Suddenly she felt herself sweating.

A faint drone, at the edge of silence. She sank her fingernails into the bench and tried to say something, but no sound came. She turned toward Hella and saw that her lips were moving, as if she were praying silently. Despite the frenzied beating of her heart, she heard the drone gradually growing louder.

"Isn't it ever . . . going to end?" Hella finally stammered.

Johanna leaned toward her, too, took a lock of her unruly hair and tenderly put it behind her ear. It seemed to her that an evil force had decided to punish them. She wanted to scream, "I haven't done anything. *I haven't done anything!*" But to whom? To what? To that empty sky?

Hella stood up and lifted the hem of her torn skirt. Johanna thought she was about to begin running.

"There's no use running, Hella," she said matter-of-factly. "We won't have time to get home."

"There hasn't been a siren for the end of the alert," said Hella. "You were right: the station . . . they always try to hit the station. That's why they're coming back. Why are you sitting there? We have to find shelter! Hurry!"

Johanna shook off her torpor, stood up and looked at her watch. It was ten past one. When had it begun? Three hours ago? Four?

They left the raised square, walked unsteadily down the steps to the sidewalk and began running along a deserted street that gleamed from the rain.

They knocked at the first in a row of almost identical doors with brass knobs. No one answered. They tried other doors. Their knocking resounded dismally in deserted entrance halls. Finally they gave up, their knuckles aching. Little by little, the distant sound was growing louder. They sat down on a step and wept.

"We're going to die in a street we don't even know," said Hella.

Johanna dried her tears and stood up.

"I'll go look for the name on the sign at the corner," she said, "if it will make you feel any better."

"No, don't leave me! Don't leave me!" Hella begged, clinging to her.

"What's going on?" a voice cried.

Two men holding flashlights were running toward them. From a distance they looked like the men who had told them not to cross the bridge, but at closer range they looked like bandits, their faces masked. One of them shined his flashlight at Johanna and lifted his mask.

"What are you doing here? Don't you have any sense?"

"We heard the planes coming and we've been looking for shelter," Johanna said, half-blinded by the light in her eyes. "Who are you? Policemen?"

"There's a shelter for two thousand people in the hospital on Poststrasse," the man said. "Follow us, it's straight ahead."

"Come on, girls; get moving!" said the other man.

As Johanna ran, the sight of people running in the same direction helped her resist the temptation to stop again. The crowd seemed to have come out of nowhere. At the Wall-strasse intersection (now she knew where she was) it became so dense that she and Hella lost their guides. She didn't care; she worried only about losing Hella.

Some of the people in that crowd, rushing through a long, nightmarish maze, wouldn't survive. Johanna felt that, heard it in the chorus of lamentations around her—what a contrast with the great silence of Friedrichstrasse a few minutes earlier!—and in the overheard fragments of stories that filled her with horror. ". . . and at the Altmarkt they all jumped into big tanks full of water to get away from the heat," a man beside her was saying in a tone that was both plaintive and detached, "and then they realized there was no way for them to get out of the tanks, and . . ." He stopped, perhaps refusing to think of what had happened next. Johanna turned her head to see what he looked like, but she couldn't tell which man had spoken.

"I have to stop," gasped Hella. "I've got a stitch in my side."

Bent forward, she tried to catch her breath. Johanna stood close to her to protect her from the crowd hurrying toward the Postplatz. Finally Hella was able to straighten up.

"Maybe it's because of the noise these people are making," said Johanna, "but the planes don't sound as loud as they did a little while ago. Do you think . . ."

"You must be deaf!" Hella exclaimed with a kind of desperation. "Why do you think these people are all running?"

When they came to the end of Wallstrasse they saw the somber expanse of the Postplatz. Two reassuring landmarks: the monument to the soldiers of 1870, and behind it the enormous metal sign advertising Yenidze cigarettes. To the right of the square, the open hospital gateway was lighted by lanterns. On all floors of the building, the glow of emergency lamps could be seen through the windows.

Holding each other by the hand, Johanna and Hella were swept along by the crowd. They all moved toward the entrance of the shelter as though drawn by a gigantic magnet.

As Johanna entered the building the sound of the approaching bombers swelled to a roar, but when she looked back she saw that the sky was still dark and empty. She squeezed Hella's hand, leaned close to her ear and said, "We've made it!" Hella responded with an exhausted smile.

The crowd pushed through a narrow entryway and into a large public ward dimly lighted by a shaded gas lamp. The beds had been hastily pushed against the walls to make room for the crowd to pass. Then came a long, shadowy staircase. As Johanna and Hella started down it, each relaxed her grip on the other's hand, and just at that moment they were separated by the jostling crowd.

"Hella! Hella!" Johanna called out frantically.

A few steps ahead, Hella turned around, called to Johanna, and waved her arms. Elbowing her way forward, Johanna succeeded in reaching her and hugged her feverishly, ignoring the people who kept bumping against her as they passed.

"Don't leave me, don't ever leave me," she said.

They continued down the stairs, side by side. Then Hella

stopped again and said gravely, "I promise I'll never leave you."

Johanna felt herself turn pale with emotion. It was as if the crowd had suddenly moved away from her, as if the terror and anxiety on all the faces around her had vanished, as if the shouts, calls, moans and murmured prayers had been stifled. She and Hella resumed their descent in the midst of a great silence.

"Do you think we'll be the same after this?" Hella asked suddenly.

"I don't know," Johanna whispered, "but here I can tell you something I wouldn't tell you at school." She put her arm around her friend's shoulder. "I love you, Hella."

At the bottom of the stairs, people were waiting to squeeze through a narrow doorway.

"I love you too, Johanna." Hella looked at her intently for a moment, and then she hurried down the last steps, smiling.

Johanna and Hella found themselves in the midst of a group of old men who, they gathered, were patients at the hospital and had been in the basement since the first attack. They spoke a drawling Saxon dialect that the girls couldn't understand very well, but from their expressions it was clear that they felt uneasy at the arrival of newcomers in what they regarded as their territory.

Johanna found a recess in the wall and drew Hella into it. They could no longer hear the roar of the bombers. For the first time since leaving the square, Johanna thought of the basement on Bernhardistrasse and wondered if Leni and Grete had left it after the bombing. If so, they must have hurried back down into it by now.

Her thoughts were interrupted when one of the old men, more pleasant-looking than the others, offered Hella a slice of gingerbread. Surprised, Hella shrank back a little before timidly refusing. The old man turned to Johanna. She smiled, took the dark, sticky gingerbread, and ate it.

"What I really wish I had," Hella whispered, "is a place where I could pee."

"That's because you're scared."

"I'm not as scared as I was in the street, when we were knocking on all those doors. And I'm not thinking about my mother as much as I did when we were in the basement of the circus."

"Now our mothers know we can't come home till morning," Johanna said.

She sighed and looked at the silent children around her. With their faces drawn and their costumes torn and dirty, they were listening to the hostile night. *They've stopped hoping*, she thought.

A colossal explosion made Johanna feel that the huge building above her must have been totally shattered. It was followed by a great silence. She found herself pressed against the cold cement floor, underneath several struggling bodies. She tried to scream but the weight on her was so great that she could only gasp. It seemed that a long time went by.

Then, as she began trying to extricate herself, she heard screams all around her. Miraculously, a lantern was still burning near her. She saw the face of the old man who had given her the gingerbread. His wide-open eyes stared straight ahead. Her revulsion gave her the strength to stand up, trembling. People around her panted convulsively, desperately trying to escape asphyxiation, their faces deformed like those of monsters.

She suddenly felt someone clutch her legs. She looked down, saw Hella lying on the floor struggling for breath, and helped her to stand up. Hella was trembling and her teeth were chattering so violently that she couldn't speak.

"Your legs . . ." she finally said. "Can you believe it? I recognized you by your legs."

Johanna hugged her. All around them, people were gradually getting to their feet. They heard more explosions in the distance, and waves of screams.

"The old man with the gingerbread hasn't stood up," Johanna remarked.

"He was lying against my leg," Hella said. "Now he's against the wall and he's not moving."

"What do they want to do to us?" a woman sobbed. "Wasn't the first time enough?"

Johanna was still hugging her friend.

"I wish you'd stop trembling," she said.

"Don't hold me too tight—you're smothering me!"

There was a brief silence, then a child began to whimper. Johanna tried to smile at him to make him stop.

Two people knelt beside the old man lying next to the wall. "He's dead," she heard one of them say, and the hospital patients began to weep softly.

"You're bleeding!" Hella exclaimed, pointing to Johanna's head.

Johanna put her hand to her cheek and was amazed to see that there was blood on it.

"Didn't you feel it when it happened?" asked Hella.

"No. I must have hit my head on the floor. I think I was half unconscious for a while."

Hella examined Johanna's wound.

"I've got an idea." She bent down, tore a piece of cloth from her skirt and used it to wipe away the blood. "With your dark hair, it's hard to see. . . . But I don't think it's serious."

"You shouldn't have torn your skirt."

"I don't care about tearing it a little more, after what it's already been through."

"You do look pretty grubby now, for a Spanish princess," Johanna said.

They giggled nervously, until an indignant voice silenced them: this was no time for laughing, they were told. A dull roar was gradually growing louder, drowning out the moans and scraps of conversation that could still be heard.

"It sounds like everything up there, above us, is on fire!" said Hella.

Just then Johanna noticed that someone at the other end of the basement was pointing toward a big crack in the ceiling. Several people had begun to cough.

"Do you smell smoke?" asked Hella.

Johanna nodded. Soon everyone was coughing. The old men from the hospital all took out their handkerchiefs and put them over their faces.

Trying to avoid the smoke, the crowd pressed Johanna and Hella against the wall. People screamed as the lamps went out. *This is the end*, Johanna thought, half smothered.

"What's happening?" asked Hella.

"Hot water is leaking," someone said.

"It's dark, I can't see anything," Johanna cried. "I don't want to be scalded to death in this hole!"

"Don't open the door!" someone shouted. "You'll let the fumes in!"

Johanna's fear gave way to revolt. She wanted to free herself from the herd. She had to get out of that basement—it was a trap.

"The door is to the right," she told Hella. "Let's try to push our way over to it."

"That's a stupid idea," said a man beside her. "Get it out of your head. The smoke won't get any worse unless little fools like you start opening doors."

The leak had evidently stopped. There were no more screams from the other end of the basement. But the smoke, probably coming through cracks in the ceiling, seemed to be growing thicker. Hella must have had the same impression because she tore off another piece of her skirt, handed it to Johanna and said, "This is to hold in front of your face."

Johanna brushed it across her cheek and remembered how carefully Hella's mother had saved that cloth to make a costume for her. She didn't understand why, but its softness brought tears to her eyes. Her fits of coughing were becoming exhausting. *If only I could sit down*, she thought.

Just then she felt Hella draw her forward. She stepped over the old man's body without thinking.

"Come on," Hella said. "Other people want to leave too."

They groped along the wall toward the door, which was barely visible at the top of a few steps. People had gathered there, arguing.

"Don't open the door!"

"Don't you realize that everything up there is on fire?"

"We can survive here, but we'd be burned to death up there!"

A tall man climbed the steps and stood looking out over the coughing, agitated crowd. He took a flashlight from his pocket and aimed its beam at himself to let everyone see him.

"Listen to me," he said loudly. "If we stay here, we'll be either roasted or boiled. Our only chance is to try to get outside the building. I'm leaving, and anyone who wants to can follow me."

"But what about the fire?" a voice objected. "You'll be putting us all in danger if you make an opening in . . ."

"I'm not going to 'make an opening,' I'm only going to open a door," the man retorted. "Listen, anyone who wants to come with me: wet your clothes in the tub of water beside the steps."

"You can't do that to the rest of us!"

"There's no reason to leave!" someone else said. "The smoke has stopped getting worse. We can—" He had a fit of coughing, then finally was able to complete his sentence: "—hold out here."

Johanna and Hella looked at each other. They splashed water on their faces and hair from the tub in front of them. It hurt the cut above Johanna's cheek but it also made her feel better.

"Let's try to be right behind him when he leaves," she said to Hella.

"I'm about to open the door," said the man. "Drop anything that might slow you down. No handbags. No furs."

"You'd better take off your skirt," Johanna told Hella. "Whatever's left of it. Hurry!"

Hella unfastened her skirt, which was by now little more than a dirty rag. She let it fall to the floor, then regretfully pushed it away with her foot.

"My coat!" a woman shrieked. "I want to keep my mink coat!"

"No reason to leave. . . . We can survive. . . . You have no right to . . ."

"Are all your clothes wet?" the man asked. "Good. When you hear me say, 'Now!,' run after me."

"We'll keep holding hands," Hella said to Johanna. "At least we'll be together if . . ."

"Remember," the man continued: "the staircase, the big room on the right, the entrance hall, the courtyard, the Postplatz. Stay away from the iron gates, they must be red-hot."

"My coat. I'd rather not come if . . ."

"Then don't," the man said brusquely.

Johanna stared at the door, smoke stinging her eyes and nose in spite of the piece of cloth over her face. She squeezed Hella's hand.

The man slowly turned the knob, then threw open the door.

"Now!" he shouted, rushing forward, his flashlight shining up the stairway. Johanna and Hella had taken only a few steps when a blast of heat struck them in the face. Through the smoke Johanna saw Hella's slender legs racing up the stairs ahead of her, and behind her she heard the door slam shut.

After they passed the landing, the heat got worse. Johanna held the piece of cloth even more closely to her face. She heard someone panting behind her, then the sound of a fall and a scream that echoed in the stairwell. Reaching the top of the steps seemed to take hours, and when she had done it she didn't have the strength to look back. She could taste blood in her mouth, and she felt as if she were suffocating.

Running as fast as they could, she and Hella followed the man through the public ward, toward the entrance hall. After opening the door, he jerked back his hand, swearing. The entrance hall was burning and a curtain of roaring flames separated it from the courtyard. He turned around, blowing on his hand.

"Girls, . . ." he began.

Then he looked back across the room. No one else was there.

"Girls, . . ." he repeated, incredulously.

Johanna was trying to catch her breath.

"Did you hear . . . that scream . . . behind me?" she gasped.

There was a cracking sound coming from the ceiling.

"My God!" the man exclaimed.

He looked around him. The heat was now nearly unbearable. He picked up a chair and broke a window with it. As soon as the glass had shattered, a billow of smoke burst into the room. Flames were already attacking the inside wall.

"Hurry!" he ordered.

He picked up Johanna and put her down on the windowsill.

"You can jump; we're only on the mezzanine," he said.

Unable to see the ground, she hesitated. But she knew that to reach safety she would have to jump. So she did, imagining an invisible thread guiding her through the blazing labyrinth.

Her knee struck the ground with a violent thud. She cried out in pain but quickly stood up and saw Hella clutching the side of the window frame, hesitating as she herself had done.

"Come on, it's not very far down!" she said.

The man had already come through the window. He took Hella by the waist and gently set her down on the ground. For a moment they stood out against the flaming background of the big room and he suddenly seemed immense.

"What about . . . the others?" Johanna asked.

"Have to . . . catch . . . my breath," he said, leaning against the wall. Then he looked at Johanna. "You're bleeding."

"It's nothing."

He stepped away from the wall and the girls followed him across the courtyard, where areas of shadow were streaked with firelight. He stopped, turned around and pointed.

"Go to the Postplatz," he said. "Then try to get to the Grosse Garten by way of the Bürgerwiese. I'll . . ."

Johanna didn't hear the end of his sentence because he had started running. She watched his tall figure move along the left side of the courtyard, beside a burning wall, then she ran after him.

"Wait! Wait for us!" she cried.

She stopped short, disoriented. He had disappeared.

"Hella! I've lost him." No one answered her. "Hella!"

She looked back. The whole public ward was now on fire.

"Hella!" she called out again in despair. "Hella!"

After a few steps she stopped again and called Hella's name, but the roar of the fire had become so loud that her voice couldn't rise above it.

As she was leaving the courtyard she felt a sharp pain: a hot cinder had struck her on the forehead. She held the piece of velvet that Hella had given her over the burn. The feel of it on her skin made her fully aware of Hella's absence. But there was no time to look for her: the flames had spread over the entire building.

Johanna went through the gate and turned right, in the direction the man had indicated. The empty street was brightly illuminated by the fire. It was incomprehensible: in the blink of an eye, Hella had vanished. "It's not fair, you shouldn't have left me like that," Johanna sobbed.

On the other side the street, deserted houses with flames reflected in their windowpanes looked as if they were about to collapse. Half-blinded by smoke, she saw people running past them, heading in the same direction she had taken.

The street had widened and she thought she was approaching the Postplatz when she saw a bright flash of light. Before she had time to wonder what was happening, the blast knocked her down. She found herself lying in a gutter. Around her a warm mist muffled all sounds and stung her nose a little, but she had no pain anywhere, not even where she had been burned on her forehead. At last she felt good again. *I'll just go on lying here,* she thought. *It would have been senseless to run like that all night.*

Then, from her left, came an inhuman cry, a continuation of the scream she had heard on the stairs. It was followed by a crackling sound that made her open her eyes. A thick liquid that gave off a strange greenish light was oozing down the front steps of a building. When it reached the bottom of the steps it spread into the street, and Johanna saw it creeping toward her. She leapt to her feet and began running again, driven by terror. The people she had seen before had disappeared. Maybe she had lain in that gutter a long time. Maybe she had dreamed that viscous incandescent tide.

She came to the Postplatz again, on the side opposite the entrance of the hospital. On the left another building was in flames, illuminating that part of the square like a vast stage. People seemed even more frightened and distraught here than at the Altmarkt. She heard screams, desperate shouts, names that rose above the tumult like bits of wreckage floating on a stormy sea: Inge, Jürgen. . . . She called Hella's name, sorrowfully, not even hoping that her friend might hear her.

"There's liquid phosphorus on Wilsdrufferstrasse," a man said, pointing in the direction from which she had come.

She still felt dazed. The scream she had heard resounded again inside her.

Beside her, a woman was talking quietly, as if she were telling a long story.

"Sophienstrasse is burning, but luckily the wind is blowing the other way now," she continued, and Johanna saw that she was talking to a little boy who had fallen asleep on her shoulders. His hair was full of ashes and his head bobbed up and down whenever the woman was jostled.

The flames of the burning building to Johanna's left suddenly flared up, revealing the postal savings bank, where her mother went every month to collect her war widow's pension. As often as possible, they went there together, and before taking the streetcar to the Bahnhofplatz they always had the same conversation; it had almost become a ritual. "You're rich this morning, Mutti." "No, not at all, darling." Johanna took Leni's arm. "But you still have enough money to go to Donner's, don't you?" Leni gave in, with a little smile, and it seemed to Johanna that happiness was her growing excitement as they approached the old-fashioned pastry shop. "I don't know how they do it, but their chocolate is almost the same as before the war," Leni always said when they came out.

Leni. . . . Safe in her basement. . . . *Are you thinking of me, Mutti? Maybe you think I'm still safe in the basement of the circus, where I ought to be. There was room to lie down and we might even have slept. Hella would still be with me now. . . .*

At the thought of being alone, without Hella, Johanna felt

chilled and nauseated. She recalled faces she had seen in the course of the long night: the little chimney sweep, the old man with the gingerbread . . . Her thoughts returned to Hella. *I just don't understand it, Hella. I saw you go through that window. . . .*

Johanna stood up, wiped her mouth with her hand and began walking alongside the wall of the savings bank, not even thinking about where she was going.

"Johanna!"

She stopped. Someone had called her in a voice so weak that she wasn't sure she had really heard it. She turned around. Hella was leaning against a tree, her bare legs pressed together and her hands behind her back as if she were tied to a stake. Johanna hugged her. but Hella didn't react; her little face, streaked with soot, was blank. Johanna felt a pain in her chest, then the questions she wanted to ask her came tumbling out.

"What have you been doing? Are you hurt? Why . . ."

It was a long time before Hella spoke.

"I saw a mother and her child lying on the pavement," she said. "At the corner of Sophienstrasse where we used to get off the streetcar to go skating." She looked at Johanna with empty eyes. "They'd been flattened on the pavement, really *flattened*. I could only see their *shapes*."

Johanna was silent for a few moments.

"I heard a scream from someone who'd been attacked by phosphorus," she said finally, as if the phosphorus were a wild animal.

Hella stared at her in bewilderment. Johanna clutched her arm and said, "Don't look at me like that! Things could be worse—at least we've found each other again."

Johanna went on, trying to bring her out of her indifference.

"Tell me where you were," she pleaded. "I kept looking for you. I was so afraid . . ."

"All at once I didn't see him anymore," Hella said quietly.

Johanna thought she must have misunderstood.

"You mean you didn't see *me* anymore?"

"I didn't see him anymore," Hella repeated, and her face became still more inscrutable.

Johanna felt a wound opening inside herself as people came from the square in growing numbers.

"Scheffelstrasse is burning!" someone cried.

"It was him you were looking for, Hella? It wasn't me?" Hella didn't answer.

"Act as if we still had the scarf," Johanna went on. "We mustn't lose each other again. Remember what we said on the stairs. It was terrible when I thought you'd . . ."

Hella's face became a little livelier. "Do you know what he said when he left me? By the way, I know his name."

"What is it?" Johanna asked reluctantly.

"Herbert," Hella replied with animation. "I told him my name and he said, 'H and H! We were made for each other!' Then he said, 'Bravo! You saved yourself. You weren't afraid to act. If you find your friend again, tell her bravo too.' So here you are, Johanna, and I'm telling you bravo from Herbert. I also told him your name."

"If you only knew how scared I was!"

"He's young," said Hella. "I realized it when he picked me up to help me through the window." For a moment she seemed absorbed in thought. "Do you think an adventure like that leaves a deep impression?" she asked. "Maybe he'll want to see us again."

"See *you* again, you mean!"

Hella looked at Johanna reproachfully.

"All right, then," said Johanna, "I'm sure tomorrow morning he'll go around to all the girls' schools in town and ask for Hella and Johanna."

"I don't think we'll have any classes tomorrow," Hella said seriously.

A great clamor suddenly burst from the crowd. An immense wall of flame had just appeared at the corner of Scheffelstrasse. It moved forward like a dragon in a fairy tale, spewing out bits of burning debris, driving everyone away from the south part of the square. Then, with incredible speed, the whole savings bank began to blaze.

The crowd headed for Annenstrasse. It was a narrow, winding street but there was no other way to escape. Around them, women and children were screaming; some fainted and were trampled by the crowd. Johanna thought only of holding on to Hella so that they wouldn't be separated, no matter what happened.

They were pushed toward the corner of the square from which there was no exit. There they stopped.

"It's never going to end, never!" Johanna exclaimed.

Hella's eyes were half closed and she was breathing heavily.

"I hurt myself," she said, grimacing.

"You've got a cut on your leg," said Johanna, running her finger along Hella's calf. "Just a minute, I'll . . ."

"Girls! Girls!" a man shouted.

Hella turned to see where the familiar voice had come from, but he was already there, holding a flashlight. He seemed to have appeared out of nowhere.

"Herbert!" she said, almost in a whisper.

Johanna was able to see his face for a moment. Hella was right: he was young, perhaps twenty, twenty-two at the most.

"What luck!" he said. "I've been looking for you two everywhere. I thought you were following me."

Hella smiled.

"You won't survive if you stay here," Herbert went on. "Annenstrasse is blocked. And people may panic if the fire keeps coming closer."

"What do you want us to do?" Johanna asked.

"I know a way out of here," he replied.

Hella looked at him, hypnotized by his sudden reappearance.

"I used to be in charge of transferring money between the post office and the savings bank," he said, "so I know this neighborhood. You can trust me." He pointed to a high wall a hundred yards away. Above it was a glass roof that formed a big marquee. "The bank's trucks are unloaded in that courtyard. There's a passage between it and Zwingerstrasse."

Johanna looked warily at the great expanse of dirty glass.

"How do you know there's no fire on the other side?" she asked.

He seemed surprised by her lack of enthusiasm.

"You don't have to come with me if you don't want to," he said reproachfully. "But I'm getting out of here. I don't want to die here like a cornered rat."

He walked away. Without a word, Hella withdrew her hand from Johanna's and ran to catch up with him. Johanna paled and ran after Hella, trying not to lose sight of her in the crowd. Finally she caught up with her and tugged at her sleeve.

"Listen, I don't like the idea of going in there," she said. "If everything suddenly collapsed. . ."

"If we hurry, we'll be gone by the time that happens," Hella replied. "Herbert knows what he's doing."

"Why not wait till the square is less crowded?" Johanna pleaded. "We said we'd stay together, and now you're going off with a man you don't even know."

Hella's face hardened.

"You're forgetting that he's already saved our lives!" she said angrily. "Can't you see that we'll never get out of here if we don't follow him?"

The crowd was jostling them so much that it was hard for them to follow. They heard cries from the direction of Wils-drufferstrasse. When they reached the entrance of the passage he was waiting for them. Behind him, several trucks were parked side by side in the murky light that filtered through the glass roof.

"Come on, girls, there's no time to waste," he said urgently.

Then, with Hella following him as if she were his shadow, he went into the passage that led to the covered courtyard. He seemed so sure of himself that other people also followed, bumping against Johanna as they passed.

"Hella!" she cried out desperately. "Stay with me! You promised! Stay with me!"

Hella didn't hear—or at least she didn't look back. Johanna saw her blond head disappear after Herbert, who had suddenly begun running.

Her eyes were drawn to the glass roof and she gasped. She tried to call Hella again but her throat was too tight to utter a sound. She stepped back. The roof had begun swaying and seemed to be melting into graceful cascades streaked with dark glowing red. The people who had gone into the courtyard were trying to escape, but she couldn't make out Hella or Herbert.

All at once the whole roof collapsed in a gigantic spray of sparks and flame. In the midst of the thunderous crash she heard shrieks of agony. She put her hands over her face, and a moment later she found herself lying on the ground beneath people who had fallen on top of her. After a struggle she stood up. Where the roof had been a few moments before, there was now open space above an enormous heap of rubble bristling with red-hot steel girders.

She turned and ran, fell and again struggled to her feet. But it wasn't really her, making these efforts to survive. Soon the real Johanna would see Hella come from behind a tree, and feel her hand in hers. . . .

Her legs weakened and she clutched a lamppost to steady herself. She didn't know where she was. In her mind she again saw and heard the glass roof collapsing in a dazzling shower of light, and she knew she would never see Hella again.

T W O

She felt perfectly content, as if she were wrapped in a soft, warm cocoon, gently swinging high in the air. A drop of water fell onto her face and she frowned. She tried to wipe it away, but couldn't move her hands. Then she tried to sit up and couldn't do that either. Finally she realized she was hemmed in by a snug down sleeping bag, protecting her from the cold and dampness.

She decided to keep her eyes closed a little longer, enjoying the warmth that enveloped her. She had no idea how she had gotten into the sleeping bag. She remembered leaving Annenstrasse—it was easier than Herbert had said it would be—and running with swirling crowds through blasts of heat, until finally, at the end of a street, she had plunged into the silence of a dark, empty space. Then, with a sense of deliverance, she had realized she was among trees.

She opened her eyes. The top of a slender poplar was silhouetted against the gray sky. The dawn seemed so pale and uncertain that she wondered if it would ever brighten into real daylight. The ashes in the air made her cough, and coughing revived the pain of the burn on her forehead. All at once the horrors of the night before came rushing back.

She pulled her left hand out of her cocoon to look at her watch. It had stopped at ten past two. Maybe that was the time when Hella . . . She shuddered. *Hella* . . . Convulsively she rolled over on her stomach. With her forehead against the damp earth, she tried to erase the image of flames from her mind.

At least today she would see Leni and Grete again. They must have spent the whole night waiting for her, and by now they had probably given up hope. Leni, Grete. It was comforting to whisper their names. *Oh Grete*, she thought, *will you like me better now? Will you stop having those secret talks with Mutti?*

She moved her hand through the wet grass and pressed it on her burn, relieving the pain for a few seconds. Then it began to hurt more than before. Why had that man come back, and why had Hella gone off with him so recklessly? *When I found you again, you promised me we'd stay together from then on!*

Johanna raised her head. Her face was wet from crying. At the foot of a tree she noticed an oblong shape like an especially thick root. Lying on the ground behind it were other similar shapes. She was suddenly revolted, thinking she had slept among corpses. Then one of the shapes coughed weakly and a tuft of blond hair popped out.

"Hello," she called.

The blond head quickly slipped back down into its sleeping bag.

"So my little nocturnal visitor is awake!" a voice said.

Johanna started. The end of a rubber-tipped cane and two old shoes covered with ashes appeared in front of her. She was imprisoned in the sleeping bag, or else she would have run away. The man laboriously squatted beside her, his blue-eyed, angular face and stubble of whiskers coming into view. He examined her calmly.

"You have a burn on your forehead," he noted.

From the look on his face, she could tell it was hard for him

to remain squatting. She wriggled out of the sleeping bag and
stood up. He, too, stood up and, seeing her shiver, went to a
pile of blankets behind the tree, took one and draped it
around her.

There were at least twenty sleeping bags on the ground,
not four or five as she had thought. A bleak, dazed silence
hung over them. Without her shell, she felt vulnerable again,
and her forehead had begun to ache.

The man took out a package of cookies and held one out
to her.

"This and the blanket are all I can give you," he said
regretfully. "I bought this package in the station. If I'd known
what was going to happen," he added with a weak smile, "I
might have bought two."

With nausea welling up in her, Johanna shook her head to
refuse the cookie.

"When I carried you last night," he continued, "you
seemed so light that I thought you were a child. But now I see
you're a young lady! I shouldn't have given you Stefan's
sleeping bag. You must have been cramped."

"I was fine."

"Well, at least you didn't protest when we slid you into it,"
he said, smiling.

She sighed and looked at him more closely. The disheveled
white hair above his deepset eyes gave him the look of a
disillusioned, philosophical owl.

"You carried me? I don't remember it," she said. "I don't
remember anything."

He laughed.

"I didn't carry you very far." He pointed to a spot near the
tree. "I found you there. You were already curled up and
asleep when I saw you. We were over there, not far away."

Johanna went to the tree that had sheltered her and stroked
its trunk with gratitude. She recalled the sweetness of certain
sensations she had had during the night, like clearings in a
forest of nightmares. They were all sensations of touch: the
soft cloth of the Bavarian scarf that had connected her with
Hella, the smooth wall of the church after they had crossed
the bridge, Hella's light, fluffy hair. . . . And now this tree.

"There are maybe ten thousand trees in the Grosse Garten," the man said, "and you chose just the right one. Believe me, you've got a bright future ahead of you: you must have been born under a lucky star!"

She shook her head.

"What are all of you?" she then asked. "I mean, what kind of group do you belong to?"

"We're like everyone else you'll meet from now on," the man said wearily. "Like you, we're castaways. But you can also say we're survivors."

Clutching his cane, he took a few steps on the lawn. He had a limp.

"The fact is that we almost didn't make it," he went on. "The whole north side of the park was bombed. We could see trees burning like torches from here."

"I almost didn't make it either. I was at the circus with my best friend . . . . She had a costume. . . ."

Johanna couldn't go on.

"You must have seen some horrible sights, poor girl," he said softly.

"We stayed together till after the second attack. Then she went off with someone I didn't trust, instead of . . . staying . . . staying with me."

He nodded. Several faces had come out of sleeping bags and were observing her curiously.

"If she hadn't done that, she'd be lying here in one of those bags, with her blond hair. . . . When I saw her going after him, I shouted, 'Stay with me!' If you only knew how I shouted. . . ."

She was shaken by sobs.

"Think of your family now," he said, putting a hand on her shoulder. "You've got to get home. You can imagine the state they're in."

"Oh, yes!" she exclaimed. "My mother and my sister are home."

"Where do you live?"

"Bernhardistrasse. Out past the station. You're right, I'd better go back right now."

"I hope nothing has happened," he said with concern,

again holding out a cookie to her. "Here, take it. I wish I could give you all of them, but I don't have anything else for my little troop to eat." He cast a protective eye over the sleeping bags strewn around them. "What you see scattered over the grass is all that's left of the most famous children's choir in Germany: the Kreuzkirche choir. I organized it long before the war, and trained it myself. In 1943 it had sixty members. Now we are only eighteen . . . but we still haven't lost our talent. When the bombing began, we were in the station singing for a trainload of refugees—I wish you could have seen their faces."

He closed his eyes for a moment. Johanna felt it was time for her to leave.

"Thank you very much for everything," she said with an awkward curtsy. "The cookie, the blanket . . ."

"Be careful when you cross the tracks: there may be unexploded bombs," he warned as she walked away, her blanket wrapped tightly around her.

She stopped, looked back and waved. With his cane under his arm, he was hastily writing something down on a piece of paper. A moment later he limped toward her.

"I don't even know your name," he said. Embarrassed, he didn't wait for her answer. "What I wanted to say is that if something has happened . . . on your street . . ."

Johanna turned pale.

"If anything happened there," she said, "I'm sure my mother and my sister stayed in the basement."

"Of course! Even so, I want to tell you about a place you can go if you do have to leave your home—which I hope won't happen, naturally. It's where I plan to take my choir. I think it's going to be impossible for us to stay here. I doubt I'll be able to find food enough for all of us. The wagon and horses we use for trips are two kilometers from here. If I can manage to get to them, I plan to take the choir to my house, about twenty kilometers from Dresden, at the edge of the Erzgebirge."

"But won't it be even harder to get food there?"

"No," he said, smiling. "As the leader of a famous choir

and the owner of a modest amount of livestock, I was given permission to kill and salt a pig!"

He held out the piece of paper.

"Take the road to Dippoldiswalde," he told her, "and turn right in front of the church. Go to Frauensteln, take the road to Altenberg, and after about a kilometer you'll see a gate on the right. That's the gate to my house."

All she wanted to do was to get back to her mother. But she politely took the sheet of paper and stuffed it into her pocket.

"Thank you, but . . ."

"I hope you won't come, of course, because it will mean that things have turned out well for you. If you do come, though, I hope you like salt pork."

"I like it all right. Well, not really. But, anyway, I have to go. And . . . my name is Johanna Seyfert."

"Seyfert!" he exclaimed. He looked at her closely. "Your father was . . ."

"Yes," Johanna said, "the archaeologist."

He nodded. Disconcerted by the sudden silence, she looked down at the ground.

"Well, goodbye," he said finally. "Maybe we'll meet again."

She curtsied again and left. It was hard for her to walk but, sensing that the choirmaster was watching her, she forced herself to keep going till she was out of sight.

She came to the main avenue of the park, which was familiar to her from the summer evenings when she had gone to puppet shows in Frau Stütze's theater. The last time, she and Grete had seen a performance of *The Brave Little Tailor;* Grete, of course, had found it childish and refused ever to go there again.

Johanna stopped to look around and eat her cookie. Mist was slowly rising in the direction of the zoo. It was there that the park looked most heavily damaged. The lawns bristled with hundreds of blackened, smoking stumps. An acrid odor hung over the main avenue and permeated the bordering thickets. She remembered having been there with Hella and Charlotte Müngerer two weeks earlier. She and Hella had

been trying to soothe Charlotte's despair over Fräulein Bodendorf, their new history teacher. Fräulein Bodendorf was
the most beautiful, understanding and admirable woman in
the world to Charlotte, and Johanna and Hella had teased her
about her crush. Then, just before the three of them met in
the park, someone had told Charlotte that a soldier came
regularly to see Fräulein Bodendorf, and that they spent
whole nights together. "Who told you that?" Johanna had
asked. "I won't tell you," Charlotte had answered, weeping
for her betrayed love, "but it's someone I see at school every
day."

*And you, Charlotte—where are you this morning? And Fräulein
Bodendorf. . . . She'll probably never know how much you loved
her.*

In the center of the path, the little obelisk erected to
commemorate the Franco-Prussian fighting that had taken
place here in 1813 was covered with a layer of light gray ash.
With bitter irony she realized that it was the morning of Ash
Wednesday.

A twig snapped behind her. She turned around and found
herself facing a motionless animal staring at the park fence.
After a moment of bewilderment she realized it was a llama
from the zoo. She went over to him and stroked his long,
arched neck.

"At least *you* escaped," she said.

Then she saw blood oozing from his thick fur. She took a
pinch of ashes from the ground and gravely put it on his
muzzle.

"Leave it on all day," she told him with her forefinger
sternly raised, in imitation of Grete.

The llama thought she was offering him something to eat;
he moved his head forward, then snorted, perhaps from disappointment, when he saw her leave.

She turned right and began following the long, deserted
curve of Thiergartenstrasse with a heavy heart. Only the
streetcars that lay on their sides, as if blown over by a hurri-
cane, showed that she hadn't dreamed the night before. The
buildings seemed undamaged. She wondered if the people

who lived in them had stayed in their basements after the second attack. She walked through the filthy fog, hearing nothing but the sound of her own footsteps, hoping she would meet someone who could tell her where they had all gone. Now that she thought back on it, there seemed to be something strange, almost fanciful, about her encounter with the choir and the llama.

The familiar shape of the station gradually became visible in the mist. She went in through the open doorway: the door had disappeared. Mist had seeped into the vast room through countless holes in the glass roof, whose blackened framework stood out against the sky like a net of barbed wire. Half-burned notice boards still bore traces of track numbers for departing trains. On the floor, a long fire hose was curved like a snake among the star-shaped craters left by incendiary bombs.

She hurried to the stairs that led to the underground part of the station. At first they seemed intact. Farther down, however, a huge crack had displaced a dozen steps, which now overlapped each other like the steps of ancient amphitheaters she had seen in her father's photographs. Above her a lantern flickered, making her feel as if she were descending into an ancient ruin. She thought of what she and Hella had said on similar stairs, only a few hours earlier. That was the last time she had talked with the real Hella. After meeting that man, Hella hadn't been the same. But it didn't matter anymore. She would always remember Hella as the blond girl who, ignoring the crowd, had stopped in the middle of the stairs and told her that she would never leave her.

At the foot of the stairs was a long room with entrances to the underground passages leading to the different platforms. Here there were even more people than had crowded into the basement of the circus. They were all asleep, and the room was hot and silent.

She tried to walk quietly, to avoid waking anyone. She could hardly see in the faint glow of the gaslight. But it was clear that many of these people had been camping here for days, living on the floor among piles of baggage that formed caves in which the families took refuge. A few children were smiling in their sleep. Maybe they were dreaming, she thought, of the carnival and the horses—which by now might be wandering like the llama among the ruins.

"How did you get in here?" asked a voice behind her.

She turned around and saw a man in a baggy jacket pushing a cart loaded with gray blankets. A dark knitted hat accentuated the pallor of his face in the gaslight.

"I always come through here on my way home," she said.

"You shouldn't have come this time," he replied. "Didn't you see the SS men guarding the entrance?"

She stared at him in surprise.

"Are you looking for someone?" he asked in a gentler tone. "If so, you'd better go to the identification service. There will be a session beginning at noon, in the Terminus hotel."

"No, I'm not looking for anyone. I'm going home. I live on Bernhardistrasse."

He shook his head.

"The passage under the tracks is blocked. You'll have to go to the crossing on Reichstrasse." He took her by the arm and led her back toward the stairs.

"What a crowd!" she said.

"The station was packed when the first attack came," the man explained. "Besides the refugees, there were hundreds of people on the platforms, waiting for two trains, and two other trains had just come in. Everyone rushed underground as soon as the attack started."

"They're all so calm."

"Oh, they're calm, all right. What can they . . ."

He looked at her and left his sentence unfinished. When they had climbed the stairs, he pointed out the direction she should take.

"I hope it turns out that you still have a home to go to," he said.

Outside in the fog, she saw that Reichstrasse had been devastated. Smoke still rose from the ruins. She put Hella's cloth over her face. She had to get home, no matter what.

At the crossing she looked for the gatekeeper's red and

white hut. She always waved to him whenever she went to the Grosse Garten by this route. But there was now a deep hole where the hut had been. She looked down into it and saw a few charred red and white boards.

She passed the wreckage of the hut and cautiously started across the railroad tracks. Her view of the station was almost entirely cut off by a burned train. She thought she saw heads and arms protruding from the windows of the cars, and began running. She didn't stop till she had reached the Bismarckplatz, where, in the distance, she could see the outlines of dozens of bodies stretched out on the ground—half naked, it seemed. Several people wandered among them like ghosts. One knelt beside each corpse, lifted its head and seemed to say a few words to it.

Again Johanna began running. From here on she knew every inch of the street, every gutter, every wall.

Winckelmannstrasse, the street that led to Hella's, seemed unscathed. *I'll go and see her mother in a little while, with Mutti,* Johanna thought. Bergstrasse was also intact. Her heart was beginning to swell with hope when, at the corner of Liebigstrasse, the last street before hers, she saw the green gate of her old kindergarten swinging in the wind. There was a huge smoking crater in the playground, and in it, twisted like a piece of wire, was the guardrail on which she had balanced so many times.

She paled. Each step now cost all her strength as she walked along the part of Schweizerstrasse where she had run so often on her way home.

When she turned into Bernhardistrasse, her heart was pounding so hard that she was afraid to look in front of her. Then . . . *Oh, my God! The Wachses' house!* A column of smoke rose through the roof, and the door had fallen onto the front steps. Frau Ackermann's house was undamaged. Farther on, a whole row of houses seemed intact.

All at once her fatigue was gone. She flew from house to house like a bird. *The Gildemeisters—nothing seems to have happened to theirs! And here's our house! It's standing! The living-room curtain is moving! Mutti!*

A short distance from the house, she stopped abruptly. In the pale winter light, her street looked exactly the same as it had each morning when she left for school, turning partway down the street to wave to Leni. For a moment she was tempted to believe she had been having a long nightmare; in a moment Mutti would kiss her and it would be over.

Her bicycle was still leaning against the shed, where she had left it the day before when she came back from school. She opened the front gate and its familiar bell tinkled. As she climbed the steps her legs trembled. She took a deep breath and pushed the doorbell button. The bell didn't ring. *No use pushing the button, you idiot: the electricity is off.* She knocked on the door. There was no answer.

She knocked again, then waited as she always did when she came back from school, with her forehead against the door. Except for the distant scraping of a shovel, an eerie silence hung over the street. She listened, holding her breath, but heard only her heart beating. She pounded on the door.

"Mutti! Grete!" she cried, shaking the doorknob.

Maybe they had gone to a public air-raid shelter. Or maybe they were still in the basement.

She had already started down the steps to shout through the basement window when she heard the doorknob turn. In one bound she was back at the top of the steps. Silently the door opened and her mother appeared.

"Mutti," Johanna said quietly.

But Leni didn't seem to see her. Her eyes were empty, her face expressionless.

"Mutti!" Johanna hugged her fiercely.

Leni didn't move either to push Johanna away or to hold her, but stayed frozen in the doorway, clutching the knob. She was still wearing the blue dress of the evening before, when she had given Johanna the scarf.

Johanna noticed that there was light in the entrance hall, which was usually dark. She slipped past her mother in the doorway and went inside.

"The stairs!" she exclaimed.

The staircase was gone. In its place a huge crack went from the roof to the basement, cutting the house in half. Wooden

steps hung from the handrail by its balusters. Daylight poured
through a gash in the roof. To the right, the wall between the
entrance hall and the living room was gone, and Johanna
could see books scattered over the floor. She turned back to
her mother.

"Where's Grete?" she asked anxiously.

Leni didn't seem to have heard. Johanna grabbed her by
the shoulders.

"Where's Grete?"

With a slight nod, Leni indicated the basement stairs. Johanna slowly started down them. She could hardly breathe.
The steps were still in place and the light coming from the
hole in the roof made it possible to see almost to the bottom.
The only dark area was where the staircase turned, just before
the door to the basement. And it was there, on the last step,
that she found her.

Grete was in a position that Johanna knew well because it
was the one she always took when she read: sitting with her
elbows on her knees. Her head was tilted forward. Her long
hair hung over her forearm. Johanna looked at her a long time
without daring to touch her.

"Grete," she finally murmured in her ear. Her voice was
choked.

Then she touched her neck. It was cold. She drew back her
hand and started up the stairs. But after each step she leaned
heavily against the wall.

Leni said nothing as she watched Johanna emerge from the
stairwell. Johanna threw her arms around her and began sobbing convulsively, but Leni remained inert.

"Talk to me, Mutti!" Johanna cried, shaking her. "Tell me
what happened!"

Leni's delicate faced tensed briefly and her body hunched
forward as if a weight on her shoulders were crushing her.
Then, holding what was left of the handrail, she leaned over
the basement stairs.

"Are you sure?" Johanna asked pleadingly, trying to exor-
cise the unacceptable. "Are you sure she . . . She looks so
. . . so natural."

Natural. She remembered all the people in the big under-

ground room of the railroad station, the long, calm frieze of
sleeping faces in the dim light, and suddenly her legs seemed
about to give way beneath her. She shook her head. "No,
that's impossible," she said aloud. Those people were going
to wake up. By now, in fact, they were already awake, and
some of them were opening their suitcases while the babies
cried. And at the foot of the basement stairs, Grete was about
to stand up and ask for her Latin book.

"I'll go down and take her pulse," Johanna said.

Leni looked at her as if she hadn't understood. And Johanna knew she couldn't bring herself to do what she had
said. She trembled at the thought of touching Grete again, of
lifting her head and uncovering her face. Then, for the first
time, Leni reacted: she shook her head. Johanna paled, as if
Grete had just died for the second time. Leni took a deep
breath and sat down at the top of the basement stairs.

Johanna looked at her, overwhelmed. Her mother's expres-
sive face, once full of dimples, smiles and mischievous winks,
was now ashen and lifeless. Johanna sat down beside her and
pressed her cheek against hers.

"I'm here, Mutti," she said softly. "I'm with you."

Leni didn't answer. Not knowing what to do, Johanna
scrutinized her face, watching for a quiver of her lips or a
flicker in her eyes. But she saw nothing. It was as if she found
a landscape she had known and loved darkened by fog, unrecognizable. Panic rose inside her.

"You can't stay like that all the time!" she cried, shaking
Leni again. "There are so many things that have to be done!
Hella's mother has to be told, and a doctor . . . Mutti, you
know I love you as much as Grete did, and now I have only
you. . . ."

Leni didn't move.

"When did you start acting like this?" asked Johanna.
"when the bomb hit? When you started worrying about me
not coming home? When Grete . . ." She stopped abruptly:
Leni had closed her eyes and her lips trembled. "It was
Grete, wasn't it?"

Her heart fell.

"Don't you realize I could easily have been killed too?" she said. "I was with Hella and now she's dead." She watched for a reaction from Leni. "But I'm here, Mutti. You still have me. I'll try to take Grete's place. I'll take good care of you."

But as she spoke, she wondered if it was possible. She thought of Grete's self-assurance, her knowing smiles, the secrets she shared with Leni, leaving Johanna out. "She looks just like you!" people often told Leni when they saw her with Grete, and both of them loved it. But Johanna was thin and had dark, curly hair like her father. After he died, she thought that maybe she reminded Leni too much of him and maybe that was why they weren't as close as Leni and Grete were. Yet she liked to be told that she looked like her father, if only because it bothered Grete. Grete once poked her ribs and said, "Papa was dark and a little skinny, I know that, but you're overdoing it." And another time: "You're too young for me to tell you what Mutti and I talk about. It's easy for Mutti and me to tell each other everything, you know, because we're so much alike, and I don't mean just physically." These last words had infuriated Johanna. But she shouldn't have had bad thoughts about her sister, not now. After all, there were times when Grete had been nice to her. She tried to remember them, without much success. Grete was never a friend the way Hella was, of course. She had *chosen* Hella.

She began crying again. "Both of them killed in the same night," she said. "I should be with them."

Leni looked at her but said nothing. Till now, each indifferent look from Leni had been like a stab in the heart to Johanna, but this one, strangely, made her feel better: her mother was sick and needed her, even if she didn't know it, and this justified Johanna's still being alive. She had been given a mission; it began with simple things.

"Mutti," she said drying her tears, " I'm going to bring Dr. Strauss, if I can find him. I'll also stop by to tell Frau Gildemeister what's happened, and ask her to come and help us. Don't you want to eat something before I go?"

No answer.

"This has been a huge catastrophe, you know," she went

on, "and there probably won't be enough doctors to go
around. Since we'll have to wait, I'd rather you had something
in your stomach."

Taking Leni's silence for agreement, she stepped over the
broken plaster that had fallen from the living room wall and
tried to go into the kitchen. The door was askew and she had
trouble opening it. Everything in the kitchen was in wild
disorder. The contents of drawers and cupboards had spilled
onto the tiled floor, and the faucet of the sink was hissing and
dripping. As she closed it more tightly, she realized that this
was the first sound she had heard since she came home.

The familiar still life of her afternoon snack was in the food
cabinet, intact: apples, ham, cheese, bread. She took it all to
Leni and put it down beside her.

"Shall I peel an apple for you?" she asked encouragingly.

Leni opened her eyes a little wider, as if she had never seen
an apple before. Johanna put it in her hand. A moment later
she heard a thumping sound: Leni had dropped the apple and
was helplessly watching it as it bounced down the stairs.

Johanna burst into tears.

"You can't stay like that," she sobbed. "What will happen
to us if . . . if you don't . . ."

She wept, leaning over the first step of the basement stairs,
her shoulders heaving. Then it occurred to her that she was in
the same position as Grete at the bottom of the stairs, and this
upset her even more.

"I'm here beside you, Mutti," she finally gasped between
sobs. "I may not have been your favorite daughter, but even
so . . . I nearly died. I love you, and you . . . you go on . . ."

Leni was staring at the dark stairwell into which the apple
had disappeared. For the time being, Johanna thought, there
was nothing she could do. *Maybe later, when she's had some sleep.*

She suddenly felt hungry. It was the first time since the day
before and for some reason it reassured her. She ate some of
the cheese and bit into one of the apples. Leni watched her.
That was already a kind of progress. Johanna wondered if she
had spent the night beside Grete's body. If so, why had she
come upstairs? Surely not to wait for her. Maybe at some point

she had just been unable to stay down there any longer and had come up to keep watch over Grete's tomb. Johanna looked at her.

"I have to go and see what condition the rest of the house is in," she said. "Maybe a tarpaulin can be put over the hole in the roof to keep out the rain."

Her words met with silence. She stood up and began climbing to the second floor, using the fragments of steps that were still set into the wall. When she reached the landing she saw that the Persian rug her father had loved was covered with red dust from broken bricks. Through the exposed roof beams, the sky looked gray and hung ominously low above the house.

Apprehensively, she went into the bedroom that she and Grete had shared. It had a deep crack in the ceiling, but was otherwise intact. She felt like weeping again when she saw the two freshly made beds side by side, prepared for the night. She sat down on hers and looked around the room where she had spent so much of her time. Seeing all her things in their usual places made her feel strange. Her pink opal glass lampshade wasn't broken. The alarm clock beside her bed was still ticking. It showed ten o'clock.

Grete's notebook was open on the table and Johanna could see the careful round handwriting in it. Since Grete's bed wasn't unmade, she must have stayed in the basement between the two attacks. Maybe she and Leni, impatient to come out after the second attack, had started up the stairs too soon, just when the house was hit by one of the last bombs. Johanna sighed. Grete would never again lie down on that bed. And yet the presence of all these things made it still seem so *possible*.

She thought of all the times they had said good night before going to sleep. It had always made them feel closer, even after they had quarreled. Grete would never go to sleep angry, so they often had bedtime conversations in which each of them got everything off her chest. *If you said mean things now*, Johanna thought, *I'd be glad to hear them because they'd show you were alive. If you'd stayed on your bed, nothing would have happened to you!*

Johanna went over to the window. On the other side of the garden, the Gildemeisters' house looked undamaged. She was tempted to call to them, but she told herself it would be better to go over to the old couple and explain what had happened. Bernhardistrasse was deserted. In the distance, columns of black smoke were still rising over the Bismarck-platz.

She went to Leni's room and cried out: the wall that separated the room from the staircase had been completely blown away, as if it were made of cardboard, and the floor had partially collapsed. The feather mattress on which her mother slept had fallen through the hole and was now draped over the piano in the living room.

She returned to the landing. Leni was still sitting on the stairs, looking down toward the basement. Johanna carefully made her way down the ruined staircase, kissed her and anxiously waited for an expression, even a fleeting one, on her face. Finally, tired of waiting, she went into the living room.

If only it doesn't rain, she thought, looking at the scattered books. This library was her father's treasure. She began piling books under the sofa to protect them. How well she knew those heavy archaeological treatises, with their gray covers! Her father used to make her try to read their solemn titles in Gothic letters and would let her look through the illustrations. Often these were covered in rice paper which she pulled aside, trembling, as if she were really approaching Knossos, or Babylon. Those real, faraway places—the places her father went to in his periodic travels—fascinated her far more than the enchanted forests in fairy tales. She liked to imagine herself going with her father to visit temples more majestic than the Japanese Palace and more ornate than the Zwinger, or to examine gigantic walls covered with mysterious writing that looked like the tracks left by birds on a beach.

She opened one of the books and read its title page:

Bruno Meissner

KÖNIGE BABYLONIENS
UND ASSYRIENS

Leipzig 1926

She remembered this book so well. She could still see her father as he was when she had watched him reading it, with his black beard and his suntanned face. "You've come to look like one of your bas-reliefs," Leni told him. "And your daughter looks as if she just came straight from the Euphrates!" He examined Johanna's face a long time and smiled. Then she put her finger on an engraving that depicted a triumphal gateway opening onto the desert. "Where is it?" she asked. "I'll take you there," her father answered. "Yes, I'll take you there, my little Assyrian girl. But I warn you, it's much hotter there than it is here." Then he laughed, something she seldom heard him do. . . . She remembered her father so vividly. One of the things she liked most about Leni was the simple idea that she had been in love with him.

She began leafing through the book, to find the engraving, but quickly gave up. *This is no time to look at pictures of ruins,* she told herself. She was about to put the book on the pile when a sheet of paper fell out. She picked it up and unfolded it.

It was a typewritten letter on engraved letterhead, dated February 3, 1938, from Professor Josef Hutka, head of the department of Oriental archaeology at Carolinum University in Prague. It was addressed to Herr Doktor Rüdiger Seyfert at 20 Bernhardistrasse in Dresden.

My dear friend,

Since you know how much time and labor my research has cost me, and under what circumstances I have had to press on to achieve my present results, I am deeply touched by your support. Judging from the letters and journals sent to me, my enemies have not relented, but I now feel I have reached the heart of the problem and am ready to receive, some radiant morning, the answer to the riddle. I am like an old Oedipus a little tired from having marked time too long in front of the Sphinx.

I hope to heaven that . . . You know what I mean.

Best regards,
Josef

P.S. Why not come and talk about all this with me? There are only a hundred and fifty kilometers and one border (for how long?!) between us, and the stories I have to tell you are worth the trip.

J.

The signature and the postscript were handwritten, in blue ink, with big, slanting downstrokes. Johanna folded the letter, put it back into the book, then went on piling up the other books until the rug was clear. Of the things her father had loved, at least these would be saved.

She picked up a book that she hadn't yet put away and read its title: *Die Orientalischen Ausgrabungen.* Her father had shown her engravings in that book, too. She remembered that one of them depicted the funeral of a young warrior prince in Ur of the Chaldees. She had liked the name of the city.

"Mutti," she called out, "who was that Professor Hutka who wanted to see Papa?"

Leni didn't answer. Johanna didn't repeat her question. She went into the entrance hall.

"I'm going out," she said calmly. "I have a lot to do. Stay here till I come back. Your Johanna will be back in a little while."

She stressed this last sentence, hoping that from now on her name would accompany Leni as she drifted in her private realm. Then maybe she would stop looking at her as if she didn't exist.

Johanna took her loden coat from the rack in the hall, picked up one of the apples and bit into it.

Columns of black smoke were still rising against the sky in every direction, and the highest seemed to be coming from the Sarrasani circus on the other side of the river. She thought bitterly of the air-raid police blocking the exits.

She went through the Gildemeisters' little garden and rang the sheep bell that served as their doorbell. She knew their house almost as well as her own, from the days when their granddaughter Suzanne was living with them. She and Suzanne first met when they were six or seven years old, and they got along wonderfully. They transformed the two adjoining gardens into settings for adventures. The lawns were continents that had to be defended against invaders, and clumps of trees were dark forests where they hid for hours. One morning, Suzanne announced that she was going back to her parents, who were both civil servants in Berlin. Johanna cried after Suzanne left, and for days she walked aimlessly in her garden, which had now shrunk back into its old narrow limits. A year later she met Hella.

She rang the bell again, then turned the doorknob. To her surprise, the door opened. She stuck her head inside. The entrance hall was dark but a little light came from the living room.

"Frau Gildemeister!" she called.

After a moment of hesitation, she went in. With its profusion of knickknacks and its printed percale curtains, the living room was as she had always known it. The porcelain stove and the copper warming pan hanging on the wall gleamed softly. It seemed as if the old lady might be hiding behind the door, about to step out in her flowered apron. Ill at ease, Johanna left the room.

She opened the door to the cellar and stood looking down into the darkness below.

"Herr Gildemeister! Frau Gildemeister!"

In the silence, her voice was unrecognizable. Panic-stricken, she bolted from the house, her heart pounding. She tried not to breathe very hard because the air was full of fumes. *They must have hurried off to an air-raid shelter*, she thought, *without even locking the door*.

As she passed the Brauners' house she was surprised not to hear Bello barking. He had always frightened her. She stopped and looked over the hedge, standing on tiptoe. A frayed rope hung from the ring to which Bello was usually tied. The street was evidently deserted.

From Bernhardistrasse, she turned right onto Leubnizer-strasse, automatically following her route to Hella's house on Zelleschestrasse. She and Hella had exchanged so many jokes and secrets on that street that, written down, their words would have made a chain long enough to connect their two houses.

Now she had to tell Hella's mother what had happened. What could she say to that woman who had never realized what a treasure she had in Hella? *I won't give her any details about her death. I'll just say I lost sight of her near the post office, after the second attack. I'll also say she was very brave last night. In fact, that's how I'll begin; "Be brave, the way Hella was. . . ." Can I say that without crying? Maybe Hella's mother will understand and help me. I need someone to take me in her arms. . . .*

Johanna broke off her thoughts. Smoke coming from a crack in the pavement was stinging her throat.

Zelleschestrasse had been devastated, including Hella's house. The rhododendron she had been so proud of was a charred stump, and corpses lay on the sidewalk. *At least she didn't have to see this,* Johanna thought.

She turned back. To her surprise, she felt almost relieved. She would have hated Frau Neumann for living when her daughter was dead.

She soon came to the street where Dr. Strauss lived. Surely he would come to see her mother and do what had to be done . . . about Grete. How often the three of them had used the slightest ailment as an excuse to visit him! Short and ruddy-faced, with a jovial, kindly manner, he always gave them cough drops and patted them on the shoulder. *"Guten Tag,* Frau Seyfert, *guten Tag,* Grete, *guten Tag,* Johanna," he said loudly, and the two girls responded with a little curtsy. The last time, he had replaced "Frau Seyfert" with "Leni." Leni was still disconcerted by it when they reached home ten minutes later. "He's in *love* with you!" Grete said disapprovingly. For a moment Leni was furious, then she laughed and said, "Too bad: I like them tall and thin!"

The thought of her mother's laughter pierced Johanna's heart. *That's one of the questions I'll ask him: "Will she ever laugh again, Dr. Strauss? Will she ever talk with me the way she used to, when she seemed to be saying everything that came into her mind?" And I'll ask him for some kind of ointment to put on my burn.*

When she came to his house she saw a handwritten sign on the fence: *Dr. Strauss has been called away.* At first she was staggered, but then she reasoned with herself: at least Dr. Strauss hadn't been killed in the bombing. He would probably be back by evening. She wondered if she should leave a note for him, but realized she had nothing to write with.

She sat down at the foot of the fence and began trying to sort things out in her mind. There had to be an order of priority in everything she had to do, but she couldn't figure out what it was. *I have to arrange for Grete to be buried. There must be some government department that will take care of it. But where shall I have her buried? In the military cemetery, beside Papa? And I have to find a tarpaulin somewhere; otherwise all the furniture will be ruined if it rains. I know where I can get one: at Hägen's house.*

"It's terrible," said a hoarse voice above her, "when you get old your arms get thin and the bones show through."

An emaciated old woman was standing directly in front of her. Johanna was about to stand up and hurry away when the woman put out her hand to stop her, looking at her intently with piercing eyes.

"Yes, it's terrible," she went on. "Things wouldn't be so bad nowadays if everybody did their share, but nobody wants to do anything, so what can you expect?" She had now rolled up the sleeves of her black dress to her shoulders and was waving her bony arms in all directions. "When they come for me on the last day, I'll stop them by swinging my arms like this, and I'll say to them, 'Let me die the way I lived, on my manure pile, like an old goat.'"

Johanna stood up, stepped sideways and felt the woman's fingers brush against her hair. Terrified, she began to run. *When I tell Hägen*, she thought when she had stopped, *that the only person I met was a crazy old woman. . .* Hägen was the retired garage owner who lived nearby and sometimes came to do odd jobs for Leni—repairs, even gardening—when she was tired. To Johanna and Grete, he was the man who replaced the brakes on their bicycles. "You wear them out so fast!" he would say with pretended gruffness. "Couldn't you ride a little slower?"

As she passed the grease-stained doors of the former garage, she heard the sound of an airplane. She stopped, petrified, and listened. It hadn't occurred to her that they might come back. What she heard, however, was quite different from the deep, thunderous roar of the night before; it seemed to be the drone of a single plane. Shading her eyes with her hands, she tried to spot it in the gray clouds.

Finally she saw it, followed by two others, slowly flying over the Grosse Garten. Then one of them turned sharply and its peaceful hum turned into an angry buzz as it swooped over the main avenue of the park at low altitude. She heard short bursts of machine-gun fire in rapid succession. An image flashed into her mind: the row of sleeping bags she had seen in the park at dawn. The plane turned, flew back over the avenue at treetop level, fired a few more bursts and then veered off to the north while the two others continued circling slowly.

Johanna's legs felt so weak that she had to sit down on the low wall that bordered the street. She kept thinking of the choirmaster and the children in the park. *I hope they're gone by now.*

Finally she began walking again. She had just passed the garden of the Zuckermann hospital when more planes appeared in the sky. Unlike those that had formed the massive armada of the night before, these flew acrobatically, climbing steeply and then diving one by one. The pilots seemed to be shooting at anything that moved.

Johanna stepped into the street, again shading her eyes with her hands, and suddenly she heard a deafening roar behind her —*immediately* behind her, it seemed. She ran to the sidewalk, jumped over the low wall and took shelter behind it just before the bullets struck. She clutched at the ground and for a moment she thought she would faint. She felt earth and fragments of shattered stone falling on her. When she opened her eyes, the blood was throbbing violently in her temples. She carefully raised her head a little and saw the plane climb at a sharp angle, then veer toward the railroad tracks. It had a white star on the underside of each wing. Bathed in sweat and trembling all over, she forced herself to lie still for several minutes even after the sky had become quiet again.

Finally she tried to stand up, leaning against the wall, but her legs gave way beneath her. In front of her, she saw where the bullets had cut a deep furrow in the pavement and pock-marked the stone wall. "I'd have been cut in half," she murmured. She sat down and sobbed, feeling as if she were about to vomit. Then she noticed a cut on the back of her left hand and began sucking the blood from it.

She looked up at the sky. She was sure they would come back. They wouldn't leave anything intact. Some buildings and monuments were still standing; she could see the dome of the Frauenkirche miraculously rising through the mist and smoke beyond the park. Surely they would come back for that, the symbol of the city.

She stood up. Her coat was splattered with mud. She felt weak, but she had made a decision.

Still sitting on the same step, Leni didn't even look up when Johanna came back. Johanna walked past her and went into the kitchen, hurriedly gathered all the food she could find, put it in a bag, went upstairs and came back with Leni's coat and gloves, two nightgowns, a few toilet articles and two blankets.

"There's no one left in the city," she said urgently. "The only person I met was a crazy old woman. And the planes will come back, for the buildings that are still standing. I was almost killed just now. Again. We can't stay here, Mutti. We're leaving."

Leni looked at her vacantly.

"Don't you understand me? We're leaving! They might be back any minute!"

Leni winced when she saw Johanna walking toward the door with the bag of food. Again she fixed her gaze on the basement stairs.

"We'll ride our bicycles," Johanna said. "I have the address of a place where we can stay."

She went out to the shed, tied the bag of food to the rack of her mother's bicycle and loaded her own with the blankets and clothes. Then she went back into the house, held Leni's coat and made her put it on, one sleeve at a time.

"Let's go," she said gently.

Looking toward the basement again, Leni shook her head and stiffened. For a moment Johanna was at a loss.

"I'm going to put up a sign outside," she said, "to make sure someone will find her and do what needs to be done."

She went to her room and came back down with a piece of chalk and the slate she had used when she was a little girl. She sat down beside her mother and began writing carefully, imitating the typography of the obituary notices in the *Freiheitskampf:*

FEBRUARY 14, 1945
GRETE SEYFERT, AGE 14½
(*In the basement.*)
HELLA NEUMANN, AGE 12½
(*Courtyard of the savings bank, Postplatz.*)

Then she looked at Leni.

"What is it they always say on the radio, when they give a list of names?"

Leni stared at the slate.

"I remember now," Johanna said.

She wrote at the top of the inscription, above the cross: "Sacrificial victims of a terrorist bombing." After reading it aloud, she hung the slate from the doorknob.

Leni stood up heavily, regretfully. Johanna took her by the hand and led her to her bicycle. Leni got on, then looked at the slate again, her mouth open.

"They'll find her and take care of her," Johanna said gently. She tried to calm down but she couldn't help saying, "Hurry, Mutti! They might be back any minute!"

Leni sighed and pushed her bicycle through the front gate. Johanna pointed her in the right direction, then rode behind her. Leni didn't look back.

II

ALL THE GIRLS

WHO FORM THIS ROUND

DON'T WANT A MAN

FOR THE SUMMER.

—Old German folk song

T H R E E

ohanna rode through a shower of raindrops heavy with soot and ashes. To keep them from stinging her eyes, she leaned over the handlebars and held her head down.

Ahead of her, Leni rode unevenly. Several times she veered suddenly and nearly went off the road.

Johanna pulled up beside her. She was tired and wanted to stop for a moment, but once they were off their bicycles, Leni might refuse to start again. She touched Leni's arm to let her know she was there. Leni didn't turn her head.

A few minutes later they passed a long column of refugees. Gusts of wind still brought acrid smells from the night before in heavy waves. In the distance, the dome of the Frauenkirche stood out against the vast black curtain of smoke rising inexhaustibly into the sky. *How can it still be standing after all that?* Johanna wondered.

As she pedaled, she touched the folded piece of paper in her pocket. It was her talisman. She tried to remember exactly when she had decided to use it. By the time she went off to get a tarpaulin from Hägen she had forgotten about the choirmaster and his little troop, and was thinking only of the mutilated house in which she and her mother would have to try to live. Then there had been the bullets narrowly missing her, and her panic. That was when she had remembered the piece of paper in her pocket.

In front of her, the rear door of a covered wagon suddenly opened, and she was so startled that she swerved and nearly fell. She glimpsed the toothless grin of an old man lying on a straw mattress that seemed ready to slide out the back of the wagon.

"You're about to lose the old man!" she said to the driver as she rode past.

He raised his hand in a weary gesture but she couldn't tell whether he had understood her or not.

People were fleeing without looking back, without speaking, all with the same blank expression, pulling a motley assortment of vehicles overloaded with valued possessions. Johanna even saw an old couple dragging a sled. They both seemed exhausted. When she passed, they were holding hands.

Now and then gusts of warm air seemed to come from the mountains in the distance—the Erzgebirge—as though from a promised land. To the right, a large humpbacked field with snow in its furrows extended to a ridge at the edge of a forest. The landscape seemed vaguely familiar. In spite of her fatigue Johanna recognized a clump of trees in which her class had picnicked the year before. Hella had worn a green dress. After the picnic they had tried to climb to the bottom of a narrow gorge called the Devil's Cauldron. When they were halfway down, a heavy rainstorm burst and, true to its name, the gorge became a devilish cauldron, with a roaring torrent at its bottom. Hella began singing "Tales from the Vienna Woods" to give them courage. How long ago that seemed now.

Leni had gotten ahead. Johanna struggled to catch up with her.

"Don't go so fast," she said, breathing hard. "We have to save our strength for the mountains. Anyway, we're out of danger now."

But Leni's face had a fierce look that made Johanna uneasy.

She was tempted to turn back and go home. Then she thought of the slate hanging from the doorknob and a chill ran up her spine. She began pedaling harder.

The people she passed on the road all looked alike to her now: weary faces streaked with black, always the same face in the same dirty mist. Overwhelmed by fatigue, she lost control of her bicycle and fell. Feeling the hard, rough pavement of the road beneath her hands, she saw Leni go on riding away from her.

"Call her back!" she shouted, but no one paid any attention. She wasn't even sure she had made any sound.

Unsteadily, she got to her feet. Her fall had loosened the blankets and clothes tied to the rack of her bicycle. She had just finished tying them in place again when she saw Leni riding back.

Leni stopped, got off her bicycle and let it fall noisily on the roadside.

"Finished," she said hoarsely.

It was the first word she had spoken since Johanna's return.

"Did you see that I wasn't following you anymore?" Johanna asked anxiously. "Is that why you came back?"

Leni kept her eyes fixed on the road, with her mouth slightly open, as if she were catching her breath.

"Finished," she repeated. "Finished."

"You already said that," Johanna replied, annoyed. "Now that we've both stopped, let's rest awhile."

She took an apple from the bag tied to Leni's bicycle and held it out to her. Leni shook her head.

"Take it, Mutti," Johanna insisted. "You haven't eaten anything since yesterday."

Leni looked at her fingernails, which were blue with cold.

"I put your gloves on you," Johanna said gently. "Why did you take them off?"

She took the gloves from a pocket of Leni's coat and put them on her again, one finger at a time. This abrupt reversal of roles between her and her mother disturbed her. She knew she sometimes acted like a spoiled child. What would happen if Leni acted the same way and refused to go on riding?

"Let's go," Johanna said firmly.

Leni didn't move. Johanna picked up her bicycle and brought it over to her.

"Let's go," she repeated, trying not to sound nervous. "Don't you hear me?"

Leni made no effort to get back on her bicycle. Johanna leaned it against a tree, tears of rage in her eyes.

"I have an address," she said. "Listen to me. You see those people who've been walking aimlessly for days and days? I have something they all wish they had: the address of a house where we can stay. And you won't go!"

"You can give me that address and I'll make good use of it," a voice said behind her.

She turned around. A woman wrapped in a shabby old overcoat had stopped on the other side of the road. For a moment Johanna thought she was the crazy old woman she had seen in front of the doctor's house.

"Come here," the woman said. "I won't eat you. As a matter of fact, it's been so long since the last time I ate that I've forgotten how, so you're safe."

Johanna hesitated, then walked across the road. The woman stood with her hand on an old baby carriage that must have been attractive in former days. Her coat was held closed by a piece of string and her face was worn but, like the baby carriage, her regular features and clear blue eyes must have been beautiful once.

"I've been walking so long," she said apologetically.

Johanna didn't know what to say. She avoided her eyes and looked into the baby carriage. It was filled with a jumble of things carelessly wrapped in pieces of newspaper. She saw a headline: FIERCE FIGHTING AROUND BUDAPEST.

"But I'm not the only one: people are out walking for their health all over Germany these days," the woman added ironically.

"I can't invite you to come with me," Johanna answered. "I don't even know exactly where I'm going."

The woman looked at her in silence. Johanna turned crimson.

"If you haven't eaten, I can give you an apple," she said, "but I don't have anything else."

A surprisingly youthful smile appeared on the woman's face, wiping away all signs of fatigue for an instant.

"I'll take what I can get," she said.

Johanna crossed the road and came back with the apple. The woman put out her hand with such natural grace that she seemed to be offering, rather than taking. She held the apple fervently for a moment, with her eyes closed, then bit into it ravenously.

"You see, he doesn't even know there are two of us," Johanna tried to explain.

The woman's eyes examined her above the apple.

"Who doesn't know?"

"The man who invited my mother and me—I mean, he invited me but not my mother, and he . . . he doesn't know I'm coming with her."

"I didn't really expect you to invite me," the woman said with her mouth full. "I was just making conversation. You get bored when you've been walking for weeks without seeing anyone you know."

She slowly finished chewing. Johanna noticed that Leni was watching her and went back across the road to give her an apple too. This time Leni held it without dropping it.

"Would you like another one?" Johanna asked the woman.

"Of course, let's have it. I'll eat it tonight."

The woman carefully hid the apple in a corner of the baby carriage. Then she took a few steps along the road, facing the dark clouds that hung over the city.

"Think of it: this was supposed to be my last stop."

"You were going to Dresden?" Johanna asked.

The woman nodded. On the road, the covered wagon that Johanna had passed was now passing her. Its rear door had been closed, hiding the old man on the mattress.

"I've been on the road for more than a month," the woman said. "I lived in Bottnitz, near the Polish border. When Koniev made his breakthrough, I tried to take a train at Beuthen to go to my daughter in Dresden, but . . ." She stopped, then raised her voice to speak to Leni: "I'm sorry—you seem upset by what I'm saying. I know it's no fun to hear about other people's troubles, especially now."

Leni frowned slightly.

"And besides that, I'm keeping you from going on your way," the woman continued.

"No, not at all," said Johanna. "We stopped here to rest."

"I had to talk to someone. I had to."

"Yes," said Johanna, watching Leni out of the corner of her eye. "I can understand that, since you haven't seen anyone you know in a very long time."

"But I haven't exactly been alone," the woman said. "At Beuthen there were no more trains. Thousands of us, thousands of women, were caught in the town just as it was being invaded by Mongolian troops. I decided to go back to my village. I managed to get out of Beuthen and started walking along country roads toward Striegau. I thought I could stay a while in a friend's house there. But it was already too late. The Soviet Third Army had outflanked us. . . . I had to go back to Beuthen."

She spoke in a dull monotone. The wind had died down and rain had begun falling again. Now and then Johanna felt particles of debris brush against her like sleet, and she wondered what building, what monument they had come from. Maybe from her own house. . . . She imagined the whole city transformed into snowflakes fluttering in the wind.

The woman had fallen silent. After crossing the road to listen to her, Leni had stood watching her lips with fascination, and now she was waiting, wide-eyed, to hear what she would say next. Maybe this encounter was doing Leni good.

"In that little town," the woman finally went on, "there were, I don't know, thirty or forty thousand refugees. . . . It was cold, about ten below. We kept hearing stories about Russian soldiers. That was all anyone talked about. Little girls were hidden in closets and basements. And even I—you can see what I look like, and yet . . . One day when I'd decided to leave by myself, on the road to Freiberg, it happened. . . ."

"*What* happened?" asked Johanna. "What did they do to you?"

The woman passed her hand over her eyes.

"It wasn't only me. What they did to me and all those other

women . . . It had to happen. We're paying for the persecutions, for the concentration camps. Did you see those pictures taken when German soldiers marched into Prague? Did you see the people's faces?"

Johanna was struck by a term the woman had used.

"The concentration camps?" she asked.

"You'll know about them some day," the woman said wearily. "Some day, even here, people will know. Their eyes will be opened. But what will it have cost? How many . . ." She stopped short and pointed to Leni. "She doesn't talk much, does she?"

"My mother," Johanna said, lowering her voice, "she's . . . she's not herself now. My sister died last night, and our house was destroyed." She took a deep breath. "Maybe you could tell her that we were right."

"Right to do what?"

"Well, to . . . to leave."

"Leave!" the woman cried. "That's not what *I* wanted to do! I wanted to arrive, to find my daughter, my Sigrid. . . . She was supposed to have been in Dresden for several days, but where . . . where? And what will I do without her, if I don't find her? What will become of me?"

Johanna stepped toward her and whispered, pointing to Leni, "Stop. Please don't talk about your daughter. I told you. . . ."

The woman nodded thoughtfully. Then, seeming to awaken from a dream, she pushed the baby carriage back onto the road and turned to speak to Leni.

"You have your daughter with you. I'd give anything to have mine with me. *Anything*, you hear?"

"Grete," Leni murmured.

The woman looked at her a long time, then turned to Johanna with a gentle smile and said, "Thank you for the apples. Everything in life is a matter of timing, and those apples came just when I needed them."

She sat down beside the road and, while Leni watched her every move, she picked up pebbles from the ground and piled them into a little pyramid.

"When you leave a place," she said, standing up, "you

should always leave something behind to show you've been there. A sign, a marker. Otherwise, no one will ever pick up your trail."

She looked down at the little mound.

"I have something for you, too," she added. She rummaged in her baby carriage, took out a greasy tube and handed it to Johanna. "I see you have a blister on your forehead. Put some of this salve on it. It works."

"Thank you," said Johanna. "What's your name?"

"What difference does it make?"

"Do you think your daughter was waiting for you in the station?"

Johanna immediately wished she hadn't asked. The woman's face tensed.

"I tried to go into the station," she said, "but there were SS men keeping everyone out. All I could see was that the big room where they sell tickets was empty. The people there must have left before. Why, were you able to get in?"

Johanna shook her head. She suddenly felt that she and Leni had to leave. Why had she mentioned the station?

She got on her bicycle and rode away. Leni followed her, pedaling like a machine. Johanna looked back to wave goodbye. The woman, leaning over the baby carriage, seemed to be talking to it.

As they moved away from the city, the smell of the fire weakened. But when the wind shifted, the acrid stench enveloped them again and the trees beside the road made Johanna think of the charred stumps in the Grosse Garten. In spite of her fatigue she pedaled faster to escape from the smell of burning that seemed to follow her. Finally she was soothed by the wintry smells of dead leaves and wet forest.

She and Leni passed a long column of prisoners of war walking slowly toward the city, carrying picks and shovels that seemed absurdly inadequate for the work they would have to do when they got to Dresden. Johanna wondered how they would feel when they saw how their friends had avenged them. Their eyes seemed as empty as Leni's. *They look as if they've suffered as much as the refugees,* Johanna thought. *But afterward, we'll be told there was a winning side and a losing one.*

Finally she spotted the half-timbered houses of Dippoldis-walde nestled in the hollow of a hill.

In front of the church, several groups of refugees had stopped to eat around a fountain that offered only a thin trickle of cold water. Johanna was relieved when she saw a sign: FRAUENSTELN 15 KM.

When she and Leni came to the first upward slope of the road, they got off their bicycles and began walking. The road turned to the right, opening up a view of the mountains. Up ahead, the slope disappeared into thick fog. Johanna wheeled the two bicycles off the road and leaned them against a tree.

"Take a deep breath," she said. "Don't you notice any-thing different? That smell is gone."

She began wiping away the soot that darkened Leni's cheeks and forehead. When she had finished, she untangled her mother's hair a little, then kissed her fervently. Leni looked at her emptily.

"I want you to be the way you were before, you hear me? Please, Mutti! Change back, and soon!" Johanna's voice ech-oed under the trees and Leni seemed shaken by it. "When we get to where we're going, you'll have a good, long sleep, and tomorrow morning I'm sure you'll say to me, 'Why are we here? How did we get here? I don't remember anything.' "

Leni, frowning, seemed to be reading her lips rather than listening. Johanna took the piece of paper from her pocket.

"Do you want to see the writing of the man who invited us to his house?" she asked. "You want to see his address? Look: Riedenberg Haus, Frauensteln. And here's his name: Hans Magnus Kerbratt. Don't you think that would be a good name for an orchestra conductor? Actually, he's a choirmaster, but that's almost the same as an orchestra conductor—they both work with music. . . ."

She would have gone on talking and talking if she had felt it was doing some good, but Leni was only staring at the ground.

"Say something to me," Johanna pleaded. "Don't leave me all alone like this." She buried her face in Leni's coat.

"Grete," Leni said in her faraway voice.

"I know, she's gone!" cried Johanna. "But I'm still here. Didn't you hear what that lady said? If you only knew how much I love you. . . ."

Leni stood caressing the handlebars of her bicycle. Johanna looked at her and wiped her tears with the back of her hand. Leni mounted her bicycle and rode away.

They saw a village up ahead, spread over a hillside. Twilight was approaching when, after pedaling up one last slope, they came into a little square. Leni sat down on the stone rim of its fountain. Johanna leaned her bicycle against it and began walking around the square, looking for a sign showing the way to Altenberg. Except for the splashing of the fountain, the silence was total. There was no trace of life anywhere. Most of the buildings around the church seemed to be empty old barns; she smelled the reassuring odor of hay. *We can always spend the night in one of them*, she thought. Then she saw a faded little sign on the steeple that read:

FRAUENSTELN, ALTITUDE 655 M
→ALTENBERG 11 KM

She ran back to Leni.

"Mutti! Mutti! Now I know which way Altenberg is! Come, we'll soon be in a warm house!"

Back at the fountain, a cow that had come to drink was breathing on the bag of food attached to Leni's bicycle. Seeing Johanna approach, the cow abandoned the food, placidly drank from the fountain and lumbered off, its bell tinkling in the distance. Johanna remembered the solemn, motionless llama in the park that morning. Two large animals appearing as silent witnesses, one at the beginning of that long day of wandering, the other at its end. Words from a children's song came into her mind:

> *Will you be kind to me,*
> *Forests and fields?*

They left the village on the little road that wound through a narrow stretch of forest. Johanna wondered if she had over-estimated her strength. The cold was biting more fiercely than before and she wasn't sure she could go on pedaling much longer. Leni seemed to be weaving back and forth across the whole width of the road.

Soon they came to a large meadow where they could see far to the north. A curtain of dark smoke was still rising from the city, spreading into a vast dome of dismal clouds. Johanna stopped to catch her breath and forced herself to look intently at the smoke. *That's where I used to live*, she thought. *I still lived there yesterday.*

She walked a few steps while Leni went on riding. Her fatigue had become so painful that she closed her eyes. She felt sick to her stomach.

She got back onto her bicycle and began pedaling again. *He said it was about a kilometer from Frauenstein*, she thought. Looking down at the road in front of her, she suddenly saw the reflection of a gate in a puddle. She stopped abruptly. The gate was partly hidden by dead ferns, as if it hadn't been opened in a long time. On it was a metal sign with engraved Gothic letters: Riedenberg Haus. She called out to Leni, who rode back to her. Johanna tried to open the gate but it re-sisted. Leni watched.

"Are you just going to stand there?" Johanna asked irritably.

Leni carefully leaned her bicycle against a tree and helped Johanna push on the gate. Finally it swung open, pulling up brambles. In front of them, a muddy, weedy lane disappeared into a stand of fir trees. They walked along it, wheeling their bicycles.

At the first bend, Johanna saw the house, a large chalet, evidently quite old, with a gray stone foundation and an overhanging balcony. On the left was a wooden barn. Both seemed gloomy and deserted. It began raining again as she and Leni were crossing the courtyard and she suddenly felt chilled and hungry. She went to a low door that seemed to be the only entrance and knocked.

No one answered, which didn't surprise her. She tried to remember how many doors she had knocked on since the day before. She knocked harder.

She was already thinking of trying to get into the barn when she heard footsteps coming toward the door. She reached into her pocket for the piece of paper. A countrywoman opened the door, holding a scarf around her head with one hand, as if she were about to go out. She looked quickly at Johanna, then at Leni.

"Herr Kerbratt invited us to come here," Johanna said hurriedly.

"You don't belong to the choir," the woman declared, examining them.

"No, but I met the choirmaster," Johanna said timidly. "He gave me his address and told me to come here if I wanted to . . . if I could . . ." She handed her the piece of paper. "Look, you can see it's his handwriting."

The woman glanced at it.

"When did you see him?" she asked uneasily.

"Early this morning," Johanna said, "in the part of the Grosse Garten that wasn't hit. The children were with him. They were in sleeping bags and I'd slept in one too. He told me he'd come here as soon as he could."

"He hasn't come yet."

Johanna wondered if she should tell her about the attack that morning. She decided not to, wanting only to go into the house and sleep.

"I'm sure he'll be here soon," she said confidently. "He had to go and get the wagon. Everyone is thinking of only one thing now: running away. There are thousands and thousands of people on the road. Because the city is . . . It was like . . ."

The woman shook her head sadly.

"I can imagine," she said. "I heard it all night. Some of us got dressed and watched it from the village. The horizon was all lit up."

"From the flares," Johanna said wearily.

The woman looked at Johanna and Leni and seemed to see them for the first time.

"You poor things! You must be starving and exhausted, and I'm standing here without asking you to come in! Let's get you something to eat, then I'll find you a place to sleep."

Johanna had to push Leni gently across the threshold and into the living room.

The woman opened a cupboard and took out what she needed to set the table. She left and came back with food on a tray: red cabbage, an omelet and two large cups of coffee substitute made with chicory. Now and then she looked at Leni out of the corner of her eye.

Johanna decided not to wait to be questioned. When the woman came near her she whispered, "My older sister was killed in the bombing last night. My mother loved her very much and she hasn't talked since it happened. I'm Johanna Seyfert, and my mother's name is Leni."

The woman's broad, ruddy face was full of compassion.

"You poor things!" she said again. "My name is Rosi. I've been Hans's—Herr Kerbratt's—housekeeper since 1920. This house is his haven. But why aren't you eating?"

Johanna began devouring her share of the omelet. Leni, who touched nothing on her plate, drank her ersatz coffee greedily. When she put down the cup, she had a liquid moustache on her upper lip, like a child. Johanna furtively wiped it off with a corner of her napkin.

"Here, you have to eat," she said sternly, holding a spoonful of omelet in front of Leni's mouth.

Leni didn't resist; she chewed, swallowed, and opened her mouth like a bird. Johanna gave her another spoonful.

"I'm not going to feed you like a baby again," she whispered. "The next time we eat, the others will probably all be here."

Rosi was watching the front door. Outside, the rain was falling harder.

"They must be late because there are so many people on the roads," Johanna told her. "It's hard to go anywhere now, especially with a big group like that."

"Do you know how long he intended to stay here, with the children?" asked Rosi.

Johanna shook her head. It was becoming harder and harder for her to speak, and even to sit up.

"It was worse than in Hamburg," Rosi said.

"I don't know how . . . how it was in Hamburg, but in Dresden everything is burning and there are . . ." Johanna was silent for a moment. "There were thousands of dead people in the railroad station."

This was the first time she had said the truth aloud.

She must have fallen asleep for a few moments because it seemed to her that the rain had stopped awhile. Rosi had sat down beside Leni and finished off the omelet. They both seemed weighed down by the same weary, resigned sadness. Finally Rosi turned to Johanna.

"How old is your mother?" she whispered as if she were committing an indiscretion.

"Thirty-six," Johanna answered.

Rosi sighed.

"I'll show you where you can sleep, upstairs," she said. "I hope you don't mind sharing a room with your mother."

Johanna thought of all the nights when she had wanted to sleep with Leni but first had to argue with Grete.

"No, of course not," she said with a sad smile. "I'd rather be in the same room with her, in fact."

Rosi took the candle and started up the stairs. Johanna and Leni followed her, more slowly. When they reached the long hall on the second floor, Rosi opened a door.

The small candlelit room seemed friendly and its big white feather mattress promised a night of warm, comfortable sleep. Rosi left, came back with a glass of water and dropped a tablet into it.

"Drink this," she said to Leni, holding it out to her. "It's very important for you to sleep tonight."

Leni did as she was told. She lay down on the feather mattress with her arms outstretched. In the candlelight her face seemed peaceful. Her eyes were closed and Johanna had the impression that her lips were moving. *Maybe she's telling Grete all the things she didn't tell me today*, thought Johanna.

"You need to sleep too," Rosi whispered to her. "I'll stay up and wait."

Johanna hesitated, then pulled one corner of the feather mattress toward her and huddled up against her mother, fully dressed. As soon as she felt Leni's regular breathing beside her, she fell asleep so quickly that she didn't even hear Rosi leave the room.

She was in a boundless ocean under a lightning-streaked sky, tossed by huge green waves. To keep from sinking she had to hold on to a piece of wood, a remnant of some long-ago shipwreck, and she clutched it fiercely as the storm grew stronger. Then, at dawn, the sea finally calmed. Still clinging to the wood, she drifted toward a beach teeming with sea birds. Their cries nearly deafened her as she drifted closer. When she washed up on shore, the birds, surprised, stopped their chatter. In the silence she heard Leni heave a loud sigh.

Johanna raised herself on her elbows and looked at her mother as she slept. She slowly moved her hand along Leni's dress, lingering over her ribs and hips, but Leni didn't wake up. Johanna felt a surge of tenderness and hugged her as she had hugged the wood in her dream. "Like the husband you don't have anymore," she murmured. She remembered one morning when she and her mother had spent the night together and awakened to find themselves clinging tightly to each other. Leni had brusquely moved away.

Johanna heard sounds downstairs: words, exclamations, the clatter of dishes around the table. She got up noiselessly, pushed the curtains aside and looked through the window. It was still dark. The ray of light she had taken for dawn was coming from the lantern of a wagon in the courtyard. Its wavering glow bathed the front of the house. She closed the curtains but a little light still came through the crack. So this was what her dream had been: the meager light of a lantern transformed into dawn, and the whispering of sleepy children into sea birds! Strange. But they had arrived safely! They were downstairs, eating. They too had escaped from the storm. . . .

She looked at her watch: five past midnight. At that same time, the night before, she had been leaving the circus with Hella. She heard the choirmaster's deep voice rise above the hum of conversation downstairs. Her heart pounding, she wondered if she should go down and see him. Rosi must already have told him.

Leni turned over, muttering. Johanna whispered in her ear, "They're here now. Everything's all right. Go back to sleep." For a long time she sat on the bed in the dark, wondering what to do. She finally decided to go downstairs; otherwise she would be awake the rest of the night.

Just then she heard noises from the staircase.

"Careful!" a voice said.

She opened the door silently and looked into the hall. Two boys carrying a stretcher were coming up the stairs. They reached the landing, paused to catch their breath, then went off along the hall.

As the stretcher bearers passed by her door, she was able to see the gaunt face and dark, tousled hair of the boy they were carrying. Just then, perhaps feeling her stare, he turned his head toward her. He looked startled at seeing her like that, a sudden, silent apparition. She quickly stepped back into the room, closed the door and stood with her back to the wall. *One of them was wounded*, she thought. *That must be why they were late*. In her mind she could still see his dark eyes looking at her.

She heard heavy, irregular footsteps on the stairs, waited for them to reach the hall, then opened the door again.

"Herr Kerbratt," she said softly, leaning out into the hall.

He stopped, came toward her with a candle in his hand and lowered it a little to examine her.

"So you've come, my child," he said wearily.

"Did Rosi tell you about . . . my mother?" she asked timidly.

She stepped aside so that he could see Leni lying on the bed. He seemed lost in thought. The flickering light of the candle furrowed his unshaven face.

"Yes," he finally said, shaking his head. "I was afraid of something like that, you know. That's why I gave you my address."

"She hasn't talked since it happened," Johanna said.

Kerbratt sighed.

"She must be in shock. I hope a good night's sleep will bring her out of it. Rosi gave her a sedative, didn't she?"

"Yes."

"Good. You need sleep too. Try to forget everything till tomorrow. We'll talk about it then, and decide what we should do."

He put his arm around her shoulders. His fatherly manner encouraged her.

"I saw a boy being carried on a stretcher," she said. "Is he hurt badly?"

"Franz?" He made a gesture that she couldn't interpret. "I don't know. I hope not. We couldn't find a doctor for him, only a young veterinarian at the zoo. He cleaned and bandaged Franz's wound." He sighed again. "Go to sleep now."

As he turned he looked more stooped than he had that morning. She closed the door. The lantern of the wagon in the courtyard had been extinguished, plunging the room into darkness. She groped her way to the bed, guided by the sound of her mother's breathing. For several moments she lay on the bed with her eyes open.

"Franz," she said quietly. "Your name is Franz."

The same plane, she thought. *The same plane tried to kill us both*. She imagined the pilot in his cockpit, clenching his teeth as he fired. *You tried to kill us both, just for fun*.

Leni moaned briefly and Johanna realized that she had begun thinking out loud. "Sleep," she whispered.

Johanna sat up in bed and looked around the little room. Sunlight was streaming through the curtains. Yes, this time it was really morning.

Filled with hope, she heard joyous exclamations from downstairs which seemed to beckon to her. It was a happy morning, and suddenly it seemed possible that there could be others like it. She thought she saw a faint smile on Leni's lips and this encouraged her.

"Good morning, Mutti. Did you have a good sleep?"

Leni, who was also sitting up in bed, appeared to be listening for something far beyond the wooden walls of the room.

"Answer me, Mutti," Johanna insisted. "How do you feel this morning? Mutti!"

Johanna stood up, went over to the window and opened the curtains. She saw the gleaming slate roof of the barn.

"Come and see," she said in an encouraging tone, turning back to Leni. "It doesn't look gloomy here, the way it did yesterday. We'll take a long walk together, and we'll go tobogganing, the way we used to do in the park. There must be a toboggan here. Don't you think so?"

She waited in vain for some sign of interest. Leni took a handful of her own hair and examined it attentively.

"I'll brush your hair for you, if that's what you want," Johanna said. "Then I'll go and make some coffee, and you'll wash yourself while I'm gone."

She began brushing Leni's long, fine blond hair and smoothing it with her fingers. It kept escaping in all directions and she had a hard time making it stay in place. It was still as lively and playful as Leni herself had been. But nothing else about her was the same. Johanna's hopeful mood vanished. The miracle she'd hoped for hadn't happened.

She took Leni by the hand, led her across the hall to the bathroom and made her open the door. At the sight of the clean white toilet, Leni stood still for a moment and then, without the slightest hesitation, lifted her skirt and began pulling down her panties. Johanna closed the door and went back into the bedroom to wait for her. A short time later she heard her flush the toilet. Then Leni came in, a little stooped, holding her hands in front of her like a sleepwalker.

"You can find it again by yourself, can't you?" asked Johanna. "Remember: it's right across the hall."

She took out the toilet articles she had brought with her, put them on the dressing table, squeezed toothpaste onto Leni's toothbrush and handed it to her. While she was making the bed she heard Leni carefully brush her teeth and rinse her mouth. With the towel, she wiped away the traces of toothpaste at the corners of her lips.

"Now I'll go down and make coffee. Didn't you notice that the coffee we had here last night tasted better than the kind we'd been drinking at home?" Johanna asked deliberately. "It didn't have so much barley in it."

Leni always made the same remark whenever someone mentioned coffee: "The taste of coffee changed in 1942." Coffee had become a symbol of all lost happiness. But this time she said nothing.

Kerbratt was beside the barn door talking with a tall blond boy of about sixteen, who held a bridle bit. Johanna thought she recognized him as one of the stretcher carriers of the night before. She walked slowly, trying to seem self-assured. The choirmaster watched her coming toward him. A pair of binoculars hung from his neck.

"You have a long face this morning," he said. "Is it because your mother hasn't made any progress?"

She stammered and burst into tears. Kerbratt put his hand on her shoulder.

"Heinz," he said to the boy, "take Helmut with you and start cleaning the horses' harness."

Freshly shaven, with his gray hair neatly combed, Kerbratt seemed less tired than the day before.

"Please don't worry," he said. "Sometimes people can be in shock for days. When I was fifteen, I had a fall in the mountains, and for forty-eight hours I didn't know my own name. Why don't you tell me exactly what happened, and we'll see what we can do."

He led her to a stone bench and they sat down. Reassured, she began telling him how she had found Leni and Grete, and how the airplane attack made her decide to get out of the city.

"The strange part of it," she concluded, "is that she doesn't seem to remember anything, but she knows Grete is dead."

Kerbratt nodded.

"Do you think your mother could have had a *physical* shock?" he asked. "Did you see a roof beam near her, or anything else that might have fallen on her?"

"No, I didn't see anything like that," Johanna replied. "She was standing at the top of the stairs looking down, where Grete was," she went on after a silence. "I'm sure *that's* why . . . Do you think she's . . ."

She couldn't bring herself to say the word.

"Crazy? Is that what you mean?"

She looked down at the yellowed grass of the courtyard.

"Here's what I suggest," Kerbratt said deliberately. "First, let's wait a few days. That will give her more time to recover. And even if it seems useless, I think you should stay with her as much as possible during that time, to talk to her. Only on the basis of everything you represent can she pick up the thread of her life again. However . . ."

Johanna looked up nervously.

". . . If we don't see any improvement in a week or two, we'll have to think of having her treated. There's a place with a good reputation, in Pirna . . ."

Johanna reacted violently.

"Sonnenstein Haus?"

He seemed surprised.

"Yes."

"That's an insane asylum! They won't let me stay with her, and . . ."

Her voice broke. Heinz, who had just come out of the barn, looked at her uneasily. Kerbratt took her by the arm and began walking with her along the lane that led away from the courtyard, trying to calm her.

"We haven't come to that yet," he said, "and I hope we never will. For now, though, I'd like her to see a doctor. I have to bring one anyway, for Franz—he wouldn't have slept at all last night if I hadn't given him sedatives. Unfortunately there are no doctors available in either Freiberg or Dippoldiswalde. They've all been called into government service. But there's an old-fashioned doctor I used to know near Freiberg.

He might not have been sent to Dresden, because of his age. But maybe he went there of his own accord. I'll find out this afternoon."

"You can ride my bicycle," she offered.

He smiled.

"And how will I bring old Dr. Wildgrüber back, if I can find him? On the baggage rack?"

Johanna laughed and suddenly felt better. They had reached the end of the lane. Beyond the little road to the village, the vast, empty, white sky glowed dimly. It seemed impossible that this same sky could have been so terrifying such a short time ago. Kerbratt was looking out over the plain, where the swirling black smoke above the city seemed so close that for a moment it seemed the forest might be burning.

He turned to her.

"Since we've come here, I'll tell you what the others already know: if you want to take a walk, alone or with your mother, you mustn't go any farther than this gate. It's a matter of group discipline as well as security. Will you promise me that?"

"Yes, of course."

He opened the gate and took a few steps on the road.

"I want to go to a place where we can see the city," he said gloomily.

He walked slowly and laboriously, clutching his cane, with Johanna beside him. After a few moments they stopped. The city was visible through a gap in the hills. He raised his binoculars.

"The Frauenkirche!" he exclaimed. "It's collapsed! When I saw it still standing, yesterday, I thought it was too good to be true."

Pale and silent, he lowered his binoculars and started back toward the house.

"You poor child," he said softly. "Growing up among ruins, how will you ever find beauty and love?"

"My future is my mother. If she becomes herself again, I'll be all right. If not, we're both done for."

"Done for? But you're just beginning, Johanna. Think of all the things you still have to see and experience."

"There are two things I'd like to see," Johanna admitted. "A Gary Cooper film, and the sea."

"Gary Cooper!" Kerbratt exclaimed. "Don't you realize it was Gary Cooper who nearly killed you yesterday morning?"

She stared at him, open-mouthed, remembering the white stars on the wings of the plane. Maybe the pilot had the same narrowed eyes as Gary Cooper gazing at far-off mountains, as she had seen him in posters.

They reached the gate. Kerbratt opened it and they started along the lane.

"As for the sea," he said, "unlike you, I've seen too much of it." He nervously tapped his cane against his stiff leg. "Till 1942 I was an officer in a submarine. Not bad for a musician, eh? I suppose it illustrates the principle of making the best use of everyone's abilities."

The house came into sight. It now seemed as peaceful and reassuring as it had seemed sinister and oppressive the night before. Kerbratt stopped and looked up at the second floor.

"I'm going up to see Leni," he said. "Let me be alone with her. She may react differently with someone who doesn't belong to her family. It's worth a try."

Johanna stared at him. He had called her mother by her first name.

The courtyard and the first floor of the house were noisy with talk and games and chores, but she didn't feel like meeting any of the other children. Not now. She slipped past them and up the stairs, hoping no one had noticed her. On the second floor she walked to the door farthest from the stairs, the one to which she believed the stretcher had been carried the night before. She listened, but heard only Kerbratt's muffled voice from the other end of the hall.

She silently opened the door and stood on the threshold, amazed at her own boldness. Franz was lying on a bed near the window, asleep. A small bedside table held bandages and ointments. She was about to leave when he turned his head.

"Cora?" he asked.

"No," she said timidly, "it's only me, the girl who saw you go by last night when they were taking you to your room."

She couldn't see him very well but she was afraid to come closer. He raised himself a little.

"You're not in the choir."

"No," she said. "Herr Kerbratt invited my mother and me to stay here awhile."

"Did he see you come in here?" he asked uneasily. His forehead was glistening with sweat.

She shook her head.

"He doesn't want me to talk," he explained.

"That's all right, I'm used to it," she said quickly. "My mother doesn't talk either. She hasn't said anything since night before last."

She sat down on a chair not far from the bedside table, where she could see him better. He looked at her with big, feverish eyes. His dark, bushy eyebrows came together over his nose, hardening his long, thin face. His dark hair hung down over his forehead. Johanna resisted an impulse to push it back for him. He seemed less handsome than when she had seen him in the flickering light of the lantern the night before. Then he had been the Assyrian prince in her father's book; now he was a pale, haggard adolescent boy with a damp forehead. For a moment she resented his failure to live up to her fantasy.

"I think I frightened you last night," she said.

"No, you didn't."

"Yes, I did. I could tell from the look on your face."

"Well, I wasn't expecting . . ."

He slid down into his original position. His profile was handsome with the light behind it, she thought. But his stern, joined eyebrows still made him look somber, even a little scornful.

"What's your name?" he asked.

"Johanna."

"How old are you?"

"Twelve and a half. How old are you, Franz?"

His eyes widened in surprise.

"You know my name!"

"Yes," she murmured.

"I'm fifteen," he told her, still seeming surprised.

She leaned closer.

"When I saw you last night . . ."

She stopped short. He patiently waited for her to go on.

"My father was an archaeologist and he used to show me pictures in books that told about his work. When I saw you on your stretcher with your lantern, you looked like one of the young warriors from three thousand years ago. You seemed to have come right out of one of those pictures my father showed me. But not anymore, of course, now that I see you in daylight," she added matter-of-factly.

Franz seemed disappointed.

"In daylight I don't remind you of anything?"

She shrugged.

"I've made you talk too much. I just wanted to pay you a little visit. I'll leave now, before your Cora comes."

"What do you mean, *my* Cora?"

"When I came in you asked me if I was Cora, so you must have been expecting her."

"If you want to know the truth, Cora dropped me when she heard I'd been shot in the leg. That's how women are: as soon as you get something wrong with you . . ."

There was a silence. Johanna felt embarrassed. She stood up and moved toward the door.

"I'll come back," she said.

He looked at her imploringly.

"Why are you leaving?"

"I'm tiring you by making you talk. You said Herr Kerbratt didn't want you to talk."

"Don't worry about that. I get scared when I'm alone. I think about my leg . . ." He sighed. "Do you want to see it?"

He pulled up the sheet and laboriously rolled onto his stomach. Johanna forced herself to look. The dark stain that showed through the bandages covering his leg was alarmingly large. Franz watched her out of the corner of his eye.

"A vet at the zoo bandaged it for me," he said. "We were lucky to find him."

"Does it hurt?"

"No. Just a twinge now and then."

"The same plane . . . The same plane almost did the same thing to me."

"Really?"

He rolled onto his back again, grimacing.

"I saw it when it separated from the others and flew low over the part of the park where I'd seen Herr Kerbratt and the rest of you. I heard it shooting, and I was hoping you were all gone. A few minutes later it dived at me. I barely had time to get behind a little wall. I saw where the bullets made holes in the pavement—if they'd hit me, they'd have cut me in half."

"I wasn't so lucky: it didn't miss me," Franz said bitterly. "In a way, though, I guess it did. . . . The vet said that if the bullet had hit the bone in my leg, the shock would probably have killed me."

"You're talking too much," she said, pulling the sheet back down over his legs. "You're getting tired."

"But I want to talk about it." He passed his hand through his hair. "It felt like a bomb had exploded in my leg. Then I blacked out. You know the first thing I remember, afterward? Waking up with my mouth full of dirt. I don't remember how my leg felt, or anything else except the dirt in my mouth. That's funny, isn't it?"

"I suppose so," she said.

She sat down again on the chair near his bed.

"As long as you're here, you may as well make yourself useful. Will you give me a glass of water?"

"Why? Do you still have dirt in your mouth?"

He laughed.

"You're needling me!"

She filled a glass and handed it to him. He drank thirstily.

"Not so fast," she cautioned him. "My mother says when you have a fever, you mustn't drown it."

"I thought she didn't talk."

"Now *you're* needling *me!*"

He timidly laid his hand on her arm.

"I'm glad you're here," he said. "I hope you'll stay a long time. Maybe you could join the choir."

"Grete used to say my singing was worse than an air-raid siren."

"Grete?"

"My sister. She died night before last."

"Oh, I'm sorry. Is that why your mother . . ."

"Yes."

"Maybe your sister was wrong," he said. "Sing something."

"You'll make fun of me."

"No, I won't."

She hesitated, then began singing a little lullaby.

"It's the only song I know," she said apologetically when she had finished.

"I have to admit it wasn't all that good," he acknowledged.

"You can't say I didn't warn you." She was touched to see how disappointed he looked. "Maybe I'll be able to stay, even though I can't sing, since Herr Kerbratt seems willing to have us."

He squeezed her hand, and she could feel his fever.

"Anyway," he said, "why would anyone feel like singing these days?"

In the hall everything was calm. She stood on tiptoe to look through a little window and saw the forest shrouded in fog. It was raining, and for a long time she stood in the shadowy hallway, listening to the soothing sound of dripping water. Even the muffled noises from Rosi's kitchen gave her a good feeling. It was as if everything she had recently gone through were being dissolved in the fog.

But then she started. The door of Leni's room had swung open, and a figure slipped into the hall. It was Kerbratt. She thought he had left long ago. She nearly called out to him, but something cautious in his movements dissuaded her. Standing in the semidarkness, she watched him start down the stairs.

After a few moments, she went to her mother's room and gently opened the door.

Leni was lying on her stomach with her arm hanging over

the side of the bed. When Johanna touched her on the shoulder, she sighed softly, as if she had just awakened from a deep sleep.

"You aren't sleeping at eleven in the morning, are you?" Johanna asked. "If you are, it's time to get up!"

Leni sat up in bed and began biting her fingernails, staring vacantly into space. Johanna had often seen her do this when she was thinking about a problem.

"It's raining," Johanna said, "otherwise I'd have taken you out for a walk." After a brief silence she asked, "Herr Kerbratt came to see you?"

"Herr Kerbratt," Leni repeated.

"Yes, the tall, thin man who walks with a limp. This is his house! He came to see you?"

Leni didn't answer. "He recognized our name as soon as I told him, because he knew who Papa was," Johanna went on.

She sat down beside her mother and watched her face for any sign of interest.

"He's the director of a famous children's choir, the Kreuzkirche choir. They're all here, so you'll have plenty of people around. Everyone will be nice to you. And when you're feeling better, we'll go back to the city and start rebuilding the house."

She realized that it had now become almost natural for her to speak to her mother slowly and distinctly, as if she were a small child.

"Bringing you here was a good idea, wasn't it, Mutti? You didn't want to come, remember? It was a good idea I had, wasn't it?"

She put her arms around Leni.

"Oh!" she exclaimed. "I forgot to bring your coffee! I'll go and get some for you right now. And you don't have to go downstairs; I'll bring you your lunch."

"Herr Kerbratt," Leni said tonelessly.

"Herr Kerbratt brought you coffee?" Johanna asked.

Leni wrinkled her forehead as if searching for an answer that eluded her.

The sound of singing wafted in from outside. Johanna went

to the window but saw no one. The sun was shining now, driving away the fog. She drummed her fingers on the windowpane, then went downstairs.

In the courtyard she passed the tall blond boy with whom Kerbratt had been talking earlier that morning. He was leading a horse back from the watering trough. When he saw Johanna he waved. She tried to think of his name and remembered it too late to call him by it. Heinz.

She traced the singing to the barn. Suddenly it stopped and the children came spilling out as if they were leaving a classroom. Kerbratt followed, walking slowly, looking preoccupied. He was talking with a red-haired boy Johanna hadn't seen before.

"Thank you, Berndt," she heard him say. "I think they're feeling more comfortable now."

"Herr Kerbratt," she said, pointing up at Leni's window. "I just wanted to know . . . How was she when you saw her?"

He looked at her in a way that seemed slightly disapproving.

"She was exactly as you described her," he answered.

She stood there feeling awkward and confused.

"I'm going to Freiberg now," he continued in a friendlier tone, "to try to find old Wildgrüber, the doctor I told you about. He'll examine your mother after he's seen Franz."

"He won't try to separate me from her, will he?"

Johanna looked troubled. Kerbratt put his hand on her shoulder.

"You know you can stay here as long as you want, don't you? Haven't I told you that?"

"But what about her?" she asked, her voice quavering. "He'll say she has to be taken away and treated in a hospital." Tears came into her eyes. "She was so full of life! She used to laugh all the time. And she talked—she talked *a lot*."

"You have to understand, Johanna. You'll stay with her only if it's good for her."

"It *will* be good for her!" she exclaimed.

"But I wonder . . ." He seemed a little embarrassed. "You've told me you look like your father. Did he and your mother get along?"

"She loved him very much. He died in northern France, in May, 1940. I even know the name of the place: Seuguelise. My mother didn't talk for several days."

"Was she the way she is now?"

"No, she acted normally in every other way. She just didn't feel like talking. Then she gradually started talking again, and laughing, and finally she was the same as before. And she not only loved my father," Johanna added defiantly, "she loved *me* too."

"I never meant to say she didn't. But you said she felt closer to Grete. I'm not trying to hurt you, but to understand your mother's condition I need to know her feelings toward you and Grete. The fact that you survived, miraculously, should have consoled her a little."

"She had the shock of Grete's death before she knew I was still alive. When I came home, she was already . . . the way she is now."

"And later," he asked abruptly, "did your mother ever say anything about . . . I don't know, about going after the war to visit . . . that place you mentioned, Seuguelise?"

Johanna thought for a moment, then shook her head.

"I liked to remember my father," she said. "He always used to say he'd take me to the places he went to, and let me see all the things he showed me in books." She paused, then went on as though talking to herself, "But my mother . . . No, I can't say she talked about him very much."

Kerbratt looked at her thoughtfully and led her back toward the house.

As she slipped into Franz's room she heard the wagon leaving the courtyard, pulled by the horses at a leisurely pace. She was sure no one had seen her. She went straight to the bed, fell to her knees and pressed her face against the sheets.

"What's the matter?" Franz asked.

She looked at him, tears streaming down her cheeks.

"I'm afraid. He went to get a doctor. They're going to take her away from me. If they take her away, I'll go with her. I'll be crazy too, if I have too."

"You can be sure Kerbratt will do what's best," Franz said, trying to calm her. "He's someone you can count on. By the way," he added, pointing to the steaming bowl on the bed-side table, "thanks for the bouillon. I hear you told Rosi it would be good for me. I thought you weren't supposed to drown a fever."

"But my mother also used to say . . ."

"Listen," he interrupted, "I don't care what your mother used to say. From looking at you, I wouldn't be surprised if bouillon was all you ever ate, but I'd rather have real food, if it's all right with you."

"Am I really that thin?" she asked.

He examined her, a look of pity on his face.

"You have to admit you don't have much of a shape."

"Have you ever seen a girl who had a shape when she was twelve? Grete was fourteen and her chest was as flat as mine."

"That's a shame," Franz said nonchalantly. "I like girls with some meat on their bones."

In the air above the bed he drew a big, rounded form, broad as a horse's rump, while she watched in disbelief.

"And you want me to be like that?" she cried, suddenly furious. "You're horrible! You're disgusting! Now I know why the others don't come to see you! I don't know why I'm stupid enough to listen to you!"

"I'm fifteen—I'm supposed to be interested in such things," he said blandly, settling himself back against his pillow.

"Then take one of those girls downstairs! I saw some at least as old as you, fat and pink, the way you like them!"

Johanna's voice had become shrill. All at once she was beginning to hate Franz. She stood up and walked toward the door.

"But they don't have a face like yours," he said.

She opened the door.

"Johanna!" he called out.

She stopped and turned around. He was even paler than when she had come in.

"Please come back, Johanna."

"Why? Since I don't interest you . . ."

"Stop being so touchy," he said wearily. "Till now, you were nice to me."

"I thought you liked me," she said. "I liked you, anyway."

He looked at her intensely.

"Come here and sit down. Not on the chair, on the bed."

She moved closer to him, but guardedly.

"You're not going to kiss me, are you?" she asked anxiously.

"Who said anything about that?"

"Nobody, but you look the way a boy looks when he wants to kiss a girl."

"So you've had a lot of experience?"

"Grete told me about it. There was a boy who used to come by for her at school. Whenever he wanted to kiss her, he just asked, 'May I?' Grete knew right away what he meant. That was in the beginning. Later, he didn't even ask."

"May I, Johanna?" Franz asked ironically.

"No," she answered, shaking her head vigorously.

He laughed.

"Maybe your sister's boyfriend would have liked something else."

"What are you talking about?"

"Can't you guess?"

She was speechless for a moment, then cried out, "Grete would never have done *that!*"

"How do you know? I'm sure she would have at least liked to be tickled a little."

Johanna's eyes opened wide.

"Tickled?"

He took her hand.

"Do you want me to show you?"

"No!" she exclaimed, jerking her hand away from him.

"I won't hurt you, I'll just show you what I mean. And then

some day . . . But I haven't known you long enough for that."

Her eyes grew larger.

"What will you do some day?"

"I'll tickle you till you scream," he said in a throaty voice.

She stepped back.

"You must be out of your mind! Is it because of your fever, or what?"

"What's the matter?" he asked innocently.

"I don't want you to say things like that to me. After all, I've only known you a few hours."

"You're right," he said scornfully, "and I should have known better than to ask a little girl to let me kiss her, as if she were old enough to know what I was talking about."

They faced each other in silence for a few moments.

"Franz . . ." she said.

"Yes?"

"Have you had many . . . affairs with girls?"

"Of course," he answered without hesitation. "Very many, in fact, now that I think of it."

"You're not exaggerating, are you?"

"No, it's true. I've really had a lot."

"And did you have an affair with Cora?"

"Don't talk so loud," he said softly. "Cora is supposed to bring me my lunch. Just imagine the scene she'd make if she heard me telling you about her when she came in."

"Franz . . ."

"Here it comes! Another question!"

"I'm sure you can answer this one."

"All right, go ahead," he said, looking exasperated.

"Is it true," she whispered, "that people take off all their clothes together when they're madly in love with each other? That's what someone told Charlotte, a friend of mine at school."

Franz fidgeted nervously on the bed.

"I'm not the one who should tell you about that. . . ."

"Then you don't know as much as I thought!"

He shrugged.

"Ask your mother. *She's* the one who should tell you about those things."

Johanna turned pale.

"But she can't . . ."

"Oh, I'm sorry! I forgot."

"There's no one I can ask about anything now," she said gravely. "No one but you."

She moved toward him and kissed him impulsively on the forehead. He started and clutched his wounded thigh.

"Did you have a twinge?" she asked anxiously.

He grimaced.

"A twinge? What makes you say that?"

"You said you sometimes got twinges, the first time I came to see you."

"I didn't expect you to kiss me, after all that."

She was still leaning down, her face close to his. She tried to seem calm in spite of the panic—and the joy—she was feeling.

"You look like a little poodle," he said.

"And you look like a . . . a . . ."

"I know, you've already told me: I look like a warrior three thousand years old!"

She laughed and sat down on the chair.

"That's the way I like to see you: smiling," he said. "Do you have any Gypsy blood?"

She looked at him in surprise.

"No."

"Or Jewish blood?"

She shook her head.

"My mother would have told me."

"But you're not like the girls from around here. You're dark, and your hair is curly."

"I look like my father, but Grete was blond, like my mother."

He was thoughtful for a moment.

"Would you tell me if you were Jewish, even just a little bit Jewish?"

"Of course."

"Even if you knew it might get you sent to a concentration camp?"

"I trust you," she said seriously, and she added, "Franz, what's a concentration camp, exactly?"

"You don't know? Your mother never told you about them?"

"No."

"Then how did you know there was such a thing?"

"I didn't, till I heard about them from a woman I met on the road yesterday. And now you."

"A concentration camp is a place guarded by SS men and surrounded by barbed wire and watchtowers. They put prisoners from other countries in them, and Germans who aren't Nazis and don't like Hitler, and Jews. And they leave them all there till they die."

"How do you know that?"

"My father told me. I have to explain something to you." He lowered his voice. "I have Jewish blood. My father's mother was Jewish. I haven't told anyone here but you."

"But you don't really know me!"

"I *feel* I can trust you," he said dramatically. Then he seemed suddenly seized with fear. "You won't tell anyone, will you? If my leg got worse and I had to leave here, no hospital would take me if they knew."

Johanna was dismayed. She had no clear idea of what a Jew was. As far as she could remember, there had never been any Jews in her class, except for Elke Abramowitz, three years ago, and she hadn't known her very well. One day Elke hadn't come to school and Frau Spitzer had said she was now in a private school in Hanover. Johanna tried to remember her face.

"I'll take care of you," she said.

She leaned toward him and kissed him blindly, not knowing which part of his face her lips would touch. It was his nose.

"You can do better than that," he said.

She kissed him on the cheek.

"You're hot!" she exclaimed.

He laid his head back on the pillow.

"Does Herr Kerbratt know . . . what you told me?" she asked.

"Yes, but he's the only one. Rosi doesn't know."

"Or Cora?"

"Forget about Cora, will you? I don't care about her! You and Kerbratt are the only ones who know. I think it's because of . . . my secret that he wanted to get me out of the city as soon as possible."

"Franz . . . The concentration camps, the Jews, all that—is that why we've been bombed?"

"Yes. You can't say we didn't ask for it."

"That woman I met on the road said almost the same thing."

"We've slaughtered people all over the place, in countries that didn't want any trouble with us: Czechoslovakia, Poland, Russia, France. Now we're getting a dose of what we gave them. It had to happen sooner or later."

She looked at Franz and scrutinized his profile. She liked looking at people in profile, without their knowing it. Free from the obligation to compose an expression, they let you see them as they really were. Only Hella had been impossible to look at that way: she always knew when someone's eyes were on her. Even when Johanna looked at her from behind, she always turned around.

"Who's Hella?" Franz asked.

Johanna stared at him, puzzled.

"How do you know about her?"

"You just said, 'Hella.' "

Before she could answer, they heard laughter and footsteps on the stairs. He grimaced.

"Here come the foolish virgins," he announced.

There was a knock on the door, then two blond girls burst into the room. One of them carried a plate of sausages and cabbage. When she had put it down on the bedside table, they both kissed Franz warmly.

"How are things going downstairs?" he asked. "It's amazing how fast everybody forgot about me when I came up here."

"We knew you had a visitor," one of the girls replied, "and we didn't want to interrupt anything."

The other girl turned to Johanna.

"By the way," she said disdainfully, "your mother is downstairs. She's sitting under the staircase, waiting for you."

"And she's not very talkative," the first girl said, laughing. They both left. Johanna stood up, pale.

"I told her . . . told her I'd bring her lunch upstairs. I didn't want . . ."

"Don't worry about those two," Franz said with gruff tenderness. "You could look all over the world and never find anyone more stupid than they are."

FOUR

he children were seated around the big table, on which a huge soup tureen had already been placed. When Johanna appeared on the stairs, all conversation stopped and she felt fifteen pairs of eyes staring at her. Rosi wasn't there. Feeling weak in the knees, she looked around for Leni and spotted her in a polished wooden armchair, half hidden under the stairs, like an owl perched in the hollow of a tree.

"I told you I'd bring you lunch," she whispered reproachfully in her ear.

Just then Rosi pushed open the door with her foot and came in carrying a big platter of sausages. She put the platter down in the middle of the table, turned to Johanna and pointed to two places on the bench, next to her.

"This is Johanna and her mother," she announced. "Their house was bombed and they'll stay with us till they can get back to it." Then she added, in a tone of commiseration that struck Johanna as somewhat false, "Come, my poor dears."

Johanna helped Leni slide along the bench, then sat beside

her. Rosi put sausages and cabbage on their plates. When she
leaned down to serve her, Johanna felt soothed by the fresh
smell of her clean dress and apron.

Conversation around the table had gradually resumed, but
the children didn't question Johanna or even look at her. She
preferred it that way. They referred to the bombing only in
brief, almost innocuous remarks, as though they wanted to
keep it buried inside themselves.

Leni wasn't eating. Instead, she sat looking fixedly at a
boy across the table from her. He was about ten, with a thin
face and tousled hair. Surprised at being the object of such
attention, he kept looking back at her, holding his spoon in
midair.

"Eat, Stefan," Rosi finally admonished him. "Don't let
your food get cold."

Johanna inwardly translated Rosi's words: "Eat, Leni, or
that boy will never finish his lunch."

"You must eat too, Mutti," she said imploringly. "If you
don't, you'll get sick."

Leni didn't respond. Through a kind of fog, Johanna saw
the two blond girls who had come into Franz's room walk out
of the kitchen, sit down at the end of the table and begin
pointing at her and whispering. Rosi stood up to take away the
empty platter and soup tureen.

"Please eat, Mutti," Johanna whispered. "Don't you see
that everybody's looking at us?"

Someone laughed and Johanna felt tears of rage welling up
in her eyes.

"Your mother still isn't eating," one of the blond girls at the
end of the table called out to her.

"Never mind about my mother!" she retorted sharply.

"Somebody who has a mother like that should at least pay
attention to her," the blond girl said.

Johanna felt herself turn crimson. Her eyes blurred and the
bite of sausage she had just eaten stuck in her throat. She
stood up and hurried outside. When she reached the wall of
the barn her legs gave way. She fell to her knees and burst out
sobbing. *Mutti! That's how they talk about you now! But you used
to get along so well with children. The girls in my class always asked*

me about you. Hella loved you. . . . If you were your old self, those idiots wouldn't talk about you that way.

"Don't be sad," a voice said behind her. "Cora didn't realize . . . She's not all that bad. She didn't know your house had been bombed. She was in the kitchen when Rosi told us."

Johanna turned around, her cheeks glistening with tears. The girl who had spoken was about her age. She had a round face, blond braids and a few freckles on her nose. Because of the freckles and the braids, she looked a little like Hella.

Johanna wiped her face with her handkerchief.

"What . . . what's your name?" she asked after a silence.

"Annette."

Johanna stood up and went over to sit on one of the low stone posts beside the barn door. *If she doesn't eat, I know what will happen. He won't let her stay here.*

"Is it true," Annette asked quietly, "that when you found your mother she'd been sitting up all night with your sister's body?"

Johanna didn't answer.

"Rosi told us about it after you left. Cora didn't know that, either."

"I'm sorry, and I apologize," said another voice.

Johanna looked up. Cora was shifting her weight from one foot to the other, looking down at the ground. Her cheeks, her breasts and her thighs were all plump and round. No wonder Franz liked her.

"It doesn't matter," Johanna said despondently. "He's not going to keep us. . . . The doctor will have my mother taken away from here."

"I came to tell you that she finally ate a little," said Cora.

Johanna brightened.

"After you left," Cora went on, "Stefan stood up and held out a spoonful of sauerkraut to her. She ate it, then she ate another spoonful, and then she went on eating by herself."

Johanna was mortified. Leni had been fed by a child in front of everyone! Cora stepped closer and awkwardly put her arms around her. She smelled of sweat and hay.

"Well, I have to go now," she said. "I've got dishes to wash."

As she walked away Johanna watched her graceless gait.

"You see? I told you she's not all bad," said Annette.

Johanna looked at her, then quickly turned her eyes away.

"What's the matter?" asked Annette. "You've got a funny look on your face."

"Nothing. It's just that you remind me a little of my best friend. You have braids like her. . . ."

"But practically every girl I know has braids!" Annette said with surprise. "You're one of the few exceptions," she added, smiling.

Side by side, they walked back to the house.

"You can introduce me to your friend when we go back to the city," Annette said, "and I'll see if I think she looks like me."

"She was killed in the bombing. I saw it happen. We'd gone to the circus together."

Annette turned pale and stopped in her tracks.

"What was your friend's name?"

Johanna shook her head and went into the house without answering. The children were clearing the table. Rosi and Cora could be heard talking in the kitchen.

"She went back there," a little girl said, pointing to the narrow recess under the stairs.

Stefan sat on a nearby stool and was trying to make Leni talk to him.

"Come, Mutti," Johanna insisted, "let's go back up to your room. You'll be more comfortable there."

Leni suddenly pointed to Annette and her eyes opened wide.

"Hella!" she cried out with a mixture of surprise and joy.

Annette paled.

"Was . . . was that your friend's name?" she stammered.

Johanna knelt at Leni's feet.

"Mutti, you know Hella is dead. I told you. And I nearly died with her."

"Hella," Leni repeated dully, keeping her eyes on Annette.

"No, she's not Hella! She's Annette, a new friend of mine, and she's very nice."

"Hella!" Leni called out again.

"Please take her away," Annette said to Johanna. "I'm sorry, but she frightens me."

Johanna led Leni to the foot of the stairs. Leni turned around to look at Annette, before mechanically climbing up to her room.

"No, I really don't think it's a pretty name," said Annette. "Ploetz. Especially for a violinist."

"On posters, you mean?"

"Yes. Annette Ploetz. Can you imagine? . . . Anyway, I don't know if I'll go on playing," she said dejectedly. "I had a good violin, an old one. It had such a beautiful tone that it brought out the best in me. But it was burned, along with all the other instruments in the storeroom of the Kreuzkirche, next to the vestry. Herr Kerbratt just told me."

She sighed, then took up her imaginary violin and began to play it. Johanna watched her, fascinated. It was as if Annette's long, slender fingers had a life of their own.

"Did everyone in the choir play an instrument, besides singing?" asked Johanna.

"No, not everyone, but many of us. Herr Kerbratt believed it was good training. He set up a little conservatory. Franz, for example, played the clarinet."

"How old were you when you started?"

Annette smiled.

"I was about four. One day I saw my father listening to a Kreisler record. I still remember everything: the light in the room, the way he was leaning toward the phonograph, how happy I felt. Later I kept telling my father how much I wanted a violin, till he finally bought me one."

Annette felt silent.

"What's the matter?" Johanna asked.

"I shouldn't complain to you, since you've lost everything. But I can't believe my violin is really gone. It's a terrible thing, for a musician, not to have an instrument. It takes a long time to get used to a new violin."

"You'll get another one, I'm sure," Johanna said confidently. "I'll come to hear you play, and applaud louder than anyone. And I think your name will look very good on posters."

"It's not time to worry about posters yet!" said Annette, laughing. Then she became serious. "I feel like you and I are already friends, Johanna. And do you know what I think? Maybe, from where she is, your friend saw you were lonely and sent me to you."

"Where is she . . . I wish I could at least be sure she didn't suffer, but really it must have been . . . Oh. . . ."

Johanna moaned, startling Leni, who sat up in bed.

"I'm sorry," Annette said. "It was stupid of me to mention that."

"Where is she . . . Where is she . . . And where do you think my mother is, right now?"

"If only we knew what she *sees*," Annette said.

Johanna nodded sadly.

"One thing is sure," Annette went on, "having your mother in this condition is better than not having her at all."

"Is your mother dead?" Johanna asked.

"She was killed in a car accident in 1937. I've never gotten over it."

"And your father was drafted anyway?"

"Yes. The last letter I got from him was in December. He was in the Ardennes, with von Luettwitz. Since then, I haven't heard anything from him. But if I lose him," Annette continued, as though talking to herself, "it won't be as bad as losing my mother. I've never seen him very much."

"But he gave you the violin," Johanna said softly.

They were both silent for a moment, then Annette said, "It was because I don't have my mother that Herr Kerbratt kept me as a boarder and lent me the other violin, the good one. Otherwise I'd have gone home long ago."

"And we would never have known each other."

Annette smiled weakly.

"That's true of everyone here: you'll get to know them because they had to stay."

"Were they sad at having to stay in Dresden?"

"Oh, no! We liked it there, right up to the end. We had the

reputation of being the best children's choir in Germany. And we liked Kerbratt, too. It was lucky, in a way, that he got wounded soon after he left and was able to come back."

"Do you know how it happened?"

"He was on a submarine and I think a torpedo tube blew up when he was standing close to it. He never talks about it." Annette paused, then said, "There used to be sixty of us. I really liked some of them. I don't even know what's become of them. . . . We're paying for something we didn't do. By 'we' I mean people our age, and even little children. You, your poor friend, Franz, me—look at what's happened to us. We didn't deserve this."

"Franz told me . . ."

"I know what Franz thinks. He thinks we all had it coming. But he's wrong! Not *all* of us! People Kerbratt's age, or your mother's, can say to themselves, 'It's our own fault.' But it doesn't make sense for people *our* age to say that. We haven't done anything."

"Sometimes in school your whole class is punished, and even if you haven't done anything you still get the same punishment as everybody else."

"What I wanted," Annette said bitterly, ignoring Johanna's remark, "was to play the violin. I felt I was made for that, and only that. It was all I asked."

"Do you ever think about the time before the bombing?"

"It seems so far away, even though it was only two days ago."

"I mean *just* before the bombing. Our lives were about to change completely, but we didn't know it, nothing gave us any hint of it. I think that's strange, don't you? When we got up that morning, the last morning of our old lives, there should have been *something*, maybe . . . I don't know, maybe a different smell in the air, something that would at least have given us a little warning."

"What were you doing whan the air-raid sirens went off?"

"I was at the circus. And I was a little bored. I said to . . ."

"Don't say her name," Annette interrupted, with a quick look at Leni.

"My friend loved Mutti even more than her own mother,

and Mutti loved her too. She used to spend most of her time at our house. I'm sure you would have loved Mutti too, she was so cheerful and friendly."

Annette smiled sadly. Leni was facing the window as if she was listening to something. Moments later Johanna heard the gate open and the wagon roll along the lane. Then sounds of footsteps and voices came from the stairs. She held her breath. The footsteps passed in the hall and she heard the door of Franz's room being opened.

"Oh, Johanna," said Annette, "I hope they won't take him away!"

Twenty minutes later, Kerbratt came in without knocking.

"Johanna," he said brusquely, "Dr. Wildgrüber would like to see your mother now."

He stepped aside to let the old doctor come in. Bent forward by the weight of a wooden box hanging from his shoulder, and clutching it as if he was afraid someone might try to steal it from him, Dr. Wildgrüber wore a gray overcoat and a purple velvet hat that reminded Johanna of pictures of peddlers in village squares offering all sorts of wondrous objects for sale.

He took off his hat and bowed to Leni with comical slowness, revealing a half-bald head and a wrinkled face with watery blue eyes and a hooked nose. He went to the armchair beside the bed, grunted as he lowered himself into it, and looked at the two girls. They stood up.

"This is Johanna, Frau Seyfert's daughter," Kerbratt said, "and Annette Ploetz, my violinist." He turned to them. "And now, girls, please leave us."

But Johanna didn't move. Kerbratt came over to her. He seemed nervous and tired.

"Your mother may be more inclined to answer Dr. Wildgrüber's questions if you're not here," he said into Johanna's ear. "She mustn't feel you can answer for her."

"You know it won't make any difference," said Johanna.

"Don't you understand that we can't afford to neglect anything that might help?" he said irritably. Then he became stern. "And this morning you made Franz talk too much, with the result that he's now exhausted."

She turned pale.

"But he told me it made him feel better."

She walked toward the door, and Annette followed. On her way out, she saw the hunchbacked doctor leaning over Leni, like an old sorcerer trying to awaken a sleeping beauty. She and Annette waited in the hall. Now and then they heard the two men's voices. Johanna was able to make out only a few words at a time, some of which meant nothing to her: aphasia, traumatic, anorexia. Sometimes Dr. Wildgrüber asked a question and Kerbratt answered.

"I'm afraid. I'm afraid they won't let her stay here," Johanna said nervously.

A few moments later she frowned. She had just understood one of Kerbratt's answers distinctly: "No, her body shows no sign of injury. It's completely unmarked, like her face."

Annette moved closer to her and whispered, "How does he know?"

Johanna motioned her to keep quiet and tried to hear more, but the two men had stopped talking.

Annette led her away.

"There's no use letting them find us here when they come out," she said.

They slowly started down the stairs.

"If your mother wasn't hurt in the bombing," Annette said, "it means her trouble is all in her mind. She must have really loved your sister. Do you think she'd be the same way if you'd been killed instead?"

Johanna felt the blood drain from her face.

"How should I know?" she said, clutching the banister.

Leni sat against the headboard of the bed, looking out at the tops of the wet fir trees. A gentle rain was falling.

"What did the old doctor say?" asked Johanna. "He doesn't want to take you away, does he?"

Leni turned to look at her in silence, evidently sorry to give up her contemplation of the firs.

"He came to take care of Franz," Johanna went on. "Franz is one of the boys in the choir. He was hit by a bullet yesterday morning. He seems to like me."

Leni turned back to the firs. Johanna stepped closer to the bed.

"You don't care about anything I say, do you? You're not interested in hearing that someone likes me!"

She felt an urge to attack Leni, to make her even more distressed than she already was.

"Mutti, how does Kerbratt know there are no signs of injury on your body?" she said, speaking softly but vehemently. "Tell me! What was he doing when he was alone with you all that time this morning? I saw him come out."

The gray light from the window accentuated the blankness of Leni's expression. Johanna's voice rose almost to a shout.

"Tell me what happened! Tell me! Did he undress you?"

The question had slipped out against her will. She stopped to listen, afraid she might have been overheard. But there was no sound from the hall. She leaned down till her face was almost touching Leni's.

"You take an interest in what's being said when Kerbratt or Annette is here, but when I'm alone with you it's as if you were all by yourself! If *I'd* been killed the other night, instead of Grete, you'd still be talking and laughing the same as before, wouldn't you?"

"Grete," Leni said dully.

"That's right, Grete is dead! You'll never see her again! You hear? You'll never see her again!"

Leni slowly hunched forward, and stayed that way, her head bowed. It was the same position in which Johanna had found Grete, only Leni's hair hadn't fallen away from the back of her neck, as Grete's had. Johanna's anger vanished.

She took Leni's head between her hands and gently pushed it back. Tears flowed steadily along the wrinkles on either side of Leni's mouth. How deep those wrinkles had become! Johanna covered her mother's face with kisses, eager to taste her tears, as if they could somehow make it possible for her to understand.

When Johanna left the room she restrained herself from going to see Franz again, because of what Kerbratt had said. She could hear his voice downstairs, sarcastic and irritated, along with Rosi's and the doctor's. It seemed to her that there had been an evil feeling in the house ever since the doctor had come. She must let him know that Leni had reacted, that she wasn't always inert. Mayhe then he would decide not to take her away.

Downstairs Johanna saw Kerbratt and the two others leaning over a big map crisscrossed by colored lines. They stopped talking as soon as she came in. She knew she was disturbing them, but she decided to speak before they could say anything.

"She suddenly started crying," she announced.

In the candlelight, the doctor's bald head gleamed like polished ivory.

"Did you say something she didn't like?" he asked gently.

"I mentioned Grete, my sister, by mistake."

"That was clever," Kerbratt remarked caustically.

"First you tire Franz, then you get your mother all worked up," Rosi said. "You'd better get a grip on yourself, Johanna."

The doctor hesitated, then said, "I'll go up and see her."

"You don't have to," said Johanna. "She's not crying anymore. Now she's the same as she was before. I just wanted you to know."

He nodded. "It's a good sign. There was a break in her mind, but if she cries it means she remembers. And if she remembers, she can recover."

"But it's the memory of what happened that makes her the way she is!" Rosi objected.

"It's an anchorage," the old man said mysteriously. "Maybe we can go from there to solid ground."

"All right, now leave us," Kerbratt said to Johanna, drumming his fingers on the map. "And let your mother get some rest."

Johanna avoided his eyes.

"She'll stay here, won't she?" she asked the doctor, almost in a whisper.

He gave her a kindly look.

"Yes," he answered. "For the time being, at least."

Relieved, Johanna ran up the stairs and quietly went into her mother's room. Leni had sunk further into her bleak sadness. Johanna sat down beside her and hugged her.

"We're staying here," she said in her ear. "Together! Isn't that wonderful?"

"I mean it, Hans," Rosi said as soon as Johanna had left the room. "If it's really true, we have to get out of here as soon as we can. Think of our girls. . . ."

Chewing on a pencil, Kerbratt scowled at the doctor, then turned to Rosi.

"Do you want us to start off with eighteen children, including one who's wounded, and just wander along roads full of refugees? Are you crazy?"

"No, thank goodness," she retorted. "We already have one crazy woman here, and that's enough."

"Never say anything like that again!" Kerbratt snapped, glancing toward the stairs. "What if Johanna had heard you?"

"Do you think she doesn't know?"

"Let's try to talk calmly," Dr. Wildgrüber interrupted. "I didn't mean to upset you. I just wanted you to be on your guard."

Kerbratt leaned over the map.

"It's impossible, Wilfrid. You must have confused Czech with Russian. Here, look." He ran his finger along the penciled line that was farthest to the west. "Last week's army communiqué says that the front is at the Polish border. And according to Schörner it seems to have stabilized."

"Army communiqués!" Rosi exclaimed. "You still believe them?"

"If you go on talking like that, you'll wind up in Ravensbrück," Wildgrüber said, laughing unpleasantly.

Kerbratt moved a ruler across the map.

"Two hundred kilometers. They couldn't have made such a breakthrough. It's just not possible, Wilfrid."

The old doctor shook his head.

"It was Russian, Hans. I'm sure of it. I speak it fluently, as you know."

"I'll start packing tonight," said Rosi, standing up.

Kerbratt pounded on the table.

"You'll do as I say! Sit down! I'm the one who makes the decisions here."

Rosi sat down, looking sullen.

"I don't understand you," she said. "He's given you all the details—the time, the exact place. What else do you want?"

Kerbratt slowly folded up his map, took his cane and walked out without answering, followed by Dr. Wildgrüber.

"You should have talked to me alone," Kerbratt said as Wildgrüber was about to climb onto the footboard of his wagon. "Rosi is going to give me more trouble than all of Koniev's divisions put together."

Dr. Wildgrüber looked at him almost imploringly and said in a low voice, "But I *saw* them."

Johanna slipped into Franz's room, where he lay with his eyes half closed and his wounded leg on top of the covers.

"Why didn't you come sooner?" he asked reproachfully. "You weren't exactly in a big hurry to find out what the old charlatan said about me!"

"Herr Kerbratt didn't want me to come and see you. He said I made you talk too much this morning. And it's true—you look terrible. But I won't talk to you now. I'll just stay with you awhile."

"It doesn't matter," he said. "The doctor won't let me stay here. He's afraid of gangrene, and in spite of that big medicine chest he carries he didn't have any sulfa drugs. I'm supposed to leave for Freiberg tomorrow, to be treated. And maybe I'll go to Chemnitz afterward. There, now you know."

Johanna couldn't think of anything to say. The doctor had decided. Her mother was staying. Of course that was what mattered most. But Franz was going to leave.

"At least he put on a new bandage," she finally said, looking at his leg.

"Don't pretend to be interested," he said bitterly. "You'll forget me the minute I'm gone."

"Why do you say that?"

She sat down on the chair beside his bed.

"You haven't told anyone my secret, have you?"

"About your grandmother? Of course not. Anyway, who could I . . ."

"Like I told you, they wouldn't let me into a hospital if they knew."

She stood up from the chair and awkwardly sat down on the bed.

"But if they didn't let you into a hospital you'd come back here, and then I could be with you."

"You don't understand!" he said angrily. "I want to keep my leg! I don't want to be a cripple when I'm only fifteen!"

"Please, don't get excited. Kerbratt will say I'm making you tired again."

She went back to her chair and sat without speaking. She was even afraid to take his hand.

"I wouldn't have minded going away if I hadn't met you," Franz began hesitantly, as if he were ashamed of what he was about to say. "After all, I may as well get good medical treatment, and it won't take all that long. But what makes me sad is the thought of not seeing you again. You were just the girl I wanted to meet. I could at least tell myself that the bullet that hit me was good for something, since it brought us together."

She felt herself tremble.

"But you won't be gone very long, you just said so yourself. I'll still be here when you get back. We'll take walks together. I'll show you the barn in the village where I wanted to sleep when I couldn't find the way to this house."

"Do you know what I'll do during those walks?"

"No."

"I'll kiss you," he said.

She smiled sadly.

"When you say something like that, I don't really know how to act . . . I think you need someone much older than I am, who could do things I don't know how to do. You know, someone . . ."

Unable to think of the word she wanted, she raised her hand and drew a curve in space.

"I can get *that* whenever I want it," he said casually.

"Some day I'd like to be that for you, too."

He took her hand. Suddenly she wanted to guide his hand all over her body, and at the same time she knew she would never do such a thing.

"It seems to me that all the girls like you, including Annette," she said. "They do, don't they?"

He didn't answer and she was afraid to ask again.

"I'm glad you're dark, Johanna," he said abruptly, "and not like all those towheaded blonds. You make me feel that I finally have a girl who's more . . ."

"More what?"

"More . . . passionate."

"Passionate?" she asked, surprised. She was silent for a moment. "What do you mean by that?"

"A passionate woman is one who makes a man want to go off with her and . . . When I think of passionate women, I think of hot countries, bright sunlight. . . . Wouldn't you like to go and see the countries your father visited?" Excitement came into his voice. "I'd like to go there with you and get sunburned all over! I'm tired of fog!"

"Well, I'm sure of one thing: I don't want to go back to Dresden."

"Then it's settled: we'll go away together. Johanna," he said, and his tone moved her, "before I leave, do you think we could promise each other . . . Oh, Johanna, it wouldn't make me so sad to leave if . . ."

He stopped.

"Go on."

"If you promised to marry me some day," he said quickly.

She stared at him in disbelief.

"Marry you?"

"Several years from now, of course."

He seemed so solemn and sure of himself that she burst out laughing.

"You'll fall in love with at least ten other girls before I'm old enough to get married!"

"That's not true."

"Girls with big breasts and everything!"

"You'll have beautiful breasts some day," he said with certainty.

"But Franz . . . You don't even know me. Oh, I'm tiring you again, and Herr Kerbratt will be angry with me."

"Will you say yes?"

She looked up at the ceiling, desperately trying to think of a way to evade the issue.

"We don't have any witnesses," she said, "so our agreement wouldn't be valid."

He looked so disappointed that she quickly gave in. "All right, Franz, if that's what you want. What *I* want is for you to get well fast."

His face became more peaceful and he lay back on his pillow.

"Here's how our engagement ceremony will go," he said. "One, the magic words. Two, the kiss. Three, the mingling of blood. Four, the nuptial rest."

"You expect me to go through all that?"

"There's nothing to be afraid of."

"I'd better go back to my mother."

"Go, then," he said in a detached tone. "Forget everything I said."

He rolled over on his side, facing away from her.

"What are the magic words?" she asked hesitantly.

"Never mind!"

"Tell me what they are."

"They're part of a whole. I can't say them to you unless you agree to everything that goes with them."

She looked at the door again, then at the bed.

"Go on, tell me."

"Then you agree to everything else?"

"All right, if you insist!"

"Repeat after me; lakabu lakabu lamanschikabu, glup-glup."

Her mouth fell open. "Those are the silliest words I've ever heard in my life!" she exclaimed indignantly.

He kept her eyes on her, without responding.

"Lakabu lakabu lamanschikabu, glup-glup," she repeated finally. "There, is that all?"

"Step two: the kiss. A real one, not a baby kiss on the cheek. It's getting dark in here. Light a candle so I can see you better."

In the candlelight, the face of the first boy she was going to kiss was white as a sheet.

"How do you feel?" she asked, to buy time.

"Much better than I did a little while ago. Come, step two."

He gently drew her toward him. She looked at his face and his expression, to engrave them in her memory. Then she leaned down, rounded her lips and pressed them to his, trying to imitate a kiss she had seen in a film called *The Cabin on the Moor*, at the Rex. A kind of electric shock spread all through her body, even to her fingertips. Franz, expressionless, took her by the shoulders and held her firmly. They looked into each other's eyes, then she couldn't hold back a nervous laugh.

"I feel like we're playing a game," she said, "but I don't know what it is."

"It may not seem that way when we do step three."

"What's step three again?"

He looked at her intently and stroked her curly hair.

"To me, you're a Gypsy girl. We're going to have a Gypsy wedding."

He took a pocket knife from the bedside table, opened it and briefly held its blade in the flame of the candle. Then he made a little cut in his wrist. A drop of blood welled up.

"Of all the blood that's flowed in the last few days, only this is a symbol of happiness and hope," he said, turning to Johanna and holding out the open knife to her. "Now it's your turn."

She started.

"Are you crazy? That must hurt!"

"It's only a little pain, to win great happiness."

Grimacing, she pricked herself with the tip of the blade, then closely examined her wrist.

"Nothing's coming out."

"Squeeze it and wait."

A crimson droplet finally appeared. He took her hand and pressed his wrist against hers.

"We are now united," he said in a low voice, and repeated it twice: "We are now united. We are now united."

He let go of her. She licked her pink-stained wrist.

"There, that wasn't so bad either, was it?" he asked.

She shrugged.

"Step four: the nuptial rest," he went on. "This one is really nothing. All you do is lie down beside me and stay there till the blood is dry."

"Mine is already dry."

"Mine isn't."

"What if somebody comes?"

"We'll hear them."

She sat down on the bed.

"You won't touch me, will you?" she asked apprehensively.

He didn't answer. They lay side by side. She felt him breathing next to her. She wasn't as nervous as she had feared.

"Franz . . ."

"Yes?"

"Are you feeling better?"

"Yes. I really am. I wasn't joking. What about you? Will you be sad when I'm gone?"

"Of course, but it won't be for long. Listen, Franz . . ." She hesitated. "Don't tell Annette. She wouldn't understand. I think she likes you a lot, and she's my only friend here, so . . ."

"They'll all have to know. I *want* them to know."

"Then tell them it was, I don't know . . . something like a game."

He sat up and looked her in the eyes.

"You know it was more than that, don't you?"

"Yes, I do," she said.

In the silence she heard dishes clattering downstairs. It surprised her to realize that the house still existed around them, that they were not in a world of their own.

Leni was sitting in the armchair with her head tilted back, evidently asleep. Johanna gently closed the door without waking her and went downstairs. Annette was setting the table, which she had decorated with little fir branches.

"Have you heard about Franz?" she asked.

"Yes," said Johanna. "I went to see him and he told me." She put her finger to her lips and pointed to the kitchen door with her other hand. "I wasn't supposed to go to his room," she whispered. "If Rosi finds out . . ."

"Especially since she's nervous right now," said Annette. "Her little darling is on the road, and from the way she mutters to herself she seems to be afraid of something, I don't know what."

"Her little darling? Who's that?"

"Kerbratt, of course. She's adored him since he was born, which was quite a while ago."

Johanna sat down and watched her putting candles into the candlesticks. Annette finally looked at her questioningly.

"Are you sad that he's leaving?" Johanna asked.

"He won't be gone long, I hope. Just long enough for his wound to heal. Rosi thinks it will be about ten days."

"Annette," Johanna said in a tone that made her new friend look up in alarm. "He told me he wanted to marry me, later. I'm telling you so it won't seem like I'm trying to hide anything. I had nothing to do with it, I . . ."

Annette had turned deathly pale.

"What did you answer?"

"He has a fever and he's got nothing to do but let his imagination wander. I think he needs something to hang on to. So I said yes. Annette!" Two big tears rolled down Annette's cheeks. Johanna stood up and took her by the shoulders.

"Look, Annette, I'm not *really* going to marry him! Or at least not for years and years! I just said it because I thought I should humor him now."

"He . . . he loves you. I could tell he did."

"He loved Cora last week. Next week, when he comes back, it will be you! Annette! Please listen to me!"

Annette shook her head sadly.

"I decorated the table with these branches so it would look pretty for his last dinner."

"You mean he's coming downstairs for dinner?"

"Yes. I asked Rosi to let him come down. This will be his last evening here, and it would be wrong to make him spend it all alone!"

The kitchen door was thrown open and Rosi burst into the room.

"I told Iris and Evi to come and help me peel the potatoes, and naturally they haven't shown up!"

"I think they're resting in the barn," Annette said timidly. "I know they didn't get much sleep last night."

"I came to help you," said Johanna.

Rosi turned to her.

"I was looking for you a little while ago. Where were you?"

"I was . . . with my mother."

Johanna followed Rosi into the kitchen, where a pile of damp, dirty potatoes lay on a spread-out newspaper on the kitchen table.

"I've been keeping them for months," said Rosi. "They're all moldy, so cut deeply when you peel them."

"I'm used to that," Johanna said.

She went to work. Rosi watched her awhile, then began to pace back and forth in the kitchen, moving lightly despite her size. Each time she passed the window she looked outside and sighed loudly. Finally she sat down beside Johanna and stared at the table.

"Why are you so worried?" Johanna asked. "Are you afraid he won't be able to find his way home in the fog?"

"Of course not. He could find his way from Dippoldiswalde blindfolded. No, it's not that. It's what people are saying, and what the old doctor saw."

Johanna's eyes opened wide.

"What did he see?"

Rosi gestured impatiently.

"Forget what I said. When I'm upset I'm liable to say anything. . . . But I wish he were here."

She clasped her hands nervously. Johanna looked at the cut on her wrist. It was now crusted over with dried blood. A short time later she stood up.

"I've finished, Rosi," she said, carefully folding the newspaper so that she could take it outside to shake the dirt from it.

"Good for you, Johanna. Go and tell your mother it will be time for dinner soon. And try to get her to eat on her own. Stefan won't always be there to help her."

Already in the doorway, Johanna stopped and turned around with a frown. But Rosi was leaning over her soup pot. Johanna saw only her broad backside, covered by a dark skirt that blended with the color of the stove.

Johanna was brushing Leni's hair when she heard Franz coming down the hall, hopping on one foot. Leading Leni by the hand, she went out to meet him. Heinz was supporting him on one side while Annette watched him attentively on the other.

"Franz," said Johanna, "this is my mother."

He abandoned Heinz's shoulder for a moment and, balancing on his good leg, bowed ceremoniously. Leni's face remained expressionless.

Franz winked at Johanna and whispered in her ear, "She's not bad at all, my future mother-in-law!"

He seemed transformed. Quickly looking at Annette to see if she had heard, Johanna put her finger to her lips. The little procession started cautiously down the stairs. Johanna saw

Franz's sharp profile against the glow of the candles on the first floor. Struck by the sight of the long table adorned with fir branches, he stopped to admire it.

"It would have been a shame to miss that," he said.

"I decorated it!" Annette announced proudly.

He smiled and she looked away, blushing. He continued down the stairs.

Heinz helped Franz to the table, where he carefully stretched his leg out on the bench. Annette slid a cushion under it, avoiding his eyes. *If you think I don't see what you're up to . . .* Johanna thought. *But I'm the one who mixed my blood with his.*

She led Leni to one of the benches and sat down next to her, almost directly across from Franz.

The kitchen door opened. Rosi came in, carrying a soup tureen and looking even more distraught than when Johanna had left her.

"Children," she said, "we'll begin without him."

Her tone was so tragic that all conversation stopped.

"What's wrong?" Franz asked. "Are you worried because of the refugees? Don't forget he has Berndt with him."

"No, it's not the refugees," she said, glancing at the window.

They all ate without daring to talk very much. Suddenly they heard a dog barking in the distance, in the village. Rosi leapt to her feet and went to open the door. A rush of icy air brought the cold smell of the forest.

"We're freezing!" Franz protested.

Rosi strained her ears, but could hear nothing. Disheartened, she closed the door.

"It's a shame your last dinner had to be spoiled," Annette said to Franz.

As Rosi slowly returned to the table, her head bowed, they heard the creaking of the wagon.

Heinz opened the door again and the flames of the candles flickered. The children saw Kerbratt climb down from the wagon and pat the horses distractedly.

"Give them a good rubdown after you unhitch them," he said to Berndt.

When he came into the house, Rosi could scarcely take her eyes off him long enough to relieve him of his suitcase and his overcoat.

"Oh, I'm so glad you're back!" she said. "I was worried sick!"

"But you knew you couldn't expect me any sooner than this," he replied. He drew her aside and said softly, "On the way back I stopped at Dippoldiswalde and Frauensteln. I didn't hear anything alarming."

"Oh, thank goodness. That makes me feel a little better."

Kerbratt bowed to Leni and sat down heavily in his usual place at the table. Everyone watched him in silence while he unlaced his muddy gaiters. Finally he raised his head and slowly looked from face to face. When he reached Johanna he said, "I asked Dr. Minsch to take care of having your sister buried. He goes to Dresden every day and he'll do what's needed." She nodded, thanking him.

"I can't tell you how glad I am to have my whole little troop here, with no one missing," he went on. "They say that in Dresden it's . . . it's horrible. Thousands of corpses are being taken away by the cartload. As for the city itself . . ."

He stopped and cleared his throat. He seemed about to sob.

"We've escaped from a great catastrophe," he said.

Rosi pushed a bowl of soup in front of him.

"Eat this while it's still hot. We'd just sat down when you came."

Kerbratt ate a few spoonfuls, which seemed to soothe him.

"I see our patient has come downstairs," he said, looking at Franz. "Do you think that's wise, Rosi?"

"We couldn't let him spend his last evening here alone," she answered. "He rested this afternoon."

Kerbratt scrutinized him.

"It's true that you look better than you did this morning. You see, as soon as you get a little rest . . ."

Franz gave Johanna a quick glance.

"It's all arranged for you," Kerbratt continued. "You'll stay with Dr. Minsch in Freiberg. He's overwhelmed with work, of course, but he's an old friend and he promised me he'd treat you like one of the family. Meanwhile I have sulfa drugs for tonight."

"How long do you think I'll be gone?" Franz asked.

"You'll stay till your wound heals. About two weeks, I'd say."

"That's not too bad," said Franz, relieved.

"It will be safer for you to go to Freiberg, believe me. Old Wildgrüber didn't like the look of your wound. And speaking of medicine, I've brought another form of therapy. I have a surprise for you, Annette."

Berndt had just come in, carrying a small trunk, which he rested on the table. Kerbratt opened it, revealing a crimson padded lining. He took out a violin and a bow and handed them to Annette.

"When Dr. Wildgrüber heard that all our instruments had burned, he was as sick about it as I was," he said. "He used to play chamber music."

"Franz," he continued, taking a cylindrical case from the trunk. "So far I haven't been able to find a clarinet, so you'll have to be satisfied with this recorder. There's also a harmonica, a viola without an A string, and a little package of sheet music, which we'll all share."

Annette was caressing the violin tenderly, almost timidly.

"I'll tune it right now," she said, not even trying to hide her emotion. "I feel almost as if nothing had happened—no, as if everything were beginning again! Oh, I'm so happy!"

Dinner was nearly over. Franz was more animated than Johanna had ever seen him. As before, everyone avoided talking about the bombing. But Leni showed no sign of sharing the general lightheartedness. Johanna held her hand under the table and sometimes guided her spoon to her mouth. Leni would go on eating by herself for a time, then stop with her spoon in midair, staring into space, as though waiting for Johanna to guide her again.

Franz tapped on his glass with his fork and the talking stopped. Johanna suddenly felt the blood drain from her face.

"Herr Kerbratt, Rosi, my friends," he said, "something important happened to me this afternoon. I decided that some day I'm going to marry the girl sent to me by heaven, or by American fliers: Johanna Seyfert. I know you're all thinking, 'But you've only known her since this morning!' But that's been long enough for me to find out that there really is such a thing as love at first sight. Some day Johanna and I will go off to a warm, sunny country. I want Annette to play her new violin in honor of our future together."

Annette seemed thunderstruck.

"You mean . . . in honor of your future with Johanna?" she asked.

"Yes," Franz said firmly.

She stared at him blankly, letting the bow of her violin touch the floor.

Johanna leaned across the table to whisper, "I asked you not to tell them like that. Not so seriously." She glanced at Annette. "What's the matter with you, Franz, are you blind?"

He hesitated.

"You'll find other boys," he told Annette awkwardly, "and they'll be ten times better than I am."

"That won't be hard," Cora remarked.

"Nobody asked for your opinion!" he said angrily.

Annette hadn't moved. The candlelight made dark shadows around her eyes.

Johanna stood up, went over to her and said, "Play your violin. Play anything, but play."

"I can't," Annette said, looking down at the floor and shaking her head dejectedly. "Really, I can't."

She seemed about to cry. Johanna looked at Kerbratt, who felt it was time for him to intervene.

"Why don't our two virtuosos play together?" he suggested affably.

"That's a good idea," Franz said, quickly following Kerbratt's lead. "Come, Annette, we'll play together, the way we used to."

Annette looked at Johanna, who nodded vigorously, then at Franz, who had already picked up his recorder. With a sigh, she put her violin to her shoulder and began tuning it. When she was ready he beat time with his left hand and they launched into a lively, high-spirited polka. Johanna remembered the summer evenings when she had watched people dancing under linden trees. She could almost smell the heady odor of the leaves.

Caught up in the music, Annette was transformed. *Probably because she's playing with him*, Johanna thought. Her heart skipped a beat.

After the polka, Franz and Annette went directly into a waltz and Rudi joined in with the harmonia. Berndt and Evi began dancing, a little tentatively at first, then faster and more confidently as Annette quickened the rhythm. Kerbratt also stood up and Rosi blushed when he asked her to dance.

Johanna was surprised by the agility with which he twirled on his good leg. Rosi gazed at him delightedly. *She really seems to love him*, Johanna thought with astonishment, because signs of love between older people always struck her as incongruous and vaguely indecent. The children were all dancing now, the boys pairing up awkwardly with the girls, who were giggling uncontrollably. Stefan had taken Cora as his partner and was vigorously pumping his arms up and down.

Except for Franz, who was totally absorbed in playing his recorder, only Leni and Johanna were still sitting on the bench. With her lips parted, Leni seemed to be watching the scene in a kind of stupor. *Someone should ask her to dance*, Johanna thought. A moment later Kerbratt, who had just taken Rosi back to her seat, picked up his cane and limped toward Leni. When he stopped before her and bowed, she looked at him in dismay and shrank away.

"Dance with me, Leni," he insisted.

She didn't move but her face tensed.

"Look, Mutti: everyone else is dancing, even Stefan!" Johanna encouraged her.

For a moment Leni watched Annette playing her violin, then she watched Evi and Berndt dancing, and finally her gaze came to rest on a dark windowpane. Kerbratt looked at Johanna helplessly.

"You'll at least dance with *me*, won't you, Mutti?" Johanna asked.

She took Leni's hands and pulled them gently. Leni stood up.

"Yes, yes, good," Kerbratt said.

Holding Leni by the waist, Johanna tried to make her dance. But in spite of the exhilaration around her, the music had no effect on Leni. Johanna felt as if she were holding a lifeless puppet. Suddenly she felt completely discouraged and led Leni back to her bench.

Annette suddenly became inspired and began playing a frenzied Gypsy farandole. Holding hands, the dancers pounded the stairs as they climbed up to the second floor, then back down, led by Annette and her violin. Then the rhythm slowed and they sang an old folk song:

> *All the girls*
> *Who form this round*
> *Don't want a man*
> *For the summer.*

Franz leaned toward Johanna.

"They're singing that for themselves, and not for you," he said, "because I'm going to be with you this summer. And every other summer, as long as we live."

The others formed a circle around Johanna and Franz. For a while the rapid swirl of faces made Johanna feel dizzy, then she stood up and joined the dance. And even though she could barely carry a tune, she sang with them, her voice quavering with emotion and fatigue.

The celebration went on and on, and it seemed better for Franz's wound than the sulfa drugs Kerbratt had brought. But Annette's arm finally became tired. She made a sweeping motion with her bow and stopped playing, suddenly bringing everyone back to earth. There was a moment of silence, of suspension in the void, when they no longer knew where they were. What was this calm place that had just appeared, like an island in the sea? They separated regretfully from one another.

Johanna walked back toward the bench, wanting to try to make her mother understand what she had just felt. But Leni was gone.

For a few seconds she stared incredulously at the empty bench gleaming in the candlelight.

"Mutti!" she cried in a choked voice.

All eyes turned toward the corner of the room where Leni had been sitting several minutes before.

"This is too much!" Cora exclaimed.

Johanna ran upstairs. They heard her go into her room, come out, call her mother in the hall, go into Franz's room and call again. When she came back down the stairs her legs felt so weak that she had to clutch the railing.

"Go look in the courtyard," said Berndt. "I'll go and tell Kerbratt."

Just then Kerbratt and Rosi came in. Berndt pointed to the bench and said, "Johanna's mother is gone."

"She was sitting there?" asked Kerbratt. "And no one saw or heard her leave?"

"We were making so much noise . . ." Berndt said sheepishly.

Johanna was crushed. She should never have stopped watching her mother, but she had completely ignored her—while she danced and sang!

"Let's go outside," Kerbratt said brusquely. "Put on your coats, all of you. We'll meet at the gate in five minutes. Berndt and the girls will search the thickets on the right. The boys and I will search on the left."

Outside, Johanna slipped away from the others and began walking toward the gate. Something told her it was unlikely that Leni would be found close to the house.

She looked back. The dim lights of the house had vanished. Around her, she heard muffled exclamations and the sound of people pushing through the underbrush.

"Frau Seyfert!" someone to her left—it sounded like Berndt—called out. Did he expect Leni to answer, "Here I am," and pop out from behind a tree?

The chill of the woods might make Leni go back to the house. But what would happen if she became hopelessly lost and, at the end of her strength, lay down on the ground without a coat to protect her from the cold? She might fall asleep and never wake up. Johanna stopped and braced herself against a tree. *Oh, Mutti, you were in another world, but I could talk to you and hold your hand. Annette was right: that was what really mattered.*

She could now see the white wooden gate, standing out against the dark background of trees.

"Is that you, Johanna?" Kerbratt asked.

Her chest felt so tight that she was barely able to whisper. "Yes."

They gathered in a disorderly cluster around Kerbratt's lantern. Rosi had also joined the group. It disturbed Johanna that Franz had been left alone.

"The gate was open," Kerbratt said.

Johanna leaned against her tree. It felt cold and rough. To her right, the road sloped up toward the mountain, gleaming faintly. She tried to imagine Leni disappearing into the night.

Kerbratt moved closer to her.

"Don't worry too much," he said awkwardly, as if he were trying to hide his own anxiety. "Things could be worse. It might be much colder."

"We'll search along both sides of the road," he went on. "Berndt and the girls will go to the left as far as the village square. I'll go with the boys to the wayside cross at the edge of the forest. We'll meet here—look at your watch, Berndt—in half an hour. Remember that Frau Seyfert may be very hard to see, especially if she's sitting down."

"Be sure not to go any farther than the wayside cross," Rosi urged.

"I said that was as far as we were going, and I meant it," he snapped. "Berndt, if your group has a problem, shout and I'll come to you. Rosi, I'd like you and Stefan to go back to the house, so Franz won't be alone."

"But I want to go too," Stefan protested.

"This isn't a game, Stefan," Rosi told him sternly.

The two groups separated. On the way to the village, Berndt's lantern cast an eerie glow on the trees along the road. Johanna followed him, walking between Annette and Cora. She kept her eyes on the ground, thinking, like Kerbratt, that Leni was probably huddled at the foot of a tree. They stopped every minute to call her name but their voices were swallowed in the fog.

They came to the dark, silent houses of the village, walked around the church and started back. As they neared the gate, they saw Kerbratt's lantern swaying in the darkness. He and his group were already there, waiting.

"There's nothing more we can do tonight," he said wearily when they were all together.

"Oh, no!" Johanna exclaimed. "I'll go on looking for her by myself."

"I'll stay with you," Annette said determinedly.

Johanna felt Kerbratt firmly grip her shoulder.

"You'll come back to the house with us and try to sleep," he said calmly. "I'll look at a map of the region and decide on the best way to search for your mother. We'll start in the morning, at dawn. But not before."

There was a long silence.

"Meanwhile," he added, "we'll call her once more."

"Leni!" they all shouted at the top of their lungs. "Leni!"

They listened. This time it seemed that their call must have carried all the way to the city, but there was no answer except the patter of raindrops on the road.

F I V E

ans Magnus Kerbratt went out into the courtyard
and stood against the wall of the house. The sky had
cleared and the night now seemed less dark and
humid, but it also seemed colder, and that worried him. He
scrutinized the edge of the forest, then walked toward the
trees. A soothing smell of straw came from the barn. He
thought of the children sleeping there, scattered as they had
been on the lawn of the park at dawn the day before, when
the mist had risen above the catastrophic ruin of the city. But
his children were alive. Thanks to him, they had escaped.

He thought of the little concert they had given on platform
B, for the arrival of the last train from Breslau. He remembered how people with exhausted, pathetic faces had gotten
off the overloaded train and suddenly smiled, because eighteen children were greeting them with a song. For most of
them, it must have been their last joy. When the air-raid
sirens sounded, they all went down into the vast underground
room. No one panicked—it was just one more alert, after so
many others. With Kerbratt leading the way and Berndt bring-

ing up the rear, the children followed the crowd. Then came
waiting and, for the first time, fear. For long minutes they felt
the bombs coming—they weren't surprised when they heard
the first explosions.

Later, when the bombing stopped, the children wanted to
stay where they were. It didn't seem strange to them that the
station hadn't been hit. The people around them seemed
determined not to move. Kerbratt wanted to shout, "They'll
be back!" But he knew it was useless: no one seemed willing
to believe him.

A little before midnight, he made his decision. He called
out the children's names and, when he was sure they were all
there, told them to hold hands. Then they climbed the stairs.
Outside, they stood in the Bahnhofplatz, looking at the enormous curtain of flame that cut across the city to the north.

He instinctively led them toward the open space of the
Grosse Garten. On the way they stopped to take their sleeping bags from the storehouse on Wienerstrasse where they
kept the equipment they needed for going on tour. They had
just laid their sleeping bags under the trees when they heard
the faint sound of distant airplanes that Kerbratt had been
expecting. They listened, pressing together, while it grew
inexorably louder. Calmly, Kerbratt explained that it was too
late to go somewhere else, and that they were in less danger
here than at the station. Stefan, half asleep, didn't understand
what was happening. When he saw the station brightly lighted
by parachute flares, he thought they were fireworks set off to
welcome another trainload of refugees.

Kerbratt shivered. Memories were racing through his mind.
In 1942, when he had come back to civilian life after a brief
naval career ended by an explosion in a torpedo tube that
smashed his leg, he had found the choir reduced to thirty-four
members. And, having been badly conducted by a trembling
old chaplain, the marvelous instrument he had spent ten years
forging had already lost some of its unity and power. He
began working tirelessly to bring the choir back to its former

excellence. But to achieve that, he had to wrap himself in forgetfulness and indifference. Indifference to the war, to the outside world and all the dark, booted shadows that moved through it; indifference to everything except his young singers, who were now sleeping in the barn. There was still something worth attempting, as long as they were all together.

But now there was another child, who had come to entrust her mother to him. That was enough to turn everything upside down.

He thought he saw something in the lane. He took a few steps forward, peering into the moonlit night.

"Leni," he called softly.

There was no answer. He walked past the clump of firs and saw what had caught his attention: a half-broken birch branch quivered in the breeze. He broke it off completely and kept it in his hand as he walked back toward the house.

He noticed a pale figure in front of the door and frowned. It was Johanna.

"I heard you calling her," she said.

"Go back inside, before you catch cold," he ordered.

"How do you know her body shows no sign of injury?" she asked abruptly, a hint of hostility in her voice.

He looked at her in silence.

"Well, don't you think she would have complained?" he said finally. She didn't answer.

They went into the house together. At the foot of the stairs he stopped.

"Since you're so observant," he said, "maybe you'll remember something about what happened tonight. When you saw your mother last, was it before or after you began singing?"

She thought for a moment.

"Before."

"So it was *while* you were singing that she disappeared."

"I'm not sure. But I don't see what . . ."

"Go to bed now," he interrupted, putting his hand on her thin shoulder.

"What time will we start looking again?"

"As soon as it's light. I'll wake you up."

"We'll find her, won't we?" she asked.

"I can't say. I hope we'll find her. I think we will. Now go to bed."

He waited at the bottom of the stairs till she had closed her door, then he went outside.

He kept his flashlight turned off until he was out of sight of the house, and when he came to the gate he opened it cautiously, in case Johanna might be trying to spy on him from her window. He turned right, onto the forest road. Still a good distance from the wayside cross, he turned onto a path bordered by ferns.

His limp became more pronounced as his leg tired, and soon he had to stop and catch his breath. He could see the plain through a gap in the trees. The horizon was so bright that he knew the city was still burning. He imagined the flames gnawing at the lacy stonework, turning the delicately colored paving stones to gray pumice, casting blood-red reflections on the river.

"I've seen too much!" he said aloud.

At least Johanna wasn't there to hear him talking to himself, he thought. Whatever made her act so insolently toward him? And furthermore, she had been eavesdropping.

Finally he went on. The path, barely visible, sloped uphill between tangled, stunted vegetation and tall trees that towered oppressively overhead. Kerbratt had turned on his flashlight; now he turned it off again. *I can see well enough without it,* he thought, *and there's no use making myself conspicuous if I'm heading into something unpleasant.*

The path gradually became wider and less steep. He began putting more and more weight on his cane. Now and then he stopped to get his bearings.

Finally he came to a flight of stone steps that took him to a level stretch of high ground bathed in moonlight. Nothing had changed. The monument was still there, on top of its mound, as pale in the moonlight as if it had been carved from alabaster.

He moved his hand over the damp, smooth surface of the stone to find the letters of the inscription. In some places they were covered with lichen. *That wasn't there before*, he thought. *I'll have it cleared away.* He remembered the color of the stone in the setting sun, and the shapes of the letters. *How does the inscription go? It's a quotation from the Book of Job. "God is clothed in splendor"? No, that comes at the end.*

He looked up at a luminous patch of sky. The tall trees formed the sides of a deep pit, with him at the bottom. The whole quotation suddenly came back to him and he recited it aloud.

" 'There are times when the light vanishes behind darkening clouds; then comes the wind, sweeping them away, and brightness spreads from the north. God is clothed in fearful splendor.' " He laughed bitterly. "My memory hasn't failed me," he went on, still speaking aloud, "and the quotation is apt: 'Brightness spreads from the north.' I wouldn't have thought that the light from a burning city could be seen from so far away, even at night! What do you think of that, Leni? It's a calamity that our gentle, stubborn Halina didn't foresee!"

He stepped back from the little mound and slowly walked around it. As he passed a big rock, almost hidden in the underbrush, he absent-mindedly drew his hand across it.

"Do you hear me, Leni?" he said. "Answer me, Leni. I know you're here."

He reached the opposite side of the mound. Sitting on the ground with her back against a stump, Leni watched him come toward her.

He sat down beside her and touched the back of her hand.

"You're shivering, of course," he said. He took off his heavy loden cloak and put it over her shoulders, but she didn't seem to notice. "So you found your way here, at night, even though it's been years. . . ."

She looked at him with her big, motionless eyes.

"What happened?" he asked. "Why did you suddenly run away like a frightened deer? And why did you come *here?* I know why," he added quickly.

With the help of his cane, he stood up.

"I should have thought of it sooner," he said. "It was the singing, wasn't it? Yes, it was the singing, I'm sure." He leaned down and touched her hair. "It was a long time ago. Johanna was still a baby, remember?"

She threw back her head and looked away.

"There must have been something you didn't like," he said unsteadily. "Tell me . . . Was it that I asked you to dance? Was that it? Or maybe everyone seemed so happy that you wanted to come back here to . . . to think about old times when . . ." He pointed to the trees near the big rock. "Remember . . . It was night then too—though I must say it was warmer." A little laugh died in his throat. "You were over there, with people on both sides of you. You looked at me while I conducted the singing. I could see your white blouse in the darkness, in the first row. I can still see it. . . . Do you remember my cantata on a theme from *The Firebird?* The children were so wrapped up in it that at the end they almost thought they saw the bird flying away. Those little faces looking up . . ." He hummed the theme softly, then sighed. "In those days I really thought I could take you away from that kingdom of tents and sand! But now you've come back to me, brought by that child. . . . He couldn't disown *her!* A real daughter of the desert! But in life there are sometimes . . ."

He tried in vain to think of the right word. Leni had curled up inside his cloak and it covered her almost completely. He knew she was looking at him but he saw her eyes only as two dark pits.

"If you came here to remember happy times, why do you look so sad? Oh, Leni, in the last ten years I've given so many concerts for you, dedicated them to you, as if you could hear them. But now you *will* hear them."

Leni's weary, melancholy face seemed to acknowledge him for the first time.

"The singing," she said in a hollow voice.

"Yes, the singing, you'll hear it again! I'll have the children do the pieces you like best: Mozart's last cantata, Bruckner's psalm. You'll sit in an armchair and we'll all sit around you, just as we did for that poor boy's mother."

"The singing," she said again. "The road."

"Yes, we're going back to the house now. You may not be cold anymore, with my cloak on, but I'm getting a chill."

He tried to draw her toward him but she resisted with a deep, powerful inertia. He might as well have tried to lift a boulder. He took her face between his hands.

"Listen to me, Leni. We're going back to the house together, and I promise you'll be happy again." He brushed his lips against her hair, then kissed it; its smell was still the same. "Look at me. My face hasn't changed any more than yours. And I hurried to you in spite of my bad leg."

He stroked her shoulder slowly, but she broke away from him and curled up still more, until her knees nearly touched her shoulders.

"You found your way here at night—don't you think that shows there's still something between us, an old, unbreakable bond?" he asked.

He turned on his flashlight, hoping to get a reaction from her. But its beam illuminated the monument and the mound in an eerie way that seemed to frighten her. He turned it off again, and in the darkness that followed he could no longer see her at all. It was as if she had disappeared all over again. He felt a pang of loss. Then he heard her voice: it was harsh and almost disembodied, as though it didn't belong to her.

"The singing," she said. "The road. The horses."

He frowned. "I didn't come in the wagon, Leni. We have to walk back."

"The horses . . . the horses," she repeated anxiously.

"You met horses on the road? With riders?"

She had sunk back into silence. But he had to know. "Horses? Or riders?"

She didn't answer. "With me," he said, gripping his cane, "you don't have to be afraid of anything."

Trying not to seem nervous, he took her hand. This time she stood up. He listened intently for a few moments, then took her firmly by the arm and, without looking back, led her down the stone steps.

When they came to the path, she started walking with long, mechanical strides, bent forward slightly with her eyes on the ground. At each turn in the path he made her wait while he went on ahead and peered into the darkness. Once he heard something that alarmed him; he seized Leni's shoulder as she walked ahead of him, and she turned around. She looked distressed, but his own alarm had vanished and he was almost happy to be there in the heart of the night and the forest, in silent communion with her.

They set off again. Cold and tired, Kerbratt was becoming impatient to get back to the house. His leg hurt so much it made him grimace. And to his surprise, Leni suddenly seemed in a great hurry. She had taken the lead and was walking faster than he could follow.

"Not so fast," he said.

She slowed down obediently. Seeing her follow his instructions with such good grace, he thought for a moment that if he could only get her to discuss even a minute part of what they both felt at being together again in their old territory, she would remember everything. She must feel something too, he was sure of it.

Later—they hadn't yet come to the gap in the trees through which they would be able to see the plain—she stopped abruptly. He felt her face close to his.

"The horses," she whispered.

They were blocking the path, almost invisible in the darkness. Kerbratt could hear the metallic sound of their bits. He began to sweat. He looked left and right but saw no one. He took Leni by the hand, intending to lead her around them.

"The horses! The horses!" she cried out in a voice made shrill by anguish.

He put his hand over her mouth and firmly pushed her off the path. Slowly and quietly, they made a detour around the horses. Just as they came back to the path, one of the horses began pawing the ground. Kerbratt quickened his pace, pushing Leni in front of him.

"Halt!"

The order came from behind them as a flashlight clicked on, illuminating dense rows of tree trunks, like the bars of a gigantic cage.

For an instant he wanted to grab Leni and run. But his leg would slow him down and he didn't know if Leni would follow him. In any case, the sound of a cartridge being chambered in a rifle made up his mind.

He turned around slowly. Blinded by the flashlight, he stood still, clutching Leni's arm. Her mouth was open in a kind of silent scream as she held her forearm in front of her eyes.

"Look, Boris!" a voice exclaimed in surprise. "It's the crazy woman again! Maybe she hasn't had enough."

The man spoke in German, but with a heavy accent. He walked toward them, his face partly hidden by his fur-lined cap.

"Stop shining that flashlight in our eyes," Kerbratt snapped. "There's nothing suspicious about our being here. We live nearby."

The man ignored him. He pulled Leni's arm away and shined the flashlight in her face.

"I'm starting to wonder if you're spying on us," he said menacingly. "But maybe you just want some more of what you got. That's right, isn't it?" He laughed. "You want more!"

A muffled wail, like the distant cry of a night bird, came from Leni's lips. The man brutally seized her by the shoulder and Kerbratt felt her shudder violently.

"Let go of her!" he shouted.

The man turned to him with contempt.

"Who asked *you* to say anything?"

Kerbratt saw stubbly whiskers and narrow eyes beneath the visor of the fur-lined cap. He felt a wave of fury rising inside him.

"I'm telling you to let go of her," he said as calmly as he could.

The man laughed.

"Boris," he called out, facing the horses, "come and listen to this!" A tall, bareheaded man with thinning blond hair stepped onto the path, carrying a flashlight. He wore a long, mud-stained military overcoat that hung almost to the ground. Kerbratt noticed a faded cloth emblem on his left shoulder. It was a St. Andrew's cross.

"Vlassov!" he exclaimed. "You belong to Vlassov's army! I should have known! We're on the same side!"

He took a step toward Boris and forced a smile. "I'm Ober-leutnant Kerbratt, of the Kriegsmarine," he said, standing stiffly at attention.

"I'll tell you what I think of Vlassov," Boris said. His breath smelled of strong vodka and cheap tobacco. "Vlassov is a piece of shit."

That's not exactly what I wanted to hear, Kerbratt thought bitterly.

"But judging from that emblem on your shoulder," he said, "there was a time when you . . . felt differently."

Boris looked at Leni.

"Vladimir Ivanovich, bring me my riding whip."

"Yes, sir."

A third man appeared, barely visible against the trees. Kerbratt heard his heels click before he did an about-face and disappeared. Boris now held a small whip.

"The emblem of that son of a bitch . . ." he began, snapping the whip against his boot. "Mikhail, tie her hands," he ordered.

The man with the fur-lined cap seized Leni's wrists and tied them together.

"Let go of her!" Kerbratt roared.

With all his strength, he swung his cane at Boris, who leapt backward, dropping his flashlight. The cane glanced off his cartridge belt and struck Mikhail on the hand. Mikhail swore furiously. A moment later Kerbratt felt an explosion inside his head. The night became black and red, and something warm and sticky seemed to flow over him. He clutched the trunk of a tree but couldn't keep from falling. Far above him, voices were shouting in a language he didn't understand. He tried to stand up. He had succeeded in raising himself to his knees when a kick between the shoulders sent him sprawling.

"Stay down this time, you dirty Nazi!" a voice said.

With damp moss pressing against his cheek, Kerbratt began moving his hand across the ground, hoping to find his cane. A sharp pain seemed to pierce his skull behind his ear.

"He's showing signs of life," Mikhail said mockingly.

"We may as well let him watch," Boris said.

Kerbratt was pulled to his feet. His mouth was full of blood. While he was wiping it with the back of his hand, his legs buckled and he would have fallen if he hadn't been held firmly. The flashlight had been replaced with a lantern like the one he used for his wagon. In its yellow light he saw a clearing and, at its edge, three more horses tied to a tree.

"Leni," he called weakly. "Where are you?"

Someone laughed jeeringly. A short distance away from the path, Leni stood with her hands tied in front of her, holding them as if she were praying. Kerbratt's cloak had fallen off her, and she was shivering.

Boris, the blond giant, began tearing the top of her dress with careful, precise tugs, baring her pale, bony shoulders. Kerbratt struggled furiously to free himself but couldn't break the grip that held him. Boris went on ripping the top of Leni's dress into shreds that hung down over her skirt. Finally her back was completely bare.

"Hold her," Boris said to Mikhail.

He raised his whip. Kerbratt tried to shout, but only an inarticulate moan escaped his swollen lips. The whip hissed briefly, then struck. Leni screamed and lunged forward, so violently that Mikhail let her go and she fell to her knees. Kerbratt cried out and a hand was clapped over his mouth. Mikhail roughly pulled Leni to her feet. The whip hissed again. Leni shrieked in pain and slumped against the man holding her wrists. She stayed there, whimpering like a child.

"Show him," Boris said.

Mikhail turned Leni around so that Kerbratt could see her back. "Bring the light closer," he said to the man holding the lantern.

Leni was trembling convulsively. The whip had left two

purplish-blue welts that formed a St. Andrew's cross. The flesh around them was already swelling.

"Now that I've told you what I think of Vlassov," said Boris, "you can see what I think of his emblem. But you were right when you said I once felt differently. I was foolish enough to believe that Hitler was going to help White Russians recover their privileges. But there's something our good friend Vlassov forgot to tell us: that you Germans are going to lose the war. We came to help the Teutonic Knights, and all we found were rabbits running away like Italians!"

As Boris spoke, Kerbratt examined him closely, seeking a tinge of madness in his eyes. But there was none.

"Vlassov knew what kind of a hornet's nest he was taking us into," Boris went on. "He misled us from beginning to end. The Red Army is not far behind us, and I know it won't be long before I'm caught between the hammer and the anvil. But in the meantime, *Herr Oberleutnant*, you miserable excuse for an officer, whenever I come across any of the people responsible for all that, I get even. You haven't seen anything yet."

Kerbratt shuddered at the bitterness of the expression on Boris's face.

"Alexei Dmitrievich!" Boris called.

"Yes, sir."

Another man wearing a long gray overcoat stepped into the circle of light. He had the delicate face of an adolescent.

"You were on duty when we had our fun a little while ago. Now it's your turn," Boris said, pointing to Leni.

She had collapsed onto the ground and was still crying softly. Her bare back formed a patch of pale color at the foot of the tree. Alexei Dmitrievich looked at her and shook his head.

"I can't," he said finally, as if to himself.

"It's an order."

The young man shook his head again, his face showing a mixture of disgust and, to Kerbratt's surprise, pity.

"Mikhail, get her ready," Boris said.

Mikhail pulled Leni up and brutally bent her forward.

"You can do better than that," Boris complained. "You've got her looking as if she were hunting for mushrooms!"

"I don't care how she looks," Alexei Dmitrievich said with calm determination. "I'm not going to do it."

Boris pressed his lips together, then slowly took a pistol from his pocket.

"Is that your last word?"

Alexei Dmitrievich looked at him contemptuously.

"Do you really think that threatening a man with a gun is a good way to make him get an erection?"

When the shot went off, the horses raised their heads and whinnied. The bullet struck the young man in the face. He sank to his knees, moaned for a few seconds, pitched forward and lay still.

Boris looked down at him impassively and touched him with the toe of his boot. *Now it's my turn,* Kerbratt thought. He looked at Leni; Mikhail had let her go. The sound of the shot seemed to have had no effect on her.

Boris took out the magazine of his pistol and examined it. He led Mikhail a short distance away. They had a brief exchange, then Boris came back to Kerbratt.

"You're lucky," he said. "We're so short of ammunition we can't afford to waste any on you." He pointed to Alexei Dmitrievich's body and added, "Let's say he got the bullet that was meant for you."

He untied one of the horses, mounted it and rode away without another word, and without another look at Leni. The others followed, one of them leading the extra horse by the reins. They quickly disappeared into the woods.

Leni had stopped crying; now and then she heaved a little sigh that was almost musical, as if something were tinkling inside her. Kerbratt picked up his mud-stained cloak and tried to put it on her, but she cried out when it touched her lacerated back. To give her something softer next to her skin, he took off his jacket and shirt and put the shirt on her so carefully that she only moaned once when he buttoned it. Then he put his cloak on her again, keeping only his undershirt and jacket for himself.

Suddenly remembering the corpse on the ground, he took his flashlight from his pocket and turned it on. The young man lay face down. Kerbratt was tempted to search him for papers, but his sense of decency restrained him. Knowing a little about him wouldn't change anything. He would simply try to remember his face, and his expression when he refused to obey Boris's order.

With the help of his flashlight, Kerbratt found his cane on the path. Feeling its knotty, polished wood in his hand again was a small resurrection for him. He went back to where Leni was leaning against a tree, draped in his cloak, the shreds of her torn dress hanging from her waist. He felt guilty for wanting to take her tortured, wounded body in his arms.

He led her around the corpse. Later, he remembered nothing from then until they reached the gate, except walking in a mist so dense that it seemed to be seeping into him to keep him from suffering.

He held Leni's hand throughout their long walk back. As they neared the house, he laughed nervously when he realized how they both were dressed. The house, behind the moonlit courtyard, looked so serene that it seemed unreal. He opened the front door, stood aside while Leni went in, then followed her inside. Someone appeared in the darkness.

"Is that you, Rosi?"

"Oh, Hans . . . I fell asleep while I was waiting for you."

She struck a match and looked at them in dismay, her hand over her mouth.

"Don't make such a face," Kerbratt said, trying to sound jovial. "It turns out that old Dr. Wildgrüber was right—and so were you."

He guided Leni to the stairs. She climbed them with difficulty, with Rosi supporting her. Kerbratt opened the door of his room, led Leni to his bed and made her lie on it face down.

"Her back," he said to Rosi. "But first, bring her some kind of sedative."

Just then his head began to throb. He dragged himself to the washstand. In the mirror he could see his lips swollen to twice their normal size and a streak of dried blood below his ear. Then his eyes blurred and he nearly fell.

Rosi had brought a little porcelain jar of the ointment she had used on Franz and was now applying it to Leni's back with a deft, gentle hand. The two crossed welts had grown darker. The purple swellings on either side were still expanding. Leni moaned and shuddered like a taut bowstring while Rosi lightly massaged her spine and shoulder blades.

When she had covered Leni's whole back with ointment, she unfolded one of the bandages brought by Wildgrüber, placed it over the welts and took her by one arm to make her sit up on the edge of the bed. Leni did as Rosi wanted. She sat motionless with her eyes closed, her breasts pale in the amber candlelight, as Rosi began methodically wrapping a strip of cloth around her torso to keep the bandage in place.

"When I see her smooth skin and her pretty, slender figure," she said, "I'm not surprised that those animals pounced on her as soon as they saw her."

"It wasn't the ones you thought," Kerbratt said, seeming to rouse himself from a trance. "They weren't Reds."

Rosi turned to look at him.

"What? Weren't they the ones Wildgrüber saw?"

"Yes, but they were deserters from Vlassov's army."

Rosi shook her head incredulously as she finished securing the bandage. She made Leni lie face down again, and covered her with a quilt. All that she and Kerbratt could see of her was her long golden hair spread out on the quilt.

"She ran away because she heard the children singing, I'm sure of it," Kerbratt said. "Rosi . . . I knew her once."

Rosi turned pale and was silent for a moment, then she asked, "Was there some connection with the Polish boy who died?"

"Yes. The boy's mother, Halina Makowska, was a close friend of Leni's. She had that monument put up at the place where the boy fell. For the inscription, she chose a passage from the Book of Job because, she told Leni, 'The Book of Job shows us how grief can lead to serenity.' The accident affected Leni more deeply than you can imagine. She had the idea of having the children's choir go there every year, on the anniversary of the boy's death. She came to discuss it with me and I thought it was a beautiful idea."

"You're talking too much," Rosi said. "You'd better try to get some sleep."

"It does me good to talk about it."

"It was always early in May."

"Yes, on the eleventh. Then in 1938 the ceremony was forbidden for reasons . . . Do you remember the reasons, Rosi?"

She shook her head.

"They sang a choral transcription of Mahler's *Kindertotenlieder*," Kerbratt said. "Honoring the memory of a Polish boy with music written by a Jew—that was considered going too far. But I didn't really mind, because the ceremony was beginning to get out of hand: it was turning into a mystical pilgrimage to the shrine of an angel. More and more people were coming to it. If it had been in Italy, there would already have been miracles. Actually, though, from what I've heard, the boy was rather pigheaded and conceited."

"Even so," said Rosi, "he fell there, all alone, and died of it. He must have spent at least an hour watching the moss soak up his blood . . . That's enough to make someone a saint, you know."

"I found Leni at that same place."

"She didn't seem to recognize anything when she came here."

"No, and she didn't recognize me either. I'm not even sure she recognizes Johanna. Yet something happened inside her: the children's singing stirred her, and she left the house and found her way to the monument."

"It might have been enough to bring her back to herself," Rosi said, "if she hadn't come across those brutes."

"One of them wasn't a brute, and he paid for it with his life.

If the others weren't still in the forest, I'd go there tomorrow to bury him, with Berndt's help."

For a few moments neither of them spoke. Kerbratt, reliving the ceremony, began to hear the singing in his mind. Leni was always at the head of those who made the climb to the monument, to watch him conduct the choir in the long, poignant lament of the *Kindertotenlieder*.

"You can't imagine how attractive she was," he said.

"Don't tell me that!" Rosi reproached him. "I'm getting jealous."

"Don't worry, Rosi. I could have seen her again after the ceremony was forbidden, but I didn't. And she never came to the church, or anywhere else, to hear us."

"Why not?"

His face seemed to sag.

"I don't know. She was married. . . ."

"To Johanna's father?"

"Yes. An archaeologist. He worked with Koldewey at Babylon for a long time, if I remember right. He was seldom at home—though Johanna looks exactly like him, so he was there long enough to . . ."

"And to think that Johanna brought Leni back to you!" Rosi said with an enigmatic smile.

"Life sometimes plays odd tricks like that."

She put her arms around him.

"You were like a lovesick adolescent, Hans. You went off to rescue your fair lady from the dragon."

He looked at Leni as she lay sleeping.

"I don't know if I loved her," he said. "Maybe the reason I didn't want to see her again was that I was afraid to find out if I loved her or not. And I still don't know, after everything that's happened." He pursed his lips, then added, "We can't keep her here, Rosi."

"You want to put her in a hospital? But where? Sonnenstein Haus, in Pirna?"

He shook his head.

"Johanna won't accept being separated from her, I know that. What's needed is an institution where they'll let her be with her mother. I think it would be good for Leni, and Wildgrüber agrees. In any case, I won't keep Johanna here by herself. She's too hostile to me." He suddenly seemed dejected.

Rosi lightly stroked his swollen face.

"I'm going to take care of you now," she said tenderly.

He leaned toward her and kissed her with the uninjured side of his mouth, and she accepted his kiss with weary dignity. He caressed her ample breasts slowly.

"I'm too old for that," she protested.

"And what about me? I'm too old to get beaten up in the forest in the middle of the night."

He unbuttoned the top of her dress. Leni murmured something in her sleep.

"I may finally start to believe I'm the only woman you'll always stay with," Rosi said.

Johanna awoke with a bitter taste in her mouth that she had never known before. She put out her arm. Leni's place in the bed was still empty. Reality gradually came back in uncertain bits and pieces. Looking through the gap between the curtains, she saw that it was still dark. *My God, he drugged me!* she thought, suddenly sitting up. *He drugged me because he didn't want me getting in the way of his sneaky little schemes.*

She got up and groped her way out of the room. She heard none of the usual sounds in the hall. No clatter of dishes from downstairs, no voices or footsteps from the courtyard. Yet she felt as if she had slept a very long time.

When she came to the bottom of the stairs she sat down on the last step and wept. Hearing a sound behind her, she looked around. Rosi was coming toward her in her dressing gown, holding a candle.

"What are you doing here, at this time of night?" she asked.

Johanna stopped crying but didn't answer.

"I was wondering who would be creeping around like a little mouse at four in the morning," Rosi said playfully.

"Four o'clock!" Johanna exclaimed. "My mother's probably dead by now!"

She began crying again. Rosi leaned down, put her arm around her shoulders and said, "Your mother is back."

Johanna shook her head.

"No, she isn't. I just left her room and she's not there."

"She's sleeping in Herr Kerbratt's room," Rosi said. "She's very tired."

Johanna started.

"Why in *his* room?" Her next words were a cry of distress: "Did she really go away?"

"Yes, she really did," Rosi answered gently. "She went so far away, in fact, that it's lucky she was able to come back."

Johanna stared at her, shivering.

"How did Herr Kerbratt find her?" she asked. "I saw him go off to look for her."

"He didn't really find her," Rosi said mysteriously. "She was waiting for him. But he had to go a long way and he got very tired, so he'll probably sleep late too."

"Is he . . . sleeping in his room, with my mother?"

"No, he's sleeping in my room," Rosi said with an expression of mingled satisfaction and pride. She smiled and began slowly stroking Johanna's hair. Johanna closed her eyes.

When she awoke, it was broad daylight. She quickly got dressed and went to Kerbratt's room.

She knocked on the door, then tried to open it. It was locked. She stood there for several seconds, feeling alone and abandoned. Then she ran off and burst into Franz's room. He looked at her in surprise. She immediately noticed the half-open cloth bag on the floor beside his bed.

"It's true, you're leaving this morning," she said.

She had forgotten how soon he would be gone. She sat down on the bed and pressed her face against the covers.

"Now I'll have no one . . . no one at all," she murmured.

He put out his hand.

"Why are you talking like that? Your mother came back.

Rosi told me when she brought me my breakfast. And I'll be back in a few days.''

"They won't let me see her,'' she said, raising her head to look at him. "She's in Kerbratt's room and the door is locked.''

"I'm sure it's locked to keep her from running away again, not to keep you from seeing her.''

Johanna hadn't thought of this.

"You really think so?''

He nodded.

"I wonder if I'll still be here when you come back.'' She sighed. "You're right: Kerbratt won't want to keep my mother here, not after she tried to run away.''

"I never said that!''

"You said he'd locked her in to keep her from running away. He'll always be afraid she's about to try it again.''

"That only shows he cares about her.''

Johanna stood up and began pacing the floor.

"I don't know if he cares about her. I have a feeling there are things he hasn't told me. He said there were no signs of injury on her body. How could he know that unless he'd . . .'' She hesitated. "I want my mother to be protected and looked after. But I can't stand him hiding everything from me, and I especially can't stand him not letting me see her! How can he do that, Franz? It's not right!''

Her voice broke and tears came into her eyes. Franz looked at her, not knowing what to do.

"Don't be upset, Johanna. Think of the celebration we'll have when I come back—it'll be even better than last night!'' His voice became serious: "Listen, Rosi will soon be here to help me get dressed, so . . .''

"But *I* can help you!''

"No, I'd rather have Rosi,'' he said. "She's used to it.''

"What do you mean, she's used to it? You've only been here since the night before last!'' The look on his face told her not to insist. "All right, I'll leave when she comes.''

"I didn't mean . . .'' he began. "I didn't sleep well last night. I don't feel the way I did yesterday,'' he said apologetically.

"You mean you wish we hadn't . . ."

"Oh, no! I'm glad we did! But it's just . . ." He shook his head despairingly. "I was so happy here with you!"

"Franz, do you *really* think we'll get married some day?"

He smiled in a way that she couldn't interpret. Then there were footsteps on the stairs and Rosi opened the door.

"Am I interrupting a love scene?" she asked playfully.

"You're in a cheerful mood today," Franz said.

His remark seemed to surprise her. Her face darkened.

"Can I have the key to Herr Kerbratt's room, so I can see my mother?" Johanna asked.

"You're forgetting what I told you last night," Rosi said firmly. "She mustn't be waked up."

"I want to see her," Johanna said in a choked voice. "I won't wake her up."

She thought Franz would back her up but he said nothing. Rosi began helping him take off his pajama top. Seeing the look he gave her, Johanna knew she had better leave.

Kerbratt found her sitting on the floor in front of the door of his room.

"What are you doing here?" he asked.

She looked up and saw him silhouetted against the skylight over the staircase.

"I want to see her," she said stubbornly.

"You can see her when I come back from Freiberg, but not before. She had a very hard night and I don't want anyone to disturb her till I get back."

"But I won't disturb her," Johanna pleaded. "I'll be quiet. I won't even move. I'll just be there beside her."

"No one is going to see her till I come back, and that's final," he said emphatically.

When she stood up, quivering with fury, she was able to see Kerbratt's face. She stared at him in bewilderment. His lips were swollen to twice their normal size and a big purplish-blue bruise covered his whole left cheek.

"What . . . what happened to you?" she asked.

He let her examine him, as though he wanted to give her time to realize the extent of the damage.

"Now maybe you'll understand a little better why I'm keeping her locked in my room," he said.

He turned away, evidently intending to go to Franz's room. She grabbed his arm.

"My mother too?" she asked in an anguished voice. "Is her face . . . like yours?"

He didn't answer.

"Let me see her!" she shouted, lunging at him.

Startled, he shoved her aside. A door was thrown open. Rosi came out of Franz's room.

"What's going on?" she said indignantly. "Be quiet or you'll wake her up!"

Kerbratt turned to Johanna. She had never seen him look at her like that before, with something like resentment.

"Since you were interested in whether she had signs of injury on her body," he said between his swollen lips, "I'll tell you that she does *now*."

He went into Franz's room and closed the door behind him.

Rosi came and put her arm around her. "There's one thing you should know, Johanna," she said. "There aren't many people who would have done what he did for your mother."

The wagon, driven by Berndt, stopped in front of the door and all the children gathered around it. When Franz appeared, leaning on Heinz, the boys patted him affectionately on the back. The choir launched into a farewell song in his honor, but Kerbratt, pointing to the second floor of the house, gestured for them to stop. Just then Franz leaned toward Johanna and whispered, "If I say lakabu, what do you answer?"

For a moment she felt the same as when they had been together in his room the day before, as if they were alone, clinging to each other. She bowed her head to keep him from seeing her tears.

"You know how I answer," she told him.

"Let me hear it."

"Glup-glup," she said very softly. Then she raised her head. "Give my your wrist. Hurry, we don't have much time."

He held out his wrist. She pushed back his cuff, took her pen and rapidly drew a little mouse with a pointed head and a long, sinuous tail. He watched her warily.

"When you see it in the morning," she said, "pretend it's me, paying you a visit."

He nodded thoughtfully.

"I won't wash, to keep from losing it," he said.

Berndt helped Franz up onto the seat of the wagon and wrapped a blanket around his legs. Franz's hand hung near Johanna's face; she took it and impulsively pressed it against her cheek. Then Kerbratt and Berndt climbed onto the front seat. Without touching the reins, Kerbratt clicked his tongue and the horses started off.

"Come back before twilight," Rosi couldn't help calling after him.

He nodded. Johanna walked a few steps beside the wagon while Franz squeezed her hand, then they parted. When the wagon reached the clump of trees he looked back. Standing a short distance from the others, Johanna was the only one who wasn't waving.

It began snowing just as she reached the gate. Although she was sure no one had seen her, she hesitated when she remembered Kerbratt's orders. Then, decisively, she opened it and took the road that led toward the forest.

Soon she came to the wayside cross. It was partly disjointed and the plaque bearing the words *Iesus Nazarenus Rex Iudaeorum* had fallen to the ground, where it was already partly covered by snow. There were endless low thickets on both sides of the road. Everything around her was cold and deserted, but the hostility of such an environment made her feel closer to the two people she loved most, both suffering. When she thought back on the night before—the singing, everyone's spontaneous joy at being together, and especially the combined presence of Leni and Franz—for a brief, miraculous moment a little of its warmth was rekindled in her. She sang aloud:

> All the girls
> Who form this round
> Don't want a man
> For the summer.

She stopped short. *I'll have you this summer, Franz. I'll have you all to myself.* She imagined him looking at her with his big, bright eyes, his face as pale as the snow. The illusion was so strong that she held out her arms and ran toward him, and cried out "Franz!" Then the face disappeared and she held her hands against her cheeks while she collected her wits.

Suddenly she found herself on a path she didn't remember taking. Around her, gray rocks were scattered through the underbrush, half buried in the ground. She went on walking. Now, instead of Franz's face, she saw his body. He had wanted Rosi to undress him because he didn't want Johanna to see him naked. But she imagined him anyway, his skin pale and translucent. The woods seemed transfigured by his presence. Each tree she brushed against seemed like his touch.

"Franz," she said. "I'm yours. I'm giving myself to you."

What's the matter with me? she thought when she realized that she had spoken aloud. *I must be as crazy as Mutti.*

She leaned against a tree and looked at the footprints she had made in the snow. The strip of undisturbed snow on either side of them seemed too wide and empty: Leni's footprints should have been beside them.

"I want you to come to my wedding, Mutti!" she said aloud. "If you want to go into the mountains afterward, we'll go with you. We'll all get lost together, and if anyone wants to hurt you, they'll have to hurt me too. And then Franz will get revenge for both of us."

She looked at the tops of the trees. She was drifting far from Kerbratt's house, where her mother was being kept locked in a bedroom after going through something terrible that no one would tell her about.

She began walking again and told herself she would keep going till she dropped. She heard the harsh, brief cry of a bird close by. In front of her, the trees were thinning out and she could see that she had almost reached the plain. Then, to her left, she heard a twig snap. Instinctively she hid in a thicket away from the path.

Scraped by frozen branches, she waited anxiously, not daring to move. A hundred yards away, four horsemen rode across the path in single file, outlined against the plain, the last one leading a riderless horse.

For a long time she stayed where she was. Her hands were numb but she was afraid to clap them to bring the circulation back. Finally she crept out of her hiding place. Where the riders had passed, another path crossed the one she had been following. The horses' hoofprints were still clearly visible in the snow. Farther on, the second path curved to the left; evidently it too led toward the edge of the forest.

She decided to leave the path and walk through the underbrush. Her hallucinations of a short time before were gone now. Each tree stood out distinctly, with the precision of an etching. She remembered the knights in armor she had dreamed of seeing at the circus. She didn't imagine them pointing their swords and lances at her, but she envisioned her mother's body, naked in the snow, being slowly pierced by a lance inflicting a fatal wound.

She took a deep breath of cold air. She was so tired she couldn't walk in a straight line. All her senses seemed to be concentrated in her hearing. Suddenly she worried that she had let herself go too far.

All at once the horizon beyond the last trees broadened into a vast expanse of gentle hills. Johanna stopped and looked out over that serene landscape. To her right, cutting straight across the fields, she saw the four riders, followed by the riderless horse—five black dots in a row—moving toward the hills. She suddenly felt lighter. For a long time she couldn't take her eyes off their slow caravan.

S I X

omeone was knocking.

"Open up! What do you mean, locking yourself in like that?"

Lying in bed, Johanna put her hand to her cheek. It was hot.

"He slapped me!" she cried out. "First I go away because of him, and then he slaps me!"

"You deserved it," Rosi said through the door. "He was looking for you for hours!"

"But I went away only because he wouldn't let me see my mother!" Johanna protested.

Footsteps in the hall, then a violent blow shook the door.

"Open this door, damn it! This is *my* house!"

Kerbratt. She hadn't heard him come up the stairs. She stood up and looked around the room. The small dresser beside the bed. She pushed it against the door.

Kerbratt pounded.

"What's going on in there? What are you doing? Open the door, you hear me? If you don't, I'll get a ladder and come through the window, and then you'll wish you'd let me in!

That slap I gave you just now was nothing compared to what you'll get if you don't open the door!"

She closed the shutters and locked them.

"Now let's see you try to come through the window!"

"That little bitch . . ." Kerbratt began, but she couldn't hear what came next.

After a brief discussion with Rosi, he spoke to Johanna again.

"Listen, Johanna," he said, "if you want to go away from here, I won't try to stop you. And you can take your mother with you. All I want is to be rid of you both, and all the trouble you've been causing me."

"You're the one who told me to come here! I wouldn't have done it if I'd known what you were like!"

"I told you not to go past the gate," he said, anger coming back into his voice. "Don't you understand that it's dangerous out there now? Wasn't it enough for you that I'd spent a good part of the night looking for your mother? And didn't you see how my face looked when I came back?"

"How do you expect me to know it's dangerous?" said Johanna. "You don't tell me anything. I have to guess everything a little bit at a time. I don't even know what happened to my mother. I don't even know what you did to her when . . ."

"I've had enough of your insinuations!" Kerbratt thundered.

"I'm not insinuating anything. You told me that now you *know* she has signs of injury on her body."

Johanna heard movement on the other side of the door, then Rosi's pleading voice: "Be calm, Hans." She gathered the few objects she had brought to the house and put them into her bag.

"All right, my mother and I will leave," she said. "If you go back downstairs, I'll come out and get her, and then you'll be rid of us."

"Don't you understand, you little fool, that I can't let you leave now because there's a group of dangerous men wandering in the forest?"

"Dangerous?" Johanna said scornfully. "No, Herr Kerbratt, you can't call them that."

"What . . . Why . . ." he stammered, taken aback.

"I saw the men my mother met in the forest."

"How did you see them?" Rosi asked skeptically.

"First of all, how many of them were there?" Kerbratt asked.

"I'll only talk to Rosi," Johanna said. "Since you won't let me see my mother, I won't answer you."

"Tell us how many there were," said Rosi, exasperated. "This is no time to make us drag every word out of you."

"Four men on horseback, plus one horse without a rider," Johanna answered after a long wait.

There was another whispered discussion on the other side of the door.

"Are you just trying to make us think you were in danger so we'll forgive you?" Rosi asked suspiciously.

"Of course not," said Johanna. "They were very nice to me."

"What did they say? What did they *do* to you?"

The anxiety she heard in Rosi's voice gave Johanna a vengeful feeling of superiority.

"They let me ride their extra horse," she said. "It was the first time I'd ever been on a horse. He was very gentle. Then one of the men, the oldest one, took a Russian doll in a peasant costume from his bag and gave it to me. He said that ever since he left home he'd been looking for a little girl nice enough to give it to."

"Open the door! I'd like to see that doll!"

"I lost it on the way back," Johanna said quickly. "I dropped it."

"She's telling us a stupid lie," Kerbratt said.

"We can go and look for it if you want to," Johanna said. "I'm sure we can still see it in the snow—it's dressed in very bright colors."

"Enough!" roared Kerbratt. "I'm breaking open the door!"

A formidable blow jolted the dresser that Johanna had pushed against the door. She jumped back and waited for the second blow. Then, when it didn't come, she decided to counterattack. She went back to the door and kicked it angrily.

"Tell me how you knew there aren't any signs of injury on my mother's body," she demanded, "and then later, how you knew there were?"

She realized she was speaking in the shrill, disagreeable voice that irritated Grete so much. The result wasn't long in coming. Kerbratt swore loudly, then she heard his footsteps going down the stairs. She pushed the dresser aside and opened the door, holding her bag with one hand. Rosi, pale-faced and red-eyed, stood in the hall.

"Why did you act like that?" she asked. "He wanted to help you. He really did. But now . . ."

"Now," said Johanna, "it doesn't matter anymore. My mother and I are leaving. He hates me. I don't want to stay with someone who hates me."

She stepped into the hall, dragging her bag behind her and looking down at the floor. Rosi moved to the head of the stairs to block her way.

"No, he doesn't hate you," she said. "But you seem to do everything you can to make him angry. Your story about the doll . . ." She gently took Johanna by the hand. "Look, there's something you have to understand; I didn't make myself clear enough this morning. If it hadn't been for him, your mother would be dead now."

Johanna shook her head.

"I'm going away from here, and I'm taking her with me."

"She can't ride a bicycle."

"Then I want to know what's wrong with her!" Johanna said forcefully. "I want to . . ."

She heard a moan through the door of the room in which Leni was sleeping.

"You see? Now you've waked her up," Rosi reproached her.

Johanna knelt in front of the door with a piercing wail, like the cry of a dying animal. Rosi hurried to her in alarm.

"Come," she said, taking her by the hand and pulling her to her feet. She quickly took a key from her belt, unlocked the door and opened it.

In the waning daylight, Leni was sitting on Kerbratt's bed with a vacant expression, watching an anemic sunbeam illuminating a bookcase full of books and musical scores. The end of the bandage around her chest had come loose and was hanging over the side of the bed.

Johanna sat down on the bed beside her.

"This is what I wanted," she said quietly. "I wanted to be here when you woke up."

She threw her arms around her. Leni cried out.

"Stop!" Rosi ordered. "You're hurting her!"

Johanna drew back in dismay.

"Maybe they gave you a doll," Rosi said. "If so, you were very lucky, because that's not how they treated your mother. Among other things, they beat her with a riding whip."

Hot tears welled up in Johanna's eyes.

"I don't know if she'll ever get over what they did to her," Rosi continued coldly. "And your way of being helpful was to sneak out of the house and wander around in the forest!"

Johanna unthinkingly wrapped the end of the bandage around her finger. What had come over her? Just then Leni looked down at the sheets with a sigh.

"Up there," she said hoarsely.

Johanna leaned toward her.

"Yes, Mutti?" she asked eagerly. "Up there?"

"Up there," Leni repeated.

She resumed her contemplation of the bookcase.

Kerbratt heard the steps creaking but didn't turn his head. Johanna emerged from the shadows of the stairwell, walked toward him slowly and then stopped halfway. He looked up and saw that tears had left glistening furrows on her cheeks. He motioned her closer. She sat down near him, timidly. She wished she could say something, but it was Kerbratt who finally broke the silence.

"I used to know her," he said softly. He seemed very old. "Long ago, long before the war, she asked me to bring the choir into the forest on the anniversary of a tragedy that happened to the son of a friend of hers. For years we held memorial ceremonies at the place where the boy died. That's where I found her when she ran away," He paused. "She seemed to be waiting for me. Hearing all of you singing must have brought back those memories so strongly that she was drawn there as if she were hypnotized."

"A little while ago, when she woke up," Johanna said, "do you know what she said, twice? 'Up there.' "

"Ah, you see . . . Yes, I'm sure it could have done her good, put her back in contact with reality. And maybe being with me again might also have done her some good," he said, sounding almost apologetic. "But then . . ."

"I'm very sorry I told you that story about the doll. I don't know what made me do it."

"And I'm sorry I slapped you. But you can imagine . . . Let's not talk about all that. What matters is that now you realize the harm those brutes can do."

"The harm they *could* do," she said with a little smile. "They've gone. They left the forest."

"You saw them?"

What a question! She would see them all her life.

"Yes." She stretched out her arm. "They went in that direction, away from here."

"South. Toward Czechoslovakia," Kerbratt said, as though talking to himself. "Well, that's one serious worry we don't have anymore."

"Why did they have a horse without a rider?" Johanna asked.

"They shot the horse's rider."

Her eyes widened.

"Why?"

Kerbratt seemed embarrassed.

"He refused to mistreat your mother like the others."

"Mistreat her?" Johanna repeated.

"He wasn't a brute like the others, so . . ." He shook his head. "I'm afraid your mother may have unpredictable reactions to what she suffered. She may run away again. That's why I have to keep her locked in."

"Do you think she'll recover?"

"If you mean just waking up some morning and wondering, 'How did I get here? What am I doing in this house?' as if nothing had happened, no, I don't think so. But if she could go to a hospital or a clinic and be treated by a specialist, I'm sure she'd have a good chance."

"But Dr. Wildgrüber said it was all right for her to stay here."

"That was before last night."

"But where would she go? Where would *we* go?"

"Dr. Minsch told me about a clinic that had an excellent reputation before the war. He can recommend that your mother be admitted to it." He paused. "It's in Prague. From Freiburg, it's only three hours by train."

Johanna suddenly understood why Kerbratt was so calm. Everything was already arranged.

"Prague?" she said in a faltering voice. "But why . . . why shouldn't we stay here, now that those men are gone?"

"Because the harm has already been done. Minsch had heard of this clinic because most of its patients were German. But we'll have to find out if it still exists. I think it would be good for your mother to go there, Johanna. She'd be in a city that's outside the war, and she'd have proper treatment for as long as necessary."

Johanna was no longer listening. Only the phrase "outside the war" caught her attention. She had been told that about Dresden, too.

"But what about me?"

"You'd go with your mother, of course. We'd try to find a family who would take you as a boarder. You could go see her every day."

Johanna felt resigned.

"I'll be gone when Franz comes back, won't I?" she asked tonelessly.

"I'm afraid so. Franz's treatment is going to take longer than we expected."

"If my mother and I have to go away, I'd like to see him before I leave," she said imploringly.

Kerbratt shook his head.

"Minsch wants him to have complete rest, without the slightest excitement of any kind. And I don't even know which hospital he'll be taken to in Chemnitz."

"Then it's *serious!*" she sobbed.

"If you love him even a little, remember that although not seeing him will be painful, it will help him recover. Sometimes not doing something we want to do is the best proof of . . ."

I wish he'd shut up, she thought. "Is Prague very far from here?" she interrupted.

"I've already told you it's three hours from Freiberg by train. It's not exactly on the other side of the world."

"My father had a friend in Prague," she said, "a college professor who worked in the same field he did."

"We could write to him," Kerbratt suggested.

"I don't even remember his name. I just happened to read a letter he wrote."

"Try to remember," Kerbratt urged.

She remembered the devastated living room and the big gray book, *Könige Babyloniens und Assyriens*. The letter with its signature in blue ink, with big, slanting downstrokes, fell to the floor. She closed her eyes. *I'm abandoning you, Franz, but it's for my mother's good, and not for long, you understand? Not for long.*

"Josef Hutka," she said.

"That was his name?"

"Yes. Professor Josef Hutka. The letter was from Carolinum University in Prague. I think it was dated 1938. He may be dead now. He probably is, in fact."

"It still won't do any harm to send him a letter. His answer will let us know if the clinic still exists."

"But while we're waiting," she said, "can't we try something? Can't we give my mother one last chance before we put her in a hospital?"

"What do you mean?"

"That man who was shot in the forest . . ."

"What about him?"

"We ought to bury him," she said quickly. "Now we can do it."

"Yes, I'd thought of that. I'll go there tomorrow morning with Berndt and Heinz."

She looked at him with her big dark eyes.

"I want to come with you," she said firmly, "and bring my mother. Not for the burial, but because we can go to the monument afterward."

He was dumbfounded for a moment. "You can't be serious! You can't really think that . . ."

"She said 'up there' twice when she was waking up," Johanna interrupted. "It must be important to her."

"But there's the body . . ."

"While you're burying it, I'll keep her away. I'll tell her we're going up to the place where she wanted to go."

Kerbratt seemed to be weighing the pros and cons of her plan.

"Maybe it will give her a good shock as strong as the sad shock she had," Johanna went on. "It might . . . wake her up."

"So you think it works like that, do you?" Kerbratt said with a faint smile. "Even if events could wipe each other out like that, I don't think the joy of being up there again—assuming it gave her joy—could make her forget what she's been through. But I know you mean well, Johanna."

"Please think about it, at least," she pleaded. "It's her last chance. Her last chance before . . ."

"Rosi will say it's a foolish idea, and she'll be right."

"But afterward we'll be able to say we tried everything."

He was silent for so long that she began to wonder if he had heard her. Then he turned his swollen face toward her and said, "As long as we're being foolish, there may be something better we can do."

Through the trees they could see that, four days after the bombing, Dresden was still burning. The curtain of smoke that rose over the plain was brightened by the setting sun. In some places it looked torn, as if birds had snagged it with their claws.

It had been a beautiful day, for that time of year. A foretaste of spring had scattered the mists and wiped away every last trace of snow. Gnats darted everywhere. The children climbed slowly in single file, walking through alternating patches of shadow and slanting red sunlight.

Berndt and Heinz led the way, carrying picks and shovels that reminded Johanna of the prisoners of war she had seen on the day she left Dresden. In front of her, Leni walked calmly, looking down at the ground. Whenever the leaders slowed abruptly, those behind them bumped into each other and Johanna felt Leni's hair against her face. She would squeeze her hand and whisper a few words of encouragement in her ear. Leni would look up as if she were listening for something, but not once did she turn around. Kerbratt was at the end of the line, but Johanna knew he was watching Leni. He had been watching her carefully ever since he told her they were going up to the monument with the choir, just as they had done in the past.

Finally Leni seemed to be getting tired. Johanna was thinking of asking Kerbratt to have Berndt slow down when the leaders came to a complete stop.

"What's the matter?" Kerbratt called out. He came up beside Leni and took her by the arm.

"My flashlight won't go on," Berndt answered.

Suddenly light shone on the bottoms of the trees farther up the slope, silhouetting dark figures against the path. For a moment Leni seemed to come out of her stupor. Her body tensed as one of the figures turned around.

"It's working now," Berndt said.

Kerbratt moved up the line, still holding Leni firmly by the arm. Gravely, the children watched him pass, waiting to resume their climb. Johanna followed him. Partway along the column, Annette grabbed her by the shoulder.

"I'm a little scared," she whispered.

Trying not to lose sight of Leni, Johanna pulled away without answering. A little farther on, Cora was holding Stefan by the hand.

"Forward!" Kerbratt said just as Johanna caught up with him.

The procession started off again, now guided by the sound of Kerbratt's cane striking against stones. Far above the trees was the pale, clear sky. Now and then Johanna could make out the shapes of broad, low rocks in the underbrush, and she thought of the Polish boy's fall and the cry that must have burst from him when he found himself lying helpless, all alone, his leg shattered.

They soon came to a stretch of forest where the trees were thicker. Johanna kept watching the path in the glow of Berndt's flashlight, expecting to see the corpse at any moment. "Only Berndt and Heinz know," Kerbratt had told her. "When we find it, they'll do their work and I'll try to keep Leni and the rest of you at a distance."

Johanna wanted to ask Kerbratt what the young Russian had refused to do to her mother. Had the others wanted him to hit her? She remembered Annette's anxious voice and suddenly wanted to go back to her and ask her what she thought of all that. But she was afraid to lose sight of Leni, even for a minute.

Behind her, one of the girls coughed. Probably Evi, she thought. It comforted her to feel them all around her: Evi, Cora, Annette, Berndt, Heinz, Stefan, Helmut, and the others. They still didn't know what to make of this expedition. Johanna herself had been astonished when Kerbratt told her that he had decided to re-enact the Polish boy's memorial ceremony for the first time since 1938, so that Leni would find herself in exactly the same circumstances as in the past. "But I'm not very hopeful, you know," he had added. Rosi, of course, had thought they were crazy, and was probably half-dead with anxiety at this very moment, now that darkness was falling.

"Halt!" Kerbratt ordered, raising his arm.

They had reached a place where the path widened. Kerbratt went forward alone, holding his flashlight. Berndt and Heinz joined him. They leaned their tools against a tree and began searching the ground. Finally Berndt and Heinz came back to the others, who watched them apprehensively.

"What's happening? What's wrong?" Evi asked.

"Nothing," Berndt replied unconvincingly.

Kerbratt also came back, looking preoccupied. He took Johanna aside.

"He's not there anymore," he told her. "I don't like it."

"Maybe they came back and buried him before going away for good."

"That's not their style," he said ironically.

He looked up the slope and hesitated. Johanna was afraid he might decide to cut the expedition short.

"They left the forest!" she said earnestly. "I saw them! I watched them till they were almost out of sight."

"Let's hope they didn't come back after you stopped watching, or leave other men of their kind behind. In any case, I wish I knew what they did with that poor boy's body."

Johanna took a step and felt something soft under her foot. It was horse dung. From one of the horses she had seen. She paled. Her attention had been entirely absorbed by the search for the young soldier's body, but now she suddenly imagined the scene as it must have taken place. Five men getting off their horses and surrounding her helpless mother . . . Right here, where she was now standing. She ran back to Leni and squeezed her hand.

"She doesn't recognize this place, and that's all to the good," Kerbratt said.

"But when we get to the monument, it'll be different. She'll be herself again," Johanna said with conviction.

"You're stubborn as a mule!" Kerbratt said, not unkindly. He turned to Berndt. "Let's go."

"What shall we do with the tools?" Berndt asked. "Leave them here and get them on the way back?"

Kerbratt thought a few moments, peering into the cool darkness beyond the path.

"No," he finally answered. "We'll take them with us. You never know. . . . Helmut can carry yours, if you're tired."

He waved his cane and the procession began moving again. His limp was more pronounced now. He seemed tired as they passed through a very dark area, then into a less dense part of the forest where the last glow of twilight reached them, cold and bluish, like the first light of dawn.

He leaned toward Leni and said, "We're going up to the monument, to sing in memory of little Zbigniew, the way we used to."

Johanna watched Leni's face for a flicker of interest.

"There aren't as many of us as before," he went on. "There used to be about sixty people altogether, remember? But the songs will be the same, and you'll listen to them in the same place."

Johanna wished she could keep watching her mother's face. Everything depended on what would happen at the monument. Leni, like Sleeping Beauty, might be awakened—not by a kiss, but by memories.

The pace of the climb had slowed and the line was beginning to stretch out. Everyone was breathing more heavily when Berndt saw the stone steps in the beam of his flashlight.

"The stairs!" he cried. "Here they are!"

Kerbratt took him by the shoulder. "That wipes away the years, doesn't it? How old were you?"

"I was eight the first time, in 1935," Berndt said.

Kerbratt turned to Leni.

"Berndt is the only member of the original group who's here tonight," he said.

Leni looked at Berndt in silence.

"Exept for you and me, of course," Kerbratt added without smiling.

"I remember when we made these," Berndt said. "It took us a whole afternoon, with more than thirty of us working. They've lasted well, haven't they?"

Kerbratt nodded. Then, holding Leni by the arm, he led her up the steps to the clearing. The dense, oppressive wall of firs that surrounded it stood out sharply against the light sky. He turned off his flashlight and took her hand.

"See how beautiful the sky is," he said.

He pointed. Her eyes followed his gesture and her lips seemed to form a brief, faint smile. *My God, could Johanna be right?* he wondered. Then she turned and seemed to be looking for the top of the big rock. She slowly lowered her face, and he had the clear impression that she was imagining the fall.

"Poor boy," he said. "But at least we haven't forgotten him."

The children were standing a short distance away, talking quietly among themselves.

"The monument," Berndt said without raising his voice.

Kerbratt turned on his flashlight and aimed it at the mound. The monument had been broken off at the height of the inscription. Only the last two lines remained:

AND BRIGHTNESS SPREADS FROM THE NORTH.
GOD IS CLOTHED IN FEARFUL SPLENDOR.

They were obscured with dark streaks forming a St. Andrew's cross. He stepped closer. Stone chips were strewn over the steps of the mound. The newly exposed cross section of marble gleamed faintly.

He knelt on one of the steps, shaken. That monument symbolized the bond between him and Leni: it was here that they had been united for the first time. He examined the place where the inscription had been defaced, and touched it with his finger. "A blasphemy," he muttered. "A crude soldier's blasphemy."

He stood up and turned around. Leni was still in the middle of the clearing, where Berndt and Johanna had joined her. She seemed indifferent to everything. He wasn't even sure she had seen the monument.

"It doesn't matter," he said to her. "They're gone. What matters is that we're all here together, the same as before. We'll sing, and you'll stand just where you always stood when you listened to us."

He took Berndt aside.

"They must have used some kind of metal tool to do that," Berndt said.

"Yes, and that's not all they used: the cross is drawn with excrement. They probably wanted to make the murder a symbol of revenge against Vlassov, who's very religious. . . ." Kerbratt paused. "Come with me," he said abruptly.

They circled the monument, probing into each bush with their flashlights, but found nothing.

"Go and tell Heinz to bring the children to me," Kerbratt

said. "We mustn't let all this make us forget that we're here because of Leni. Gather some ferns and try to clean off what's left of the monument, without turning on your flashlight. I'm sorry I have to ask that of you, Berndt."

Kerbratt had the children form a semicircle around the mound, with Stefan between him and Leni.

"Turn off the flashlights," he ordered. "Helmut and Cora, light the torches."

In the silence that had fallen, they all heard the matches being struck. Both torches flared. Holding them overhead, Helmut and Cora each stood at one end of the semicircle.

"The flames ravaging our city," Kerbratt said, "were such a tragedy for us that I hesitated a long time before deciding to have you light these torches. But we must regard these flames as glimmers of hope. Ten years ago, torches like these illuminated this monument for the first time. It was erected in memory of a boy killed by falling from that rock the year before. He's buried in Poland, but it was here, under these trees, that our choir first gathered to sing in his honor. It was Frau Seyfert's idea, and now that she's passing through her own personal ordeal I wanted her to come here with us. The monument has been desecrated by pillagers, but what this place represents to us is above blasphemy and violence—isn't it, Leni? It's a symbol of . . ."

"Don't talk so loud," Stefan interrupted, "or you'll wake up that man."

Kerbratt leaned toward the little boy.

"What are you talking about?"

"There's a man sleeping, over there, and you mustn't wake him up," Stefan said, pointing toward the stump against which Leni had been sitting when Kerbratt found her.

Kerbratt took Helmut's torch and walked forward.

Half hidden by underbrush, the young soldier lay on the ground, his blond hair gleaming in the torchlight. Kerbratt knelt and ran his hand over the rough cloth of the uniform.

"So this is where they put him."

The soldier was curled up as if he wanted to protect something. Kerbratt thought he must have been slung over his

horse's back, then brought here and shoved off onto the
ground. Beside his neck was a triangular fragment of the
monument. Kerbratt picked it up and, in the torchlight, was
able to read:

THERE ARE TIMES WHEN THE LI
THEN COMES THE WIND, SWE

He sighed and stood up.

The children had gathered around him in silence. Leni
looked at the young man without emotion.

"All right," Kerbratt said calmly, "go back to the monument."

The children returned to the base of the mound. One of
them was sniffling.

"Berndt and Heinz, you know what to do," Kerbratt said.
"Help them, Helmut."

The earth was loose; it took them only a quarter of an hour
to dig a hole that was big enough. Then they took the young
man by the hands and feet and gently laid him in his grave.

"Goodbye, Alexei Dmitrievich," said Kerbratt, raising his
cane. "Proshchai."

Berndt and Heinz began shoveling earth back into the hole.

"We'll sing Bach's motet *Ich will den Kreuzstab gerne tragen*,"
Kerbratt said.

They had sung it so often in the comfortable darkness of
churches that they all began as if with a single voice. At first,
in the open air and after a strenuous climb, it seemed a little
thin and unsubstantial. But soon it swelled with the serenity
of a soul rising to heaven. Johanna knew the motet from
having heard it in church, but when she tried to sing, her
voice choked. While she listened, she tried to imagine that,
instead of falling, the little Polish boy had jumped from the
rock and flown up through the trees. She looked at Leni,
desperately hoping that the music she had chosen years ago
would affect her. But Leni seemed more remote than ever.

Berndt and Heinz had finished filling in the grave and were
leveling the ground. Kerbratt began singing a slow melody set

to the Beatitudes, and the others joined in: *Blessed are the pure in heart, for they shall see God.*

Johanna smiled sadly. If Franz and the old woman were right, none of them had a pure heart. Even if it wasn't their fault, they were part of something enormously wrong, and would never see a God who had disappeared behind the black smoke that engulfed Dresden. The other children might think that music would protect them, that together they formed an unsinkable raft sailing in harmony under the guidance of Captain Kerbratt, but for her it was different. She wasn't singing, and in a few days she would be on the road to Prague. Franz was far away. She looked at the rock. From where she was, she could distinctly see the top of it through the treetops. It would be so simple to jump from up there. Up there—that was what Leni had said. And maybe that was what she had meant.

"What's the matter?" Annette asked. "Are you crying?"

They had stopped singing and were huddled together, a little frightened by the return of silence.

"Nothing," she said.

"Just remember that you and I didn't know that boy," Annette said. "And the one we love isn't dead."

Heinz had tied two sticks together to form a cross. Kerbratt planted it in the middle of the grave and put the broken fragment of the monument beside it. Then he stepped back and stood very straight. Finally he turned and looked at Leni, but she kept looking at the ground. He turned to Johanna but she avoided his gaze.

Berndt began leading the children away. Johanna saw Annette's blond head disappear around a bend in the path. Suddenly she felt a small hand take hold of hers. It was Stefan, standing between her and Leni.

"Did anybody know we were going to find that dead man there, Johanna?"

"No."

"Then why did we come here?"

III

Time is a child.

—Heraclitus

SEVEN

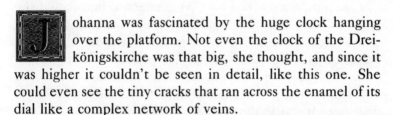

ohanna was fascinated by the huge clock hanging over the platform. Not even the clock of the Drei-königskirche was that big, she thought, and since it was higher it couldn't be seen in detail, like this one. She could even see the tiny cracks that ran across the enamel of its dial like a complex network of veins.

It was ten past five. Ten minutes earlier, they had gotten off the train and mingled with the crowd on the platform. Firmly holding Leni by the hand, Johanna had stood looking for a "gray-haired little old man wearing a black overcoat with a velvet collar," as Professor Hutka had described himself in his letter.

The people around them were talking in a language she didn't understand, which made her feel even more isolated and vulnerable. When the crowd thinned out, she had to face the fact that Professor Hutka wasn't there.

A quarter past five. She led her mother to a bench and they sat down. Leni waited calmly, with her long legs crossed. To comfort herself, Johanna touched the folded letter in her jacket pocket. It had arrived two days ago. Kerbratt had written to Professor Hutka on the day following the burial of the young Russian soldier, and his reply had come a week later. Kerbratt had gone to Freiberg as soon as he had read it, to buy the tickets, check on the train schedule and send a telegram to Hutka.

Twenty past five. It was hard for Johanna to go on sitting.

"Excuse me," she asked a porter in German, "was there another train from Freiberg that came in at the same time as this one, but at another platform?"

The porter frowned.

"Bitte, sprechen Sie Deutsch?" Johanna asked insistently.

He abruptly turned his back on her, muttering, and pulled his creaking cart away. She went back to the bench.

"He spoke only Czech," she explained to Leni, who didn't seem to care.

She sat down and looked at the clock again. *If he's not here by five-thirty,* she thought, *I'll try to get to his house by streetcar.*

That prospect terrified her. What streetcar line should she take? In what direction? And how could she ask, if people didn't understand her? Quivering with impatience, she took Professor Hutka's letter out of her pocket. When she unfolded it to reread it, she was struck by the long downstrokes of his signature, just as she had been when she saw it for the first time. It was in the same blue ink.

The letter from Professor Hutka to Dr. Kerbratt was dated February 24, 1945.

Dear Dr. Kerbratt,

I was greatly saddened by the death of my old friend Professor Rüdiger Seyfert, and what you have told me about his wife and daughter has deepened my sadness. I am, of course, willing to help as much as I can. I am acquainted with Dr. Kucera's clinic because I took a brief rest cure there, two years ago. It is now under the competent management of its founder's daughter, Milena Kucera. Since it is near my house, I could take young Johanna in as a boarder, and she could go to see her mother as often as she liked. I must tell you, however, that I will leave Prague in the middle of May for my yearly course of treatment at Carlsbad, so Johanna can stay with me only until then. But perhaps it will be long enough to improve poor Leni's condition. . . .

Johanna knew the rest of the letter by heart, but she had wanted to reread the part of it that gave her the greatest pleasure. By the middle of May at the latest, she would be back in Kerbratt's house with Leni. Only a little more than two months. Franz would be back by then.

Kerbratt had let several of the children come along when he took Johanna and Leni to the Freiberg station in the wagon. No one was sad; their departure was not like Franz's. On the way, everyone talked about plans for the summer.

The Freiberg station was a small building that must have been attractive and cheerful before the war. Exuberant groups of hikers with rucksacks and alpenstocks must have gathered here to wait for trains that would take them into the mountains. On the walls, faded posters still praised the charm of the Thuringian Forest. But under the posters there were only a few old peasant women, their faces half hidden by black scarves, who looked at Johanna and the others in unfriendly silence. Then the train from Dresden, packed solid with passengers, slowly rolled into the station.

"See you soon," Kerbratt said casually as he lifted the two suitcases into the train.

"I'll think of you when I play my violin!" Annette said.

"Liar!" Johanna retorted, forcing a smile.

Berndt pointed to the posters.

"When you come back, we'll go hiking in the Thuringian Forest!"

"Ah! Here are my two travelers!" said a friendly voice.

Johanna looked up. Professor Josef Hutka was even shorter than she had expected: he had said in his letter that he was "not very tall." Under his snow-white hair, he looked contrite.

"They gave me a wrong platform number and I went all the

way to the other end of the station," he apologized. "I thought the train was late, as trains often are these days, so I waited half an hour before it occurred to me that something might be wrong. That's what it's like to get old."

His coat had a velvet collar, as he had written, and it was dusty. He was looking at Leni with youthful blue eyes under bushy pepper-and-salt eyebrows.

"You haven't changed," he said, smiling. "I recognized you right away. Yet it's been so many years. . . ."

Leni, absorbed in contemplating the clock above him, ignored him.

"My mother is a little . . . absent-minded," Johanna said. "I have a letter from Herr Kerbratt that will explain . . ."

"Yes, I know."

For a moment, Josef Hutka seemed embarrassed. Then he examined Johanna so attentively that she began to feel uneasy.

"You look exactly like your father!" he exclaimed. "It's amazing!" Sensing Johanna's distress, he looked away and lowered his voice. "What a loss! What a great loss for science, and for friendship! That letter brought back so many memories. . . . But what made Herr Kerbratt think of writing to me?"

"I'll explain later," Johanna said wearily.

They picked up the suitcases and went through the waiting room and out into the square.

This was the first time Johanna had been in a city since her flight from Dresden. It was hard for her to believe that the massive buildings around the square were real; they seemed as if they were only part of a movie set hiding the real city, a city of corpses and ruins. She struggled to keep up with Leni and Josef Hutka, fighting back tears. Suddenly a streetcar clattered past, startling her. In her memory, the streetcars of Dresden made no sound. They silently glided back and forth across a ghost city. But this was Prague. This city existed, intact.

Black and freshly polished, Josef's little car was parked all by itself at the end of the streetcar station. Johanna watched him open its trunk, put the suitcases in, and open the front door for Leni. When she saw him sitting behind the wheel with Leni beside him, she stood staring at them through the windshield. Josef rolled down the window.

"Well, what are you waiting for?" he said. "Get in."

"What kind of a car is it?" she asked as she climbed into the back seat.

"A Skoda."

"My father had a little Adler-Trumpf. I haven't been in a car very often since he died."

"I remember your father's car! I even saw you in it, one day when he'd gone to bring you home from kindergarten."

Josef started the engine. There was hardly any traffic, only a few streetcars and bicycles. Johanna's eyes met his in the rearview mirror. They were attentive and friendly. So he had already made an appearance in her life. Maybe she had seen him talking with her father in the living room, consulting heavy books in clouds of cigar smoke.

"That's the Powder Tower," he pointed out, "which used to mark the entrance to the Old City. That building with the Gothic façade is the Carolinum, my university. I worked there with your father for quite a while."

Johanna wondered how the old professor's face could fail to remind Leni of anything.

In front of them were the spires of the cathedral and an imposing, austere building on a hill.

"That's Hradcany Castle," Josef said. He turned right and drove along the edge of a park. "There's the Mala Strana quarter. Your father and I used to walk there, in the summer, when the whole city smelled of linden blossoms. The last time he came here, in 1937, I'd just come back from Crete after going there to study a group of tablets that had recently been discovered at Knossos. One morning he showed me a letter from Grete, who must have been five or six years old. It was full of drawings and inkspots. He laughed and said, 'Look; it's not much easier to decipher than our Minoan characters!' "

"Grete," Leni said, becoming agitated.

Johanna leaned toward Josef and whispered in his ear, "You mustn't say that name. It's in the letter from Herr Kerbratt."

"Grete," Leni repeated. "Grete. Rüdiger. Rudi."

"That's the first time she's said my father's name. I mean, it's the first time since . . ."

"We're almost there," he announced.

They were driving along a quiet street lined with two- and three-storied houses. He stopped, got out of the car and went to open the door for Leni.

"You're going to like it here," he said. "The clinic isn't far and Johanna will come to see you every day."

He took her by the arm and led her toward the front door. Johanna followed. Even before she stepped into the vestibule, the smell of floor polish reminded her of Frau Gildemeister's house. Opening from the vestibule was a staircase with a skylight at the top. The shelves on the walls were covered with statuettes.

"Martha!" Josef called out, putting down the two suitcases.

A door opened on the right and a woman appeared.

"Here are our travelers, Martha," he said.

The woman's ageless face, framed by gray hair drawn tightly against the sides of her head, was not welcoming.

"Dinner will be ready in an hour," she said.

Leni was absorbed in looking at a copper barometer. Josef picked up her suitcase.

"You'll have time to rest, Leni. Come, I'll show you to your room."

"I thought she was going to the clinic as soon as she got here," the woman said.

He turned around.

"No, Martha. I went to see Milena and we agreed that I'd bring her tomorrow morning at ten o'clock."

Josef took Leni familiarly by the arm and led her toward the stairs, but the carpet wasn't wide enough for both of them and Leni made dusty footprints on the freshly waxed floor. Martha rushed forward with a rag in her hand.

"When I go to all that trouble," she muttered in heavily accented German, "I don't expect . . ."

Josef started up the stairs, gently pushing Leni ahead of him. After a few steps he turned around and said something in Czech. Martha stood up, opened a door and disappeared.

He led Leni to a musty, dark little room with striped wall-•
paper and a window facing the street. Johanna followed him,
carrying the other suitcase.

"This is where your father used to sleep," he told her as he
opened the curtains.

She tried to imagine her tall, dark father in this cramped
room.

"Would you like to stay here and rest till dinner?" he asked
Leni.

There was no need of an answer. Leni was already stretched
out on the bed, like a felled tree.

Josef showed Johanna to a bright little room on the other
side of the landing. She saw that it overlooked a small enclosed garden. In the distance, the cathedral and Hradcany
Castle rose above tiled rooftops. To the left, the river was
partly hidden by mist.

"Is that the Elbe?" she asked.

He didn't answer immediately. Seeming lost in reverie, he
stood looking at her as she was silhouetted against the light
from the window.

She was about to repeat her question when he answered,
"No, it's the Vltava, a tributary of the Elbe. I'm a member of
the old school: I still call it the Moldau."

He sat down and she sensed that he wanted to talk.

"For an old man like me, it doesn't seem so long since our
language was given formal recognition."

"You speak German so well. . . ."

"It was my main language till 1918. We weren't officially
allowed to use Czech till our independence. And although I
loved my old oppressed Czech language, until the invasion I
went on speaking German a good part of the time, even in the
street."

"The invasion?" she asked. She thought she had misunderstood. "What invasion?"

He looked at her in surprise.

"You must know that we were attacked and that we've
become a protectorate of the Reich."

"But I thought the Czechs had *asked* the Germans to come
in."

"No, that's not true," he said sadly.

She felt overwhelmed.

"They told us that the Czechs had welcomed our soldiers," she said, "and we believed it. We believed we were liked."

Josef shook his head, remembering the day he had stood with a tearful, angry crowd watching the procession of German tanks.

"Hitler wanted to destroy the Czechoslovakian state," he said, "using the pretext that the German minority in the Sudetenland was oppressed. With the complicity and cowardice of the great powers, he came into Prague. He slept in Hradcany Castle. But no one welcomed him, I can tell you that."

Johanna stood near Josef, with her head bowed, unable to speak.

"You had nothing to do with it, Johanna," he said gently. "Nothing at all. You couldn't know. You and other children were kept in ignorance."

"But to you, I'm an enemy. I don't understand why Herr Kerbratt wrote that letter, unless he didn't know either. But if he doesn't know, who in Germany does?"

Somewhere in the world there must be a place where Mutti and I can stay, she thought. Josef was looking out the window.

"I think my mother and I had better leave," she said.

She had already picked up her suitcase. Josef took it from her and put it back on the floor.

"Johanna, you're the daughter of a man I admired, a friend who gave me encouragement just when I needed it most. You're not an enemy to me; I could never regard anyone from your family as an enemy. But I want you to understand why I'll ask you to take certain precautions when you go out. Some people may be hostile if you speak to them in German."

"That's why that porter didn't answer me, in the station!" she exclaimed. "And Martha," she went on, lowering her voice. "She seems so . . ."

Josef nodded thoughtfully.

"To me, Johanna, Germany isn't the country of Nazism. In spite of the terrible things happening now, I still regard Germany as the country that taught me everything about my occupation, the country that's produced men like your father."

"But other people here will hate me because I'm German," she said.

"Not all of them. There are many Germans in Prague who've been living here since long before the war. Some of them came from the Sudetenland or Silesia; others came from Germany itself, simply because they liked our city." He stepped back and examined her. "To the people who see us, you'll be a girl walking with her grandfather, that's all."

"We'll take walks together?" she asked.

"Of course. I don't intend to hold you prisoner here. Prague is a very beautiful city, as you'll see."

"As beautiful as Dresden was?"

The past tense in her question touched him.

"Some places will remind you of Dresden," he said. "The churches, the gardens. Then there are little streets where you feel as if you're in the Middle Ages, with signs and emblems above the doors. There's the house of the key, the house of the two suns, the house of the three violins . . ."

"Can I walk alone?"

"No, I'll go with you. As long as you're with me, you'll have nothing to fear," he answered firmly. "Furthermore, I don't think there will be any incidents between Czechs and Germans as long as the German commander maintains control over the city. That will be only as long as there's no break-through on the eastern front, but it seems likely that there won't be one for at least several weeks."

"But what if the Russians attack the city?" she asked anxiously. "Will we have time to leave?"

"We'll have a few days' warning. Remember that I have a car to take you away in, or, if worst comes to worst, a basement where you can hide."

"No! No more basements!" she cried.

Josef evidently understood. He gave her a kindly smile, which soothed her.

"Don't worry," he said. "You'll be as happy here as your

father was. You mustn't think that people always have to be unhappy in troubled times."

They entered a big room with floor-to-ceiling bookshelves and glazed cabinets containing dozens of clay tablets covered with ancient writing. Between the two windows overlooking the garden, fragments of bas-reliefs formed a frieze of human figures.

"The most beautiful pieces are on the shelves in the vestibule," Josef said. "The ones here are mainly for use in my studies."

Johanna slipped between two desks piled with folders to look at the books.

"Are you looking for a particular book?" Josef asked.

"Yes," she said, "and here it is."

She put her finger on it. He read its title aloud: "*Könige Babyloniens und Assyriens*, Bruno Meissner."

"My father had a copy of this same book. . . ."

"That's not surprising," Josef interrupted. "It's a classic."

"When I came home after our house had been bombed, I tried to put away all the books that had fallen on the floor, and I found this one. A letter from you was in it, thanking my father for supporting you in some kind of research you were doing. I told Herr Kerbratt about it when he mentioned the clinic in Prague. That's how he knew to write to you."

Josef picked up a thin book from a shelf near the door and handed it to Johanna. She looked at its title page;

JOSEF HUTKA
Professor at Carolinum University

CRITICAL INTRODUCTION
TO THE DECIPHERING OF
THE MINOAN WRITING
IN CRETAN INSCRIPTIONS

"I remember that letter to your father," Josef said. "It refers to the book you have in your hand, which I published at the end of 1937 to sum up my first research in an area that was still partly unexplored. Many of my colleagues had disparaged my work and I was discouraged, but your father wrote me that he was sure I was on the right track. I can't tell you how much that meant to me."

"Did you know my father before that?"

"We'd met at Babylon in 1924. Your father was getting ready to go and work with Woolley's team at the site of Ur. He had the reputation of being a promising young archaeologist. We got along from the start.

"Your father was a radiant man in every sense of the word," he went on. "He loved the sun more than anything else. And to think that he died in all that cold. . . ."

Johanna let her eyes wander over the clay tablets in the cabinets.

"What were you and my father looking for?" she asked.

"The same thing you'd look for in those circumstances," he said. "What would you do if you came across a secret message? You'd try to find a way to understand it, and . . ."

Just then they heard a loud crash in the vestibule.

Josef ran out of the room and Johanna followed. Leni was standing stock-still in the middle of the vestibule, looking haggard. On the floor in front of her were the sand-colored fragments of a shattered statuette. Josef bent down, touched a few of the broken pieces with his fingertips and exclaimed, "The Parthian horseman!"

Johanna could still make out the horse's neck and one of the rider's parted thighs. She bent down and began putting some of the pieces together.

"No, never mind," said Josef. "I'll have to do it myself."

She straightened and looked reproachfully at her mother, who hadn't moved.

"It came from Masjid," Josef said. "My colleague Hoesch found it. It was twenty-three hundred years old."

"Twenty-three hundred years," Johanna repeated dully.

"And then it was shattered by a lunatic," said a voice from the doorway.

Martha was standing on the threshold of the kitchen.

"Martha!" Josef thundered.

Her thin lips formed a mirthless smile. She went back into the kitchen and Josef followed her, speaking Czech. His voice was cold and cutting. Martha answered shortly in the same tone, and Johanna heard no more.

She turned to Leni.

"Why did you do that?" she asked vehemently. "Professor Hutka is going to so much trouble for us because he worked with Papa. And look what you've done!"

"Horses," Leni said, growing agitated.

"Don't quarrel with her about it, Johanna," said Josef, coming back into the vestibule. "I don't hold it against her."

He had brought a whisk broom, a small shovel and a padded wooden box that he must have used for transporting fragile works of art. He got down on his knees and began sweeping the fragments into the shovel. His fingers trembled as he put them in the box. He seemed so sad, and was so obviously trying to hide his sadness from her, that Johanna burst into tears.

"I'll pay you for it," she sobbed. "Even if I have to work all my life, I'll pay you. . . ."

He carefully set the box down on a table.

"We'll put it back together," he said, laying a hand on her shoulder. "It will take an enormous amount of time and patience, but it can be done."

Leni was standing against the wall, looking up at the skylight.

"Take her back to her room," Josef said, "but be gentle with her. We'll bring her downstairs when it's time for dinner."

Johanna realized miserably that he was no longer trying to speak directly to Leni.

The little Skoda rolled into the paved courtyard, skirted a carefully maintained flowerbed and stopped at the foot of the front steps of the clinic. All during the trip, Leni had con-

stantly watched Josef drive, her hand nervously toying with
the catch of the glove compartment.

When the three of them had gotten out of the car, Johanna
drew Josef aside. "Are you sure she'll be all right here?" she
asked.

"When I came here two years ago," he said, "they took
very good care of me."

"What was the matter with you?"

"Nothing much," he answered evasively, "but it was
enough to let me form an opinion of the place. Ah, here's
Saint O."

A nun had just appeared in the doorway of the building.
She came down the steps to meet them.

"This is Sister Saint Odilia," Josef said, "the only saintly
soul in this good city to whom I can talk about my little
ailments."

"But you don't do it often, professor—your health is too
good!" she said, glancing at the two newcomers.

"I hope you'll forgive me for that, Saint O.," he said teas-
ingly.

The floor of the vestibule was polished so brightly that it
might have been done by Martha herself, Johanna thought.
Two people in pajamas were pulling a handcart down the long
hall. Johanna grimaced at the smell of disinfectant. Josef
looked around him.

"It seems awfully calm," he remarked.

The nun started down the hall and Josef and Johanna began
to follow her. But Leni backed into the vestibule and stood
pressing her palms against the wall, her mouth half open in
fear.

"Professor!" Johanna called.

Josef came back while Saint O. stood waiting.

"We're taking you to meet Milena, your doctor," Josef
said. "She'll take care of you, and she's very nice. You'll be in
good hands."

Leni didn't move.

"Saint O., can you go and get Milena?" he asked.

The nun disappeared around a bend in the hall. *Maybe*

Mutti's afraid to be separated from me, Johanna thought hopefully.

Saint O. returned with a slender young woman of about thirty. She had blond hair, high cheekbones and a calm, strong face, and she wore an immaculate white coat.

"Excuse me, professor," she said, "I was expecting you a little later."

"My fear of being late always makes me early," Josef said. "Dr. Kucera, this is Frau Seyfert and her daughter Johanna." And he added in an undertone, "We're having problems getting through the hall."

"You'd better leave her alone with me," Milena said.

Josef took Johanna by the arm.

"All right," he said, "we'll go and wait in the courtyard." Johanna rebelled.

"I won't abandon her like that! She'll never go with you if I'm not here."

"I only want to talk to her," Milena said, "and try to persuade her to go to her room. You can come to see her in a little while."

Johanna gave in. Leni still stood next to the wall, looking frightened.

"Let's go to your room, Leni," Milena said gently when Johanna and Josef were gone. "I've chosen a very pleasant one for you."

Leni went on staring apprehensively down the hall. Milena could see nothing that might upset her.

"Let me try," said Saint O.

She approached Leni cautiously, then seized her by the arm.

"No!" Milena cried.

Leni swung her free arm and slapped Saint O., who stepped on her long skirt, slipped and sprawled on the floor in a flurry of petticoats. Leni watched the nun floundering on the floor in bewilderment, laughed shrilly and bolted for the front door.

"Professor!" Milena called out as she helped Saint O. to her feet.

Josef and Johanna were strolling around the courtyard when

they saw Leni throw open the door. Johanna ran to block the gate but Leni went to Josef's car, opened it and slipped into the driver's seat.

Milena followed her into the courtyard. She, Johanna and Josef stood beside the car in silence, watching Leni turn the steering wheel back and forth, like a child.

"Does she know how to drive?" Milena asked.

Johanna shook her head.

"Get in beside her," Josef said quietly, "and take the key out of the ignition without doing anything sudden."

Johanna went to the other side of the car, opened the door and got in beside her mother. With both hands on the steering wheel, Leni stared sadly through the windshield.

"The picture," she said.

Johanna knew very well which picture Leni had in mind. It showed Grete at the age of three or four, sitting on her father's lap in his car, clutching the steering wheel. Johanna had seen the picture in its usual place on Leni's bedside table just before they left Dresden, and it was probably still there, in the silence of the deserted house.

"We've had a long trip, Mutti," she said, "and now we're here, and Milena will take care of you."

Leni looked at her.

"Come on, let's go," Johanna said, suddenly annoyed.

Leni didn't seem to have heard. Johanna got out of the car and went back to Josef, who was talking quietly with Milena.

"It's because of Grete," she said dejectedly. "Always Grete. . . ."

Milena and Johanna were sitting on the steps, discreetly keeping an eye on the car. Inside it, Leni still hadn't moved. Josef had gone to comfort Saint O., who, Milena had told him, was greatly upset by her misadventure. Milena had asked Johanna to tell her everything about the night of the bombing, their flight from Dresden and their stay at Kerbratt's house.

"For a reserved little girl, you've done a lot of talking," she said when Johanna had finished.

"Reserved? Who told you I was reserved?"

"Herr Kerbratt, in the letter he sent me with the payment for your mother's stay here. Evidently it was about the same as the one he wrote to Professor Hutka."

"But if you already knew about me and my mother, why did you have to question me?"

"Because only you can give me certain details," said Milena. "Only you know how your mother behaved before. I couldn't have understood, for example, why she's sitting frozen behind that steering wheel if you hadn't told me about the photograph on her bedside table."

"Do you think you can bring her back to normal in two months?" Johanna asked.

"We'll have to begin by bringing her out of that car," Milena said jokingly. "And for that, I've got an idea. . . ."

Milena went to the door on the driver's side, opened it and asked Leni to move over. Leni obediently slipped into the passenger's seat and Milena sat down behind the wheel. She drove out of the courtyard and turned left into the calm little street. After a short drive she turned left again, into a long lane bordered by neatly trimmed rosebushes. On this side, the clinic seemed less severe.

"Come, Leni," Milena said when she had parked the car. "Let's try to find some primroses to put in your room."

Leni followed her into the garden, where they found three flowers that had just barely opened.

"Now we'll go and get a vase to put them in," Milena said.

She stepped casually into the building. Leni followed her, her eyes fixed on the bouquet. Milena rummaged in a closet on the veranda.

"Ah, here we are!" she said, triumphantly holding up an opal glass vase. "It will look very pretty in your room."

"Room," Leni repeated.

Milena started up the stairs. She heard Leni coming up behind her.

"It's a pretty little room," she said without turning around. "It gets sun in the morning. I'm sure you'll like it."

*   *   *

When Milena reappeared at the bottom of the stairs, Josef put down his newspaper and Johanna was able to read the headline: FIERCE FIGHTING ON THE ODER. Milena seemed thoughtful and preoccupied.

"I'm sorry, Milena," Saint O. said. "I acted like a beginner. I feel very guilty about . . ."

"Never mind, Saint O.," Milena interrupted. "What matters now is that she's in her room and seems comfortable there."

Milena turned to Johanna. "I'd like you not to come to see her for several days," she said gently.

Johanna could hardly believe her ears.

"But . . ." she stammered.

"Let me explain," Milena said. "I'd like you not to see her because I want to begin by making her feel a *need* to see you. I want her to be aware of your absence and ask for you."

"But if she doesn't ask for me within a few days," said Johanna, "I'll come back anyway! And I'm not leaving without saying goodbye!"

"You can go and see her now, but don't tell her goodbye; just walk out as if you were coming back in a few minutes. If—maybe this evening—she begins to worry about you and says your name, that will be the first crack in her detachment. And we'll have made a start."

Johanna felt weak.

"Her room is on the second floor," Milena told her, "last door before the little hall. I hope you realize how important you can be in your mother's treatment."

Without answering, Johanna climbed the stairs.

"Wasn't that a little cruel?" Josef asked.

"I'm convinced that we must replace Leni's memory of Grete with an awareness of Johanna's *existence*," Milena replied calmly. "What I'm hoping is that Johanna's absence will make Leni feel that something is missing. Getting Johanna back may then satisfy her, and restore her taste for living."

"Don't you think you should at least give her time to get acclimated before you take Johanna away?"

"Did you notice anything unusual today?"

Josef thought for a moment.

"Yes, I noticed that there weren't as many people here."

"If I weren't an optimist, I'd say that the rats are beginning to desert the ship."

"You mean your clientele?"

"Yes, my faithful German clientele," she said bitterly. "I don't know what rumors are circulating in the city, but my German patients are leaving."

"Where can they go? The Russians are in the Sudetenland!"

Milena shrugged.

"I don't stand around in the train station to ask them where they're going. All I know is that they keep asking for their bills. Only last night old General von Sparnberg, who came here to have his gout treated, suddenly panicked and left in such a hurry that he forgot to take half his clothes."

"You make me feel as if I should put Leni and Johanna on the next train out of here!"

"I thought of that, but after examining Leni I realized that if anything can be done to help her, it must be done now."

Josef glanced at his newspaper.

"From what the paper says, the front has been stable for nearly a week. If you want my opinion, the war won't be over for several months."

"That's what I think, too. But when Leni's treatment is over, assuming I have time to finish it, you'd better send them back to their mountains as quickly as you can."

"The Russians may have captured those mountains by then. In any case there will still be quite a few Germans left in Prague—they may be safer here than anywhere else."

"Nothing's happening now because the front is holding fast and Franck has the city well in hand. But if the people decide to settle some scores on their own, can you imagine the explosion of hatred it may set off?"

"You may be one of its victims, Milena, with all the Germans you've treated through the years."

"I've taken my precautions," she said brusquely. She

paused, then went on. "As for Leni, let's say it's a race between events and me. But I'm hopeful. As soon as I find the first crack, I can begin breaking through the detachment that's probably her protection against pain."

"She's not always detached. Johanna says she sometimes reacts violently, as I saw for myself last night, when she broke a Parthian statuette of a horseman."

"What?" Milena cried.

Dumbfounded, Josef watched her run up the stairs.

Leni was standing in the middle of the room, looking at her bleeding hand. Blood was steadily dripping onto a piece of broken glass that covered an engraving lying on the floor. Johanna hurried back and forth between Leni and the wash basin with bloodstained cloths in her hands.

Milena gently examined Leni's injured hand.

"It's not too serious," she said. "But why didn't you call me?"

"For our last time together, I wanted her all to myself," Johanna said plaintively.

Milena opened a closet and took out some absorbent cotton and a bottle of hydrogen peroxide. Leni winced as Milena cleaned and disinfected the long gash in her palm.

"But how did you know?" Johanna asked.

"You told me about how she was attacked in the forest, and so did Herr Kerbratt, in his letter, but you didn't tell me about the incident last night, with the statuette. You should have, because it's important."

"I didn't think there could be any connection. . . ."

"There was a connection," Milena said.

She pushed a button that rang an electric bell. Almost immediately there was a knock on the door and Saint O. came in, holding a first-aid kit.

"Get rid of that," Milena said, pointing to the engraving.

Johanna looked at it as Saint O. picked it up. Barely visible behind the broken, bloody glass was a knight in armor on a white horse, leaning back from the apparition of some sort of mythic animal. The engraving was entitled *The Vision of Saint Hubert*. Saint O. carefully carried it out of the room.

"This is the nun who will take care of you from now on, Leni," said Milena when Saint O. had returned. "She'll bandage your hand now, and every day she'll help you to get dressed and eat your meals."

Johanna felt herself being gently pushed out of the room. She turned and saw Leni staring at the bandage Saint O. was wrapping around her wrist. On the wall above her was a dark rectangle where the engraving had been.

"What if she doesn't ask for me?" Johanna said. "What if she *never* asks for me?"

"Then Milena will know what she wanted to know, and she'll try to find another solution," Josef said. "But don't worry; the experiment won't go on too long, I'll see to that."

"My mother has been acting badly since last night."

"Try to forget all that. We're taking a walk, and you'll see that it's very enjoyable to discover such a beautiful city with such a good guide."

She laughed. *At last!* he thought. They had driven in the general direction of Hradcany Castle, crossed a railroad track and left the car on a public square, at one corner of a baroque church whose name he couldn't remember. He was beginning to notice lapses of memory.

And now they were walking along little streets near the river. The Vltava suddenly appeared at the bottom of a slope, pale, almost golden. The sun had finally broken through the mist and the whole city was bathed in light.

In the midst of that peace, Josef could pretend that danger existed only in his mind. But he knew it was a deceptive feeling; he remembered the calm September morning in 1938 when he had been in this same neighborhood with the same sense of security he had now. Newspaper and radio reporters all over the world were waiting for the speech by Hitler that would give his final decision: peace or war with Czechoslovakia. Martha had followed the news almost minute by minute but, to her surprise, Josef had left the house and strolled through the city. It had seemed even more beautiful than usual. "The city is calm," he said when he came back. "Calm!" Martha sneered. "It's calm like an animal hypnotized by a cobra that's about to strike. Hitler does that to his victims; it's one reason for his success."

He took Johanna by the arm. The soles of their shoes clattered cheerfully on the uneven cobblestones. The Waldstein Palace rose above the trees like a fairy-tale castle, and the air was so light and clear that he felt the weight of countless gray days lifting from his heart.

Soon they came to the river. In front of them, the statues of the Charles Bridge stood out against the bright sky. Johanna watched a piece of wood floating in the small eddies in the surface of the river. Maybe it would go on drifting till it reached Dresden and passed under the Augustusbrücke, the bridge she had crossed with Hella for the last time. High up on the hill, behind the long façade of Hradcany Castle, big scaffoldings masked the southern tower of the Cathedral of St. Vitus and tiny workmen could be seen above an immense pale green awning.

"It feels good to be here," she said.

Josef had exactly the same feeling.

"Yes, it does," he replied. "And now, how would you like an ice cream to celebrate your first day here? I know a place where they sell ice cream that's almost the same as before the war."

"Why don't we walk under the bridge, as long as we're here?" she proposed.

"I'm old enough to be your grandfather but you want me to go trotting around as if I were a friend of your own age," he said jovially.

"I made a friend my own age just before I came here, and I miss him."

Josef was astounded to feel a slight shadow pass over his happiness. He tried to joke.

"You do? Then why didn't you tell him to come here with you?"

"He was wounded," she said gravely. "He's in a hospital now, but it's not too serious."

"I see. . . . So I should consider myself lucky to have you all to myself."

She smiled so childishly and brightly that he was moved to tears. He turned his head away.

They stopped under the bridge, where the air was cold and damp, as if they were in a catacomb. The exposed stone surfaces were covered with inscriptions, mainly names and dates.

"Hanna–Vaclav, 9/1/31," Johanna read aloud. She turned to Josef. "Do you think those two were in love?"

He considered the two names scrawled in clumsy capital letters.

"Maybe. Maybe not. One thing is sure: on the first of September, 1931, under the Charles Bridge, they were together. That's what's called a scientific conclusion," he said, smiling. "Don't forget that I have a lifetime of experience in drawing conclusions from inscriptions."

"Yes, but you study much older inscriptions than this one," Johanna said. "Nineteen thirty-one is the year Grete was born." She pensively traced the letters with her fingertip. "Maybe that walk along the river was the last thing they thought about."

"What do you mean?"

"Maybe they're where Grete is now."

"Why do you want them dead and buried? Maybe they're alive and married now, with a lot of children."

"Maybe," she agreed, seeming disappointed. She took hold of his arm. "Why don't we write 'Jo–Jo, 3/1/45' somewhere?"

"Why Jo–Jo?"

"For Josef–Johanna. Maybe in fourteen years someone will come by here and say about us what we said about those other two."

He laughed.

"In fourteen years you'll be a charming young woman taking a walk here with your husband. He might get jealous!"

"Have you ever been married?" she asked.

"No."

"Martha was furious about that statue," Johanna said. "She must have already hated us. . . ."

"Why?"

"Because we're German."

"Martha is an old maid who's obsessed with order. And she knows how much my collection means to me. She must have thought I'd be heartbroken."

"Were you?"

"It's not so much what the statuette was worth, though it was very valuable. It's what it meant to me personally: a friend gave it to me in the days of my first excavations."

Maybe, he thought, he had been really happy only when, as a young archaeologist, he had been wonderstruck in the harsh light of the East. It was the time of the ullu bird, the time of . . .

Johanna was leaning against a lamppost, looking at the water.

"There's a story about a bird that I'll have to tell you some day," he said enigmatically.

She turned to face him.

"Why not now?" she asked.

He could tell that she loved to hear stories. It was typical of children her age. He hesitated.

"It would take too long," he told her timidly.

What he had wanted to say was, "It would be too soon." As they resumed their walk, he watched her striding over the cobblestones with her slender legs while the breeze ruffled her thick, dark hair. She looked at him and he felt as if she had caught him doing something wrong.

"Then when?" she asked.

"When what?"

"When will you tell me that story about a bird?"

He smiled and tried to calm the pounding of his heart. They were now climbing a flight of steps between two high walls. Above them, the spires of the Cathedral of St. Vitus appeared to watch over a city deserted because of some medieval plague.

"This Mala Strana, with all its steep slopes," he said, breathing heavily, "isn't for someone my age. But we're almost there."

They came into St. Nicholas square. The tearoom was on a little side street. They were the only customers. They sat down at a marble-topped table beside a faded tapestry. A young woman wearing a small lace headdress was drying cups behind a carved wooden counter. Josef ordered two vanilla ice creams and two glasses of lemonade.

Johanna sat silently looking through the window, frowning slightly. Josef discovered that she had a few freckles, and light down around her lips.

"*Na zdravi!*" he said, raising his glass.

"And what am I supposed to answer?"

"*At slouzi!*"

"*At slouzi!*" she repeated.

She felt ill at ease in that deserted, antiquated tearoom, with an old man who stared at her. The lemonade was too warm and too sweet.

She leaned toward him and whispered, "The waitress is looking at us."

He glanced toward the counter, where the young woman was indeed looking at them.

"Well, what of it? There's no one else here! She's bored, poor girl!"

"She's not looking at us in a nice way. I'm sure it's because she heard you speaking German to me when we came in."

"Just think of all the Germans who have come to this place since it first opened!"

"Yes, but that was before . . ."

She seemed nervous.

"Would you rather have had a different flavor?" he asked.

"No, the vanilla is very good."

When she had finished, he stood up.

"Let's go," he said.

She didn't seem to relax till she was outside. He watched her blinking in the sunlight as he paid the check, and his hand tightened on the door handle.

"Thank you," she said. "I enjoyed the ice cream. I hadn't eaten any for a long time. And I've enjoyed the walk, too. We've seen some very pretty sights."

He forced himself to smile. They walked back to the car in silence.

"What's wrong?" he asked as he opened the car door.

"I wish I knew if my mother has asked for me."

"We'll find out when we get home: if Milena hasn't called, it will mean your mother hasn't asked for you. I doubt that she has, because I think it's still too soon."

"Well, I think she *has* asked for me," Johanna said a little aggressively.

She was silent during the drive home. When they had gone into the house, she waited in the vestibule while he went to question Martha in the kitchen. She noticed that another statuette had replaced the horseman on the shelf.

Josef came out of the kitchen and said, "Milena hasn't called."

Johanna started up the stairs without answering. He saw her distress but felt powerless to help her.

"It's still too soon, I've already told you that," he said.

She went on climbing the stairs. A few moments later he heard her gently close the door of her room.

EIGHT

"Did the bird come at the same time every day?"

"Yes, at twilight," Josef said, as though talking to himself. "Just as the setting sun turned the ramparts of the southern palace pink. He was always there at the same time."

"Oh, look!" Johanna cried.

In front of her was a narrow street bordered by very small houses painted different colors, red and green and blue-gray.

"Those originally belonged to the huntsmen of the castle," Josef said. "Later, goldsmiths lived in them. That's why this is called the Street of Gold."

"They look like something out of a fairy tale!"

He smiled.

"This city is full of fairy tales. You'll find them everywhere, behind every door."

Johanna's face clouded.

"Do you know any fairy tales where a mother completely forgets her daughter exists?"

"In fairy tales there's always a time when everything goes badly," he replied.

Afraid she might become taciturn again, he quickly led her toward one of the castle towers.

"This is the Daliborka," he said. "It's called that because a young knight named Dalibor was once thrown into its dungeon. To pass the time, he made a violin from smuggled-in pieces of wood, and he played such beautiful music on it that the whole city was spellbound."

"Did he get out of the dungeon?"

"The story doesn't say."

She looked at the massive tower and thought of Annette's violin.

They turned away and walked in the direction of the Eastern Gate, toward St. George Street.

"In the Middle Ages," he said, "people came in through that bricked-up doorway over there, on the ground floor of the Black Tower."

She looked up. The big square structure had one high window. A single slender tree grew in front.

"Wenceslaus I had it bricked up in the thirteenth century," he continued. "It used to fascinate me when I was a child; I always imagined someone hidden behind it."

They passed under an arch and went back down by way of the castle staircase. To the left, the St. Wenceslaus vineyard stretched before them in the soft sunlight.

Josef stopped. "I'm a little tired," he said sulkily. "I'm not used to taking such long walks."

"You don't take walks with Martha?"

"Walks? With *Martha?*" He sat down on a bench facing the river. "No, I've always stayed at home, with my work."

"What about the bird?" she asked. "You'd better not put off telling me your story much longer or the bird will fly away."

"He'll never fly from my memory," he said. "I'll tell you now, and this time I won't let anything interrupt me.

"After forty-five years I can still remember that bird as if I'd seen him only yesterday. He had a tuft of feathers on his head that bobbed up and down when he walked. It was strange, seeing the same bird every day at the same time. I finally asked a friend to go with me as a witness. That day the bird didn't come. The next day I went back alone and he came again."

"And he didn't fly away if you got too close to him?"

"At first I didn't try. Then one day I got close enough to touch him. He let me stroke him a few times, then he flew away. And he never came back."

"*That's* the story?"

He smiled, seeing that she was trying not to seem disappointed.

"No, there's more." He paused. "At first, of course, I didn't know he would never come back. I happened to look at the place where he'd been standing when he flew away, and there was a word written on the sand."

"What? The bird wrote something? I don't believe you," she said seriously.

"I could hardly believe it either. But the word was there. And the most amazing part of it is that he obviously left the word especially for me, because I was the only one who could understand it."

Johanna frowned.

"Then it must have been in a language that no one else could read," she said confidently.

"You're close, but not quite."

She squinted thoughtfully, and it made her look the same as when she had blinked her eyes in the sunlight after finishing her ice cream. *My God!* he thought. *It took me almost fifty years, but I've seen her again!*

"I give up," she said.

"The word was written in cuneiform," Josef explained.

She opened her mouth in surprise, but mainly to please him, because his revelation didn't enlighten her very much.

"In that series of excavations, which had begun at Babylon in 1899, my job was to translate any cuneiform inscriptions that might be found. It's easier for a bird to write in cuneiform than in our alphabet. That's well known."

He seemed amused by Johanna's perplexity.

"Well, what did he write?" she asked.

"Hold out your wrist and I'll write it on you."

"That's strange: just before Franz went away, I made a drawing on his wrist. Maybe he still has it."

"There's nothing strange about it," Josef said. "It's a very old gesture of friendship. The Phoenicians used it to wish each other a good voyage. What did you draw?"

"A mouse."

"In ancient times, that wasn't considered a lucky animal." Johanna's face fell. "No, that's not true," he said quickly. "I must be confusing the mouse with some other animal. Let me have your wrist."

She held it out to him reluctantly. He put on his glasses, took his fountain pen and leaned over her. The point of the pen tickled as it moved over her skin. When he had finished, he took off his glasses and let go of her wrist. She looked at it and saw:

"It really does look as if a bird stepped on the same place several times," she said. "What does it mean?"

"It's the word 'ullu,' " he replied. "It means 'joy.' "

"And that's what the bird wanted to tell you: 'joy'? Why?"

He took his time, then answered.

"A short time later I met a young woman. She was the daughter of a local official, a Turk who had been brought up in England. Our work fascinated her. She ran among the stones like a gazelle. . . ."

"So you wrote that word on her wrist too?"

"No. I didn't even touch her. Don't forget that a gazelle is shy and swift."

"Then the bird was mistaken."

"Why?"

"He wrote 'joy.' But for a woman to give joy to a man, he must be able to touch her."

"You seem well informed," he said, surprised. "May I ask who put that idea in your head?"

"Franz. And since he said it, it must be true," she declared.

"How old is Franz?"

"Fifteen."

"That's how old she was," Josef said. He was silent for a moment, then continued with restrained fervor: "The bird was *not* mistaken! He was right. It was enough for me to see her now and then—I was happier than I'd ever been before, or have ever been since!"

"Then what happened?"

"Then I went away."

"You never saw her again?"

"Never."

"So it's a sad story."

"No," he said, "since what the bird predicted came true. And I felt that being able to translate the word justified all the studying I'd done. But I'm boring you."

He saw that she had stopped listening to him.

"We'll never know if the bird did it on purpose," she said hastily.

He smiled.

"No, we'll never know. Although . . ."

He stopped. She had stood up and started down toward the river, apparently impatient to move at a pace faster than his. She looked back and gaily waved the arm he had marked with the beneficent sign.

"Keep going!" he called out, waving back at her. "But wait for me down there."

When they stepped into the house they noticed a strange smell coming from the kitchen. Josef opened the kitchen door.

"What have you made for us this morning, Martha?" he asked. "I'm sure you've proved once again that your ingenuity can triumph over wartime food shortages. It seems to me that . . ."

He stepped back abruptly and the door slammed in his face. He turned to Johanna with an ironic expression, then opened the door again and went into the kitchen.

"What's come over you, Martha?"

"I'll tell you what's come over me!" she cried. She was standing in front of the stove, holding a smoking pan. "I was able to get a little lard, but because you two were late, everything's burned. It serves you right."

She swung the two halves of the casement window back and forth, trying to get the smoke out of the kitchen.

"Lard!" Josef exclaimed. "You talk as if it were foie gras!"

She spun around

"At seventy-three, you may not think you're too old to be clever and act like a ladies' man, but *I* can't afford to be so frivolous. Do you ever take a look at what's going on around us? And do you think it's easy to feed *that* with only our two rations?"

She pointed toward the vestibule. Josef was glad that Johanna couldn't understand Czech.

"For several days you've been rediscovering the joys of sightseeing in the city," Martha said sarcastically. "Suddenly you're cheerful and witty, giving history and archaeology lessons. And you've forgotten everything else, haven't you? Or rather you remember only when you're hungry, and even then you can't get here on time for meals."

"Enough!"

"You act as if our thirty years together meant nothing," she went on, not seeming to have heard him, "and all because of a little schemer . . ."

"Enough!" Josef roared, barely restraining himself.

He moved toward her, his fists clenched. Surprised, she backed up against the window.

"Martha, I know it's hard for you to see me enjoying a little . . . I won't say happiness, because that would hurt you, so I'll just say that I'm enjoying an interruption in my sense of drifting steadily toward death. I'm sure you have fond memories of days when I never left my armchair. I was never late for dinner then."

She was silent, her shoulders heaving. He suddenly turned away. He went through the vestibule and into the living room, where Johanna stood, her face ashen.

"Don't worry," he told her, "Martha is jealous, that's all, because you've burst into our tidy routine. It's ridiculous, but that's how it is."

"I think I'd better go and stay at the clinic," she said. "Otherwise she'll make life unbearable for you."

"That would interfere with Milena's experiment. And anyway, I don't want you to stay at the clinic. What would you do there? You'd be bored. If you stay here, we can go on taking our walks and rides together, and talking about things like the ullu bird. Who else could I have told?"

"If you only saw the way she looks at me!"

"Try to avoid her."

"That's not easy." Seeing the look on his face, she put her hand on his arm. "But I'll try."

"My little Semiramis," he murmured.

"You sound like my father," she said sadly. "He used to call me his little daughter of the Euphrates. He told me he'd seen little girls like me bathing in the river, near Ur."

"You liked him to tell you stories about being an archaeologist, didn't you?"

"Yes, and I liked it even more when he showed me pictures, or things that people had used thousands of years ago. Grete wasn't interested. But he told me he'd take me with him to an excavation site some day, me and no one else. And he would have, too."

"Yes, I'm sure he would have. One day, when you were about five, he said to me, 'You should see how intently she looks at pictures I've taken! Some day I'll make her my assistant!' "

"Oh!" she exclaimed delightedly. "Did he really say that? I . . . ." She stopped short: she could hear Martha nervously pacing the floor in the next room. "Have you called Milena? It's been five days now."

"Yes, I called her, and we decided that if your mother still hasn't asked for you by Thursday, I'll take you to the clinic anyway. But Milena is pleased with the daily sessions she's been having with your mother. She feels that she's becoming less withdrawn."

Johanna sighed and looked at the ray of sunlight that had

fallen across the desk loaded with piles of books and folders.

"I can't tell you when we'll have our lunch," said Josef. "I'm tempted to take you to Marosek's restaurant, down the street, for an omelet."

"Oh, yes!" Johanna said enthusiastically. "I've never been to a restaurant!"

"All right, let's go, I'm hungry." The doorbell rang and Josef looked at his watch. "That's the mail. It's been coming later and later."

As soon as he went into the vestibule, Johanna's joy at the prospect of eating in a restaurant vanished, inexplicably. She later told herself it must have been a presentiment.

"This is from Herr Kerbratt," Josef said, coming back into the room with an envelope.

She watched him open it and take out two sheets of paper, each with a different handwriting on it. He read them both and stood still for a time, staring into space. Then he turned to Johanna.

"This is a letter for you, from your friend Franz," he said, holding up one of the sheets. "Poor boy . . ." he added in a barely audible voice.

Johanna took the letter. To her surprise, Franz's handwriting was painstaking and regular; she had expected it to be erratic, like him, with big, jagged strokes moving unpredictably up and down.

Chemnitz, Feb. 28, 1945

Dear Johanna,

Don't be too sad, but they finally cut off my leg. That was on the 20th. The gangrene kept getting worse so they decided to amputate. I haven't gotten out of bed yet but I have a pair of good crutches waiting for me and everyone has carved something on them. You and I will go walking together this summer, only we won't walk as fast as we thought, that's all. Next to me is a girl who breathed burning gas. She wants to carve something on my crutches too. (That's to make you a little jealous, because she looks like Cora.) Write soon, and tell me what you're doing with all those Czechs.

Love and kisses,
Franz

Overwhelmed, Johanna looked at Josef. For a brief moment she hoped she might have misread the letter, but she saw from his expression that she hadn't.

"They . . . they cut . . ." she stammered, and burst into tears.

"You didn't tell me it was so serious," he said, gently stroking her hair.

She wept convulsively, imagining Franz's poor wounded leg, now a hideous stump. She gasped and shuddered so violently that Josef was alarmed.

"I'm going to the clinic," he said, "to get a sedative for you."

"Don't leave me!" she cried. "Don't leave me with . . ."

"All right," he said quickly. "Well, what about lunch?" he said to distract her. "A good omelet . . ."

She shook her head.

"I'm not hungry any more. I feel like vomiting."

He took her by the shoulders.

"You'll have to write him. I'm sure it will do him a great deal of good."

He was annoyed that he couldn't think of anything better to say. Her anguish disconcerted him. But it seemed clear that it would be better for her to do something to help Franz.

"Herr Kerbratt also thinks you should write Franz," he said, holding out Kerbratt's letter. She wouldn't take it.

"What can I say?" she said. "What is there to say? You were right about the mouse. . . ."

"I'll read Herr Kerbratt's letter to you," Josef insisted.

She didn't seem to have heard him.

He began reading, almost in an undertone:

Dear Professor Hutka,

I hope that things have gone well so far with Leni and Johanna. But that is not what prompted me to write. I have received distressing news from Dr. Minsch, concerning one of my choirboys, Franz Schwarzenbeck, who was shot in the left leg during the bombing of Dresden. I hoped that his leg could be saved, but unfortunately that became impossible. He has written about it in the enclosed letter to Johanna; the two of them became friends during her stay in my house. Because I know how much his news will upset her, I would not have forwarded his letter if I did not believe that an answering letter from her would console him. I know that you will support Johanna in what will be an ordeal for her also.

Faithfully and gratefully yours,
Hans Magnus Kerbratt

Johanna felt disheartened when Josef finished reading the letter. What good would it do to write to Franz? The only thing she wanted to do was to jump with him from the top of the big rock where they had held the funeral ceremony for the young Russian soldier. He would float beside her in the air, light and agile.

"So Herr Kerbratt knew that you and Franz . . . were close?" Josef asked cautiously.

"Yes. Franz told everybody. But I . . . I don't want to talk about it."

She wanted to talk to Franz, to be with him, even if she couldn't avoid seeing that *absence* under the sheets.

"I'd like to go up to my room," she said.

She had stopped crying but her face was drawn, as if she had gone without sleep for days.

"You don't want your old friend to stay with you?" he asked.

She shook her head.

"I don't know Franz, of course," he said, trying to comfort her a little, "but I'm sure that thinking of you is a great consolation to him."

Nothing he said seemed to reach her. She walked out without a word, went up to her room and sat down on the bed.

After rereading Franz's letter, she sat for a long time, looking at the floor. She thought of Franz limping along on two crutches, but quickly drove that image away. Then she remembered hastily drawing the mouse on his wrist. She glared at the sign that Josef had so carefully inscribed on her own wrist, the mark left by the bird that promised joy. . . . *Franz!* The cuneiform sign now looked like an evil insect. She angrily erased it with her thumb.

*   *   *

Milena seemed thinner than when Johanna had seen her before, and her gray eyes had dark half-circles under them. But she forced a smile.

"It seems to me that in the last week Johanna has grown until she's taller than you, professor!"

"No, Milena, she'd already had the impudence to outgrow me before she came here," Josef replied.

A bouquet of daffodils was the only patch of color in the room. Milena sat behind a desk piled with papers uncertainly held together with paper clips.

"Saint O. has been seized with a sudden mania for taking inventory," she explained.

"Why?" asked Josef. "Does she want to hide some of the clinic's sheets and tablecloths?"

"Don't you know her better than that? She'd like to be ready to bandage up half the people in the city if they should need it—God forbid, as she says."

"In the meantime, there seems to be a lull on the eastern front," he said. "I only hope Schörner can hold out for a few weeks and the Americans can get here in time to save us from the Russians."

Johanna looked at Josef indignantly.

"The Americans and English bombed Dresden, and you want them here! They killed Grete, and crippled my mother and Franz, and you're hoping they'll get here before the Russians! What harm have the Russians ever done me?"

"They . . . attacked your mother," he said timidly.

"Those weren't real Russians. Herr Kerbratt explained it to me."

"Never mind that," Milena said impatiently. "We're not here to fight the war over again. . . . Johanna, I'm sorry to say that your mother hasn't asked for you, but you mustn't take that to heart. She's still withdrawn. Something *has* happened, though, something I hadn't expected." She looked toward the window. "Did you have a garden at home, in Dresden?"

Johanna seemed surprised.

"Yes," she replied. "Not a very big one, though. Why?"

"Did your mother work in the garden?"

"No. There was a gardener who came sometimes, an old retired garage mechanic."

"Then I don't know how to explain it," Milena said, "but your mother has developed a passion for gardening. She's in the garden right now, in fact. I'd like you to go and see her. Watch very closely and tell me how she reacts when she sees you."

She stood up, went over to the window and parted the curtains. Outside, Johanna could see Leni bending over a flower bed. Catching sight of her so abruptly made her legs feel weak.

"And what makes you think she'll react at all when she sees me?" she asked bitterly. "She's forgotten me. She's forgotten me because she didn't love me."

"Professor Hutka and I will go into the hall, Johanna, so you'll know we're not watching you," Milena said.

Johanna watched Leni. Near the window, a big forsythia had bloomed in a cheerful, gaudy explosion of yellow.

"I've never seen her gardening before," she said, her nose to the windowpane.

Wearing an old coat that was too big for her, Leni was spading the soil around a rosebush.

"Mutti," Johanna said.

Leni kept working. Johanna went around the rosebush to stand in front of her.

"Mutti . . ."

This time Leni straightened up.

"Johanna!" she cried.

Johanna threw herself into her arms.

"Why didn't you ask for me?" she said, in tears. "I'd have come every day. Milena wanted to wait and see if you'd ask for me, but you never did."

Leni looked at her with a kind of dismay.

"You . . . you're gardening now?" Johanna asked, trying to sound encouraging.

Leni pointed to the spaded soil around the rosebushes.

"We'll be gone long before those bushes have flowers on them," Johanna said.

Leni seemed to have gained a little weight. She looked down at the ground, impatient to get on with her work.

"You don't have any blisters, do you?" Johanna asked. "Let me see your hands."

She took them and examined them. On Leni's left hand, at the base of the thumb, the long cut that she had given herself the first day at the clinic had nearly healed. The palm of her right hand was a little red. Johanna massaged it gently with her fingertips. After a few moments, Leni brusquely drew it back.

"Are Milena and Saint O. nice to you?" asked Johanna. "Are they taking care of you the way they should? You must not spend *all* your time gardening! Milena talks with you sometimes, doesn't she?"

Leni began working again. The garden was silent except for the sound of her digging.

"Do you remember when Hägen used to come and hoe the ground around our beets? We were the only ones on our street who had beets."

When Leni heard Hägen's name, she straightened up, and on her face was the expression she wore when she was searching for something that eluded her.

"Hägen," she repeated.

"That's right, Mutti: Hägen! He used to oil our bicycles, too. He always wore the same little blue cap."

Leni bent down again. But Johanna decided to keep trying to bring her back into a world of precise details—people, things, events—that only they knew.

"The only one in the neighborhood who really worked in her garden was Frau Gildemeister. Remember? In April, she always spaded her flower beds, the way you're doing now."

Johanna paused. Leni stopped working and looked at her.

"And do you remember Suzanne, who lived in Frau Gildemeister's house? She and I used to water the flowers with big watering cans, one for each of us. I usually came home sopping wet, and you scolded me."

As Johanna spoke, the past—the sound of a voice, a smell—

started to come back with insidious vividness. She wanted to push it away, but she had to keep remembering in order to reach Leni.

"Frau Gildemeister, our neighbor," she said. "You remember her, don't you?"

Leni suddenly stepped back with an expression of pain and anger on her face. Johanna could read the thought in her mind: *What do I care about Hägen and Frau Gildemeister? That was when I still had Grete, and I'll never see her again.*

Johanna wanted to shake her, to force her to realize that life was more important than death, that she ought to be more attached to her living daughter than to the memory of her dead one. But Leni had resumed her work. Johanna backed away, deliberately scuffling the gravel to see if Leni would notice. At the end of the lane she stopped and called out, "Mutti! I'm leaving now, but I'll be back soon."

Leni straightened up again. Johanna waved, but Leni stood frozen among the rosebushes, looking like a scarecrow in her oversized coat. For a moment Johanna had the horrible thought that birds might peck at her vacant eyes.

Johanna and Josef walked side by side. By now, she automatically adjusted her pace to his. Conversation usually flowed naturally between them, accompanied by the sound of their footsteps and inspired by things they saw along the way. But today was different. She told him what had happened in the garden, then fell into a brooding silence. His efforts to cheer her up had failed.

They said nothing till they came to the intersection of Pohranicni Straze and Narodni Obrany. For several days now, big clouds drifting in from the north had given the city the look of a threadbare tapestry.

"Did you tell Milena everything you told me?" he asked.

"Everything? That sounds as if you thought there was a lot to tell," she said caustically.

"Your mother said your name when she saw you—that's an improvement."

"She said it once. She was surprised, maybe, but then she was the same as before."

"Milena said you could come back again, didn't she?"

"Yes, she said I could come back whenever I wanted. But now that I know my mother doesn't want me, I'm not sure I really want to."

It had begun raining. They stopped to take shelter in the doorway of a clockmaker's shop.

"I thought she'd make more progress," she added.

"But she's only been there a week! You're forgetting that her treatment is supposed to last two months."

Several other people had stopped in the doorway. They listened in silence as Johanna and Josef spoke German. Suddenly their silence seemed threatening, and Johanna took hold of Josef's sleeve and pulled him out to the sidewalk.

When they had taken only a few steps, the rain stopped. Josef looked up at the clouds. High above and to the right, the dark, jagged cathedral seemed in mysterious harmony with the stormy sky.

"Did you see how they looked at us?" she said when they were far enough away.

He had noticed nothing, of course. She suddenly felt resentful.

"You haven't forgotten to write your friend Franz, have you?" he asked.

"No," she said.

What business was it of his? She had known Franz just long enough to feel, when she was with him, something she had never felt before, and when he left she had been certain that he would come back healed. And now *this*! Why did the people she loved have to be crippled, mentally or physically? What good was a mother who looked like a scarecrow and forgot her as soon as she was out of sight? How could she adore a body with only one leg?

Josef, walking beside her, hadn't said anything more. She took his silence as a reproach.

"Martha told me your broken statuette couldn't be glued back together," she said brusquely.

"If that's a roundabout allusion to Franz," he said, "I'll tell you that while you can't give him back his leg, you *can* help him to bear his loss."

"Nothing but saving his leg would have helped him," she retorted sullenly. "Now it's too late."

Then suddenly, as they were approaching the house and could already see its windows through the bare branches of the big linden tree in the garden, she burst into tears.

"Franz . . . his leg . . . It's horrible that . . . that nothing can be done about it. I'll never get used to it."

He took her in his arms and tried to soothe her.

"I said that about Franz because I thought a letter from you would do him good," he told her gently.

"Everybody in the choir will write to him," she answered, sniffling.

"Yes, but what if he's waiting for just one letter, and it's the only one he doesn't receive?"

They went inside and into the living room.

"You told me that Franz looked like a picture in one of your father's books," he said.

"Yes. It was a book on Ur. One of the illustrations showed the funeral of a young prince. When I first saw Franz in the hall, it's strange, I . . . I really *recognized* him."

"I know what you mean. Take that statuette. I'm not bringing it up because I miss it, since I'm much happier now than I was before, when I still had it. But I recognized that horseman. I knew his territory, its trails and routes; I'd drunk from the rivers in which he watered his horse. He was more real to me than the horsemen I sometimes see in the morning riding around the Letna Esplanade." He opened a drawer and took out a small notebook. "If I said that to Martha, she'd say I was escaping into the past to avoid the terrible reality of the present. But that's not true. So many things have happened through the centuries. . . ." He sighed and handed Johanna the notebook. "Read this. It's a fragment of a hymn inspired by the destruction of the writer's city."

Johanna read the paragraph he pointed to:

"In Ur, both the weak and the strong die of hunger. Old

men and women die in their houses by fire. Babies sleeping
on their mothers' bosoms are thrown into the water like fish.
O Goddess, your city weeps for you who were its protectress.
The great storm from the sky has put an end to sweetness in
this land."

Johanna looked up. Josef had dozed off in his armchair, a
faint smile on his face. She drew the curtains and went upstairs.

He felt suffocated and moaned.

"It's falling!" he cried.

The room was dark. He could just make out her face. She
was there again, her big, dark eyes filled with anguish.

"I'll go and bring help, Ishtar!" he said.

He tried to stand up, desperately flailing his arms.

"Let me help you," Johanna said. "You fell out of your
chair. I heard you shout from upstairs."

"Open the curtains! I want light!"

She quickly pulled back the curtains. The sky was clear
now. With his tie undone and his white hair tousled, Josef
seemed bewildered. Johanna was tempted to go and bring
Martha, then remembered that she had gone to buy food.

"Stay," Josef said weakly. "Don't leave me!"

"I'm not going anywhere."

She smoothed his hair with her hand and waited for him to
get his bearings.

"Are you feeling better?" she asked finally. "Would you
like me to call Milena?"

"No, I'm all right. Forgive me, I must have frightened you.
We all have our nerves on edge these days."

The tightness in his chest was easing gradually.

"Who was Ishtar?" Johanna asked.

He started.

"What? Did I say something about . . ."

"You said, 'I'll go and bring help, Ishtar.' "

"Ishtar was the Babylonian name of the goddess of love,"
he said, seeming taken aback. "The Sumerians worshiped her
as Inanna, sister of Utu, the sun god. . . ."

"Ishtar was the girl you loved, wasn't she? The daughter of the Turkish official?"

He didn't answer.

"Do I look like her?" she asked.

"You look like a typical girl from that part of the world, as your father told you," he answered evasively.

"If I didn't look like her, you wouldn't have drawn that sign on my wrist! When you look at me, you see *her* again, still as young as she was fifty years ago. That's nice for you, isn't it?"

He ran his hand over her curly hair, gruffly affectionate. He seemed relieved.

"Time is a child," he said quietly.

"What?"

"Time is a child. Heraclitus said that. It means that like children, time is irrational, impetuous, unstable and creative. It creates its own twists and turns, shortcuts, fertile and unexpected meetings. . . . And if time is a child, you are that child, Johanna. You take me back fifty years, to when I was really alive."

Johanna felt uneasy. It was just as she had thought: when he looked at her, he saw someone else, a girl he had known at the end of the last century in the ruins of a destroyed city. *Now I know how Annette must have felt when Mutti thought she was Hella.*

"It also means that, like children, time represents hope," Josef went on. "Nothing can change what has happened, but who can say what will come out of it? Roses will come from those bushes your mother is cultivating, and from those . . ."

"We won't see those roses," Johanna interrupted. "I've already told her that. We'll be gone before they bloom."

She wanted to leave, but curiosity held her back.

"Why did you say you'd go and bring help?" she asked.

Her question seemed to disorient him and she was sorry she had asked it. He murmured something and closed his eyes again. He took her hand in his and, little by little, she felt him relaxing.

Seeing his lips move, she leaned toward him to listen.

"How lucky it was for me," he said almost in a whisper, "that you found that letter!"

*　　*　　*

Holding a pair of pruning shears, Leni kept walking in the garden, stopping only to examine a plant from time to time. Once or twice she looked at Johanna with a twitch of her lips that was a caricature of her old smile. But she never called her by name. When Johanna couldn't bear her disappointment any longer, she left Leni and went to Milena's office.

"You're too impatient," Milena told her. "Remember, it's a very slow process."

When Johanna was back in Josef's house, time seemed to have taken on Leni's slow, heavy pace. Bored, she wandered from her room to the landing and from the landing to the vestibule. Josef was working in the living room, at his big desk piled high with folders. Since his angry scene with her, Martha had been sulking in her room over the coach house at the back of the garden, appearing only to cook and serve meals, in as sour and surly a manner as possible.

Johanna knocked on the living room door.

"Come in," Josef said.

He had some photographs out on the desk.

"I'm bored," she said glumly. "Am I bothering you?"

He looked up.

"No, of course not."

"Who's that?" she asked, pointing to one of the photographs.

"That's my old friend Weidner," Josef said. "He used to earn his living by composing crossword puzzles for the *Berliner Illustrierte.*" He laughed. "Now he's a professor in Vienna. The people at the *Berliner Illustrierte* couldn't get over it when they found out that for twenty years, without knowing it, they'd been working with one of the greatest living Assyriologists."

"And who's that?" Johanna asked, pointing to a robust man in a sun helmet leaning against a wall.

"That's my real teacher: Koldewey, the 'inventor' of Babylon. I joined him in 1899, when the excavation site was opened."

"Was that the year you met Ishtar?"

"No. I met her the year after that."

"Don't you have a picture of her?"

"No. In those days, taking pictures was a complicated process. The ones you see here were taken much later." He uncovered another picture. "Look at this one. I took it myself. It's Koldewey, twenty-five years later. But look at the man beside him."

She leaned forward.

"It's my father!"

There he was, with his strong, clean-shaven face and his large, intense-looking eyes. He wore a stiff collar, which made his sharp features almost boyish.

"That's not the way he usually dressed," she said.

She looked at the picture more closely. It had yellowed a little and begun cracking at the corners. *He didn't even know Mutti yet*, she thought.

"As for the man on the right," Josef went on, "the tall one with a white mustache, he's Sir Arthur Evans, one of the greatest archaeologists of all time. At that time he'd already been working fifteen years on excavating the palace of King Minos at Knossos, on the island of Crete. Do you see anything unusual? Here, look through this magnifying glass."

Intrigued, Johanna scrutinized the photograph.

"No, I can't see anything."

"Look at the clay tablet that the three of them are examining. The signs engraved on it aren't cuneiform like the ones on my tablets here. They're a different form of writing, engraved on tablets that Evans found at Knossos."

"Well?"

"Grotefend and Rawlinson had deciphered cuneiform writing, Champollion had deciphered Egyptian hieroglyphs, but at the time this picture was taken, nothing was known about the language that was spoken seven centuries before Homer. Can you imagine that?"

As he spoke, his cheeks had become flushed.

"No, not really," Johanna said.

He laughed.

"I'm incorrigible! I'm talking to you as if you were your father!"

It made her feel strange to know that he was speaking to her father through her. But it also made her father seem present, as if he were in the room, following the conversation.

"The year that picture was taken was the year I first began to take an interest in the problem," Josef went on. "In that tablet was a riddle whose solution might open up whole new perspectives in archaeology and linguistics. And the fact that your father is in the picture is symbolic, because he encouraged me to pursue my research. Both he and Evans died four years too soon, before I had the pleasure of telling them . . . before they knew. . . . But Evans had had a long and prodigiously productive career, whereas your father still had so many things to give us, to teach us. . . ."

"They died too soon to know *what?*" Johanna asked.

"That I'd found what they'd all been looking for so long. Cretan linear writing has now been deciphered, and I'm the one who did it," he said loudly.

She looked at him with a smile, feeling strangely proud, as if she suddenly shared a little of his discovery. So that was what he had devoted his life to.

"No one knows about it yet," he said. "My first published study described my preparatory work, but no one knows that I've found the definitive solution, because there are no more meetings and conferences these days, no free exchange of information. As soon as the war is over I'll publish my article, and it will be the biggest shock in the world of archaeology since Schliemann discovered the royal tombs of Mycenae!" He opened a drawer of his desk. "The article is here."

She saw a brown folder with a ribbon around it.

"It contains the whole code," he said, "and the linguistic conclusion that follows from it. The world will finally know what language the ancient Cretans spoke."

"What language was it?" Johanna asked.

"That's an important secret. I'd rather tell you some other day, when we have more time to discuss it."

She nodded.

"I like to be told secrets. Promise me that nobody will know before I do."

"I promise."

"Just now, when you were telling me about your discovery," she said thoughtfully, "you had the same expression as Herr Kerbratt when he was telling me about a cantata he composed. He said he wanted me to hear it after the war."

"In sad and terrible times like these," Josef said slowly, "it's good to be able to take refuge in something you love. If you're not comforted by anything, if you see only a barren world and a dark future, then you become like Martha."

They both listened. Martha wasn't there.

"Maybe that's why your mother has been spending so much time among flowers," he added.

"It's odd," Josef said abruptly, "but when I think back over my childhood I remember Easter better than Christmas. In my little village of Svratka, in Moravia, it was really a celebration of renewal. On Maundy Thursday, my parents and my two brothers and I would go to sprinkle the fields with holy water. We carried it in little stone jars that were used only on that one day a year. Then on the morning of Good Friday, the village children went to the brook to sprinkle one another with water. Some of us took involuntary baths. There was a legend that when the sun rose on Easter morning it celebrated by turning three somersaults in a row. We always climbed to the top of a hill behind the village to watch for the sun's somersaults."

"And did you see them?"

"Some claimed they did, and said that those who didn't were blind! There was even one boy—his name was Julius, I remember—who always saw the sun turn *four* somersaults! The rest of us called him a Slovak, because Slovaks had a reputation for exaggeration."

"What did you do afterward?"

"We went to church, where I met my mother and my sisters in their Easter clothes. Sometimes I didn't recognize them.

They wore embroidered bodices and skirts so finely made that we boys weren't allowed to touch them. They looked like pieces of fancy pastry. After church, we all went to the orchard and hung wreaths on the trees that had given the most fruit the year before. Then we all danced around those trees. . . ."

"Grete and I just went out to look for Easter eggs in the garden," Johanna said sadly. "Since my mother always hid them in the same places, we raced to see who could get there first, and Grete always won. Last year I didn't even help to decorate the eggs. I said, 'What's the use? You'll only find them all.' She decorated them all herself."

They were sitting in one of their favorite places: on a bench in front of the tennis court of the Royal Palace. A dark, overbearing statue of Night stood out from the façade, with one arm raised, presumably toward dawn.

"That statue looks like my mother standing on a stool and trimming a hedge," Johanna commented.

"Was that what she was doing this morning?" Josef asked, laughing.

"Yes. She wouldn't even come down from her stool to say hello to me," she said bitterly.

"I know you've taken a strong dislike to gardening, but it seems to me that your mother is making progress, and Milena agrees. She doesn't have that empty look in her eyes anymore."

"Not when someone talks to her about pruning shears, or grafts, or seeds, or potted plants, no! But when I talk to her about myself, about what I've been doing, she's still the same."

"You're too impatient."

"I'm tired of hearing that! That's what Milena always says!"

"Calm down. Your mother is creating a tidy, flowery little world for herself, a world that gives her a sense of security. You don't have a place in it yet, but you will. Sooner than you think." He changed the subject: "I hope you'll wear the dress I bought you when we go to Milena's Easter lunch tomorrow."

A week earlier he had told her he was tired of seeing her always in the same dress. Rosi had put another dress into her suitcase, but it was a little too big for her and she didn't like it very much. So she and Josef had crossed the river, for once, and gone to the department stores on Vaclavske Namesti. The choice of dresses was narrow but they had found one with fine embroidery and short puffed sleeves.

"It's funny that Easter comes on the first of April this year," she said.

"I never saw such a sunny March before, in Prague. Except for the day when we went to see your mother for the first time. Do you remember?"

She felt a rush of warmth for him.

"I remember everything that happened in March," she said. "I don't know what I would have done without you. I think you've done me a lot more good than Milena has done my mother!"

He put his finger to his lips.

"Don't ever say anything like that when we're at home. Martha has been on good terms with Saint O. since I was at the clinic, and she'd tell her if she overheard you. Milena's feelings would be hurt if Saint O. told her. She's trying very hard."

"I didn't mean to say anything bad about her," Johanna assured him. "I meant to say something good about you."

He laughed and affectionately patted her arm.

After coming to the end of the Royal Garden, they strolled along the river, as they had done during their first walk together, a month ago. Josef had decided to ration his gasoline coupons, so he and Johanna walked everywhere: to the Royal Garden; to the Deer Moat, overlooking the cathedral; to the garden on the ramparts where, for the past week, they had been watching the purple blossoming of the *Pawlownia imperialis* in front of the New Palace. Wanting to show Johanna a city without war, he was careful not to take her past newsstands, where the *Prager Tagblatt* might be displayed with news from the front. Except for the time when they went to buy the dress, they always took their walks in the vicinity of Hradcany Castle. Josef preferred to avoid the part of the city that lay on the other side of the river: it had signs in German everywhere, its predominantly military traffic upset him, and its noise tired him.

Both his life and the war were in limbo—by some miracle, Schörner had been keeping Koniev from going beyond the Oder for more than a month. And when this fragile, precious period came to an end, the time of his great scientific triumph would begin. But would that be enough to outweigh the vast loneliness he would feel when Johanna was gone?

Kerbratt had written a few days ago that no matter what happened he was going to stay where he was. Rosi had finally realized how foolish it would be for them to leave the house and wander along roads already full of refugees. He reported that Franz had been very glad to receive Johanna's letter, was in fairly good spirits, and would come back on April 6. But Franz hadn't answered Johanna's letter. For a week she had asked if there was anything for her each time the mail came, and then she had said no more about it.

"What are you thinking about?" she asked.

Josef had been looking at the silvery surface of the river.

"I'm thinking that boat will never get past the bridge if it keeps trying to do it that way," he said.

A small boat was attempting to pass the New Bridge by following the channel, where the river was full of strong eddies. Twice already it had come close to capsizing. Finally it slipped past and disappeared on the other side of the bridge.

"You see!" Johanna said with a playful wink.

He suddenly felt like hugging her, thanking her, weeping. *So we never change!* he thought. *We stay as fresh and excitable as we were at the beginning.*

"Why don't we go and write our initials under the Charles Bridge?" she suggested. "We can do it now that we've known each other for a month, can't we?"

"No, I still won't risk making your future husband jealous," he said, smiling. "But I've got an idea for tomorrow. I remembered the chocolate eggs we used to get as Easter presents. They were decorated in a special way, and looked as if they were wrapped in a net of gold threads. . . . I think I know where I can get some. You're going to let me give you a little surprise."

"What do you mean?" she asked a little uneasily. "You're not going to make me walk back to the house by myself, are you?"

"You'll be safe. Just do the same as when you go to the clinic: don't talk to anyone. I'll see you at home in a little while."

He walked away. She knew where he was going. She had often seen him look furtively at the meager displays in shop windows and she knew the few shops that were better supplied than the others. He looked back and waved to her, then she saw him disappear in the direction of the St. Nicholas church. He was heading for the confectioner's shop on the square. She started back toward the house along their usual route, walking fast.

NINE

he tried not to make any noise when she came in, intending to go straight to her room and wait till Josef came back. But as soon as she started upstairs the kitchen door opened.

"He's not with you?" Martha called from the foot of the stairs.

"No," Johanna answered. "He should be back any minute."

"He's not in the habit of letting you come home alone," Martha said skeptically, looking out at the street.

Johanna sensed such hostility from her that she couldn't resist taunting her.

"If you want to know the truth," she said, "he's gone to get a surprise for me."

"A surprise! What do you mean, a surprise?"

"Tomorrow is Easter and he wants to get something that will make it seem a little like the Easters he had in his childhood."

"So he wants you to have a nice Easter! That's the last straw!" Martha cried angrily.

She went back into the kitchen and slammed the door. Johanna heard her muttering vehemently in Czech. With her heart pounding, she went into her room and sat down on the bed. *What a fool you are!* she reproached herself. *Why did you have to say that to her?*

She heard Martha pacing back and forth downstairs. Then there was the sound of a door opening. She listened intently. Footsteps on the stairs. She rushed to the door and locked it. A few seconds later she heard Martha reach the top of the stairs, come to the door and stop there.

"Leave me alone!" she cried. "Go away!"

Martha replied with such fury and hatred that her voice seemed about to shatter the door. Amid a torrent of Czech that Johanna didn't understand, the same exclamation in German was repeated several times: "So he wants you to have a nice Easter!" Then Martha suddenly stopped.

"Open the door," she said calmly.

"Leave me alone. Professor Hutka will be back any minute."

"Open the door, you hear me? I just want to show you a child's drawing. It can't hurt you," Martha said with unexpected gentleness.

"Go away!"

"I have another key, and I'll go downstairs and get it if you don't open the door. But if you put me to that trouble I'll make you sorry, I'm warning you."

Frantic with terror, Johanna didn't answer.

"A child's drawing, just a child's drawing," Martha repeated. "He'd have liked to have a nice Easter too! He'd also have liked to have candy, and he'd have shared it with some of the other children. There were ten thousand of them. They hadn't even seen a lump of sugar in three years. Now . . ."

Her voice had become hoarse. She was standing against the door and Johanna could hear her breathing.

"I don't know what you're talking about! Go away! I know you hate me because I'm German, but you also hate me because I go for long walks with Professor Hutka. He's about to come back and put you in your place, and then . . ."

"My place!" Martha interrupted. "You idiot! I'll tell you one thing: my place isn't in this city that you Germans have defiled! He can take you out and show you around if he wants to, but I'll never go walking here again. That monster Hitler came here to Prague, and then he sent another monster: Heydrich. Czech patriots were able to assassinate that one. But you've never heard of Heydrich, have you? And I'm sure you've never heard of the Gestapo either! But it was from here that it spread terror all over the Reich! Yes, from Prague, from our beautiful city! The professor showed you the Street of Gold, didn't he? And the Daliborka? I'm sure he told you about Dalibor and his violin. But he didn't show you the Petschek bank, did he? If you'd gone past the Petschek bank you wouldn't have heard violins: you'd have heard screams of pain!"

Her voice had become so loud that Johanna had put her hands over her ears.

"Please leave me alone!" she begged. "You're jealous because he likes to be with me!"

"You think he likes to be with you? Don't you realize he's senile? He thinks he's in Babylon. He's as crazy as your mother. No, I'm not jealous, but having to live in the same house with you makes me sick, you filthy scum! I'll make you pay. . . ."

"Scum yourself!" Johanna cried. "I've heard screams too— screams from people being burned alive by phosphorus! The fire bombs fell on *us! We* were the ones being burned!"

"Good!" Martha retorted furiously. "It serves you right! But nothing will ever replace that boy. . . ." Her voice broke and she began sobbing hysterically. "That senile old man wants you to have a nice Easter," she said, when she was able to speak again. "And what about that boy? Don't you think he'd have liked to have a nice Easter too? But there were no Easters at Terezin! And Josef Hutka dares to speak your language! I'm speaking it now, but only because I want to hurt you as much as I can, scum!"

Johanna threw open the door. Martha was there, clutching a piece of paper, her face convulsed.

"I won't let you talk to me like. . . ." said Johanna. "What about Grete? And Hella? They used to draw too, and they won't anymore. . . . The truth is that you're jealous and mean. I'll tell Professor Hutka what you've said and he'll throw you out."

"I'm not jealous of a German girl," Martha said, stepping toward her, her teeth clenched. "Try to get this through your thick skull. I'm from Zakolany. The boy I told you about was my sister's son. After that dog Heydrich was killed, you Germans took reprisals. You rounded up all the children in our village and put them in a concentration camp where there were already thousands of Jewish children. Then they were scattered and sent to other camps, and now they must be dying there. I don't know where my nephew is. My sister doesn't even know what his registration number was at Terezin. All I have left of him is this drawing he made a little while before he was caught in the roundup."

She waved the piece of paper in Johanna's face. Johanna glimpsed clumsily drawn and brightly colored trees. She was staggered; it was as if someone had brought Grete's last essay or Hella's earring, the one she had seen shining at the circus.

"Maybe he's still alive," she murmured.

Martha gave her a look charged with hatred.

"Your friend the professor never told you about Terezin, did he? And I'm sure he never said anything about Lidice, either, where they burned the village and shot everyone in it. Women, old people, everyone! He's not interested in those things anymore, now that you're making him feel young again. Though I don't understand how a skinny little runt like you could. . . . He's senile. Senile! When I told him that partisans had been slaughtered in his dear Crete, that his precious ruins were red with blood, he told me I was spiteful! He's a dirty bastard, and so are you! I'll report you both!"

Johanna slipped past Martha and ran into the other bedroom.

"Hurry, Josef! I need you! Hurry!" she shouted through the window overlooking the street.

There was no sign of him in the street. She turned around and saw Martha staring at her.

"So you call him by his first name now?"

"Yes, when we're alone," said Johanna, determined not to let herself be intimidated. "And I don't mind telling you that he likes it."

She didn't see the slap coming. It left her dazed. Martha backed away slowly, then turned and went down the stairs. Johanna heard her stride through the vestibule and slam the front door.

"Martha."

Hearing Josef's voice, Johanna silently opened the door of her room, stepped to the head of the stairs and looked down. He was holding a big dark-red package by the string wrapped around it.

"Martha!" he called again.

"She's not here," Johanna said. "Where have you been?"

He looked up, awkwardly trying to hide his package.

"Ah, there you are, upstairs. I ran into my old friend Provost Cibulka. We got into a discussion of Gourmont's remark that the invention of writing was . . ."

"I felt sick," Johanna interrupted. "I must have eaten too much."

"You didn't eat any more than usual."

He slowly came up the stairs, looking worried.

"You still don't feel well?"

Without answering, she went back into her room. He followed her.

"My God!" he exclaimed. "You look terrible!" His eyes moved around the room and stopped at the washstand. "And you've vomited!"

She nodded.

"All right, I'll draw a bath for you," he said. "In a way, you chose a good time to be sick, because there's hot water that was going to be used to do the laundry."

She knew that hot water was a rare luxury but she didn't protest. He went into the bathroom, turned on the faucet and came back to the bedroom.

"Did your . . . sickness just come over you . . . all at once?" he asked hesitantly.

"Yes."

"You . . . didn't see Martha?"

She shook her head. He seemed skeptical.

"I really didn't," she assured him.

He put his hand on her shoulder.

"If I'm going to find you in a state like this whenever I leave you, I'll stay with you every minute from now on," he said jovially. "Your face is flushed. I wonder if you're about to come down with something."

He went back to the bathroom, tested the water with his finger and turned off the faucet.

"It's ready now."

Everything in the old-fashioned bathroom—the cream-colored tile, the steam that clouded the bamboo-framed mirror, the heady smell of beeswax that came from the closets, the strange shape of the tub, the porcelain basin decorated with flowers—made her feel that the bath she was about to take would be a rare, exotic event. The nightmarish things that Martha had told her began to recede from her mind.

"I'll leave you now," Josef said. "I'll be downstairs."

"No, no," she said quickly. "I'd rather you stayed."

She began taking off her clothes and tossing them onto a stool. A few moments later she sat down in the tub and closed her eyes. The gentle warmth of the water and the quietness of the room were soothing, but the sound of Martha's panting, hate-filled voice kept coming back to her.

Josef was sitting on a chair, looking attentively at her face. She had pulled her hair back. Suddenly her features contracted as if she were in pain. He stood up.

"What's the matter?" he asked in alarm.

She reassured him with a gesture.

"You ought to soap yourself a little," he suggested.

He stood looking down, unable to take his eyes off her. Her wrists and ankles were strikingly delicate and her ribs were clearly visible beneath her wet skin. She opened her eyes and her gaze met his.

"How do I look to you?"

"You look thin as a rail and red as a lobster," he said, forcing himself to take on a dubious expression.

"In other words you don't think I'm . . . attractive?"

"You're tall and graceful and you have a pretty face. You'll be a beautiful woman some day."

"I'd like you to wash my back," she said. She wanted the hatred Martha had poured over her to be washed off and swept away with the dirty water, into the sewer.

She stood up facing the mirror, with water streaming down her body.

"I think it would be a good idea for me to wash your hair first."

"If you want to."

He began rubbing her head with soap. After a while she turned around, blinking her eyes beneath her helmet of lather.

"You wouldn't have been able to do this to me in Babylon," she said jokingly.

"What makes you think so? The Babylonians invented all kinds of things! They had bathtubs, and even running water. . . . There, I'm finished, you can do the rest yourself," he said, patting her behind.

She turned to face him and he saw that a fleck of lather was clinging to one of her eyebrows, like a white flower on a black stem. His hands began to tremble and he quickly hid them in a towel.

"Tell me about that girl in Babylon," she said. "Did you ever . . . see her?"

"What do you mean by 'see her'?" he asked warily.

"Come on, tell me," she insisted. "Did you ever see her naked?"

He gave her an enigmatic smile.

"I'll dry you now," he said, raising the towel.

Johanna began tracing the outline of her body with her finger in the clouded mirror. She turned the outline into a silhouette by wiping away the moisture inside it, then examined her reflection with satisfaction. Finally she wrote "Jo–Jo, 3/31/45" at the top of the mirror.

"There, I've written our initials!" she said triumphantly.

"But I'm afraid they won't last," he replied, laughing.

She contemplated herself again in the cleared part of the mirror.

"I wish I could always be the way I am now: smooth as that mirror, with nothing bulging out," she said, running her hand over her flat chest and belly.

"Excessive modesty isn't one of your faults," he remarked.

"You should have seen Grete when she got ready for bed! It was really something to see! Especially after she started having her . . . you know what I mean."

He said nothing.

"You know what I mean, don't you?"

"Yes."

"I wish I didn't have to grow up," she said. "I don't like what's going to grow on me: breasts, hair on my body, all that. And I especially don't like having to bleed. It seems a little disgusting. Luckily my mother had time to explain it to me before she . . . She told me it would happen first to Grete, then to me."

She sighed. He put the towel over her shoulders.

"I don't want you to catch cold," he said. Then he added, "It's good your mother told you about that. Mothers often wait too long, till after it's already happened, and then girls think they've hurt themselves and they're worried."

Johanna huddled under the towel.

"Blood . . . I still think it's strange. Grete said the blood came pouring out, but she was probably exaggerating, like your Slovak."

"My Slovak?"

"The one who claimed he saw the sun turn four somersaults instead of three."

"Ah, yes. It's true. Grete was exaggerating. The blood doesn't come pouring out."

"I didn't think so," she said. "Even so, I'd rather not have to change and get old."

"Sun and blood," he murmured. "Yes, you'll ripen. You're made for living in countries where the sun is bright and hot. I'll take you with me when I go back."

"To Crete?"

"Yes, among other places."

"I can't go there," she said. "They'd know I was German."

"Well, what of it?"

"In Crete there's blood on the ruins, on the statues, and the people there know who's responsible."

She began getting dressed. He stared at her in silence.

"Tell me the truth, Johanna," he said abruptly. "What happened? What did Martha say to you?"

Her body stiffened.

"You can't know how much good that bath did me," she said, "but don't spoil everything now. Please."

He took her by the shoulders. His face had turned pale.

"What did she say to you? I want to know. What did that foul woman say to you?"

She was alarmed by the agitation in his voice.

"It was nothing important," she said. "Please don't be so upset."

"I know that story of hers about blood on the ruins in Crete! That's what she told you, isn't it?"

He was almost shouting.

"Promise me you won't tell her I said anything about Crete," she begged, panic-stricken. "I didn't mean to. It just slipped out. Promise me, please!"

"You were too clean; she had to dirty you," he said, his face tense with anger.

"Promise me. . . . She didn't do me any harm, but you'll do yourself harm if you lose your temper."

She hastily finished drying her hair.

"I think I make her unhappy," she said. "I think that's the reason."

He nodded reflectively. Then he left the bathroom and regretfully went downstairs.

The kitchen door, usually left ajar, was tightly closed. As a result the vestibule was plunged in semidarkness. Josef walked toward the living room, slightly bent forward. Suddenly he stopped. Silent and almost invisible, Martha stood in front of him, blocking his path.

"You're getting even worse as time goes by," she said harshly. "Now you play with little girls when they take a bath."

"You're contemptible," he said without raising his voice.

"For a man your age, those kinds of pleasures are better than nothing."

Not wanting Johanna to hear, he pushed Martha into the living room and closed the door behind him.

"You're contemptible," he repeated. "Get out. The sight of you makes me sick. Send me a bill for what I owe you."

"Do you think it's going to be so easy? Do you think that after thirty years you can just throw someone out? And I won't leave till I've told you a few things. For example, that I've treated myself to some pleasure too: the pleasure of slapping a little slut who called me a mean, jealous woman."

He felt a vibration that seemed to start in the floor and spread from his feet to every part of his body. He stepped toward her.

"You slapped her!" he cried, his voice faltering. "I'll make you pay for that."

He tried to grab her but she pulled away from him, reached out to a shelf and picked up a clay tablet covered with cuneiform writing.

"Put that down!" he ordered.

"Things are different now," she sneered, "not like the time when Frau Seyfert broke a Parthian statuette and you respectfully knelt at her feet to pick up the pieces."

"Put it down, immediately!"

"You stopped just short of telling her you were glad she'd broken it!" Martha went on. "The poor *lady* was tired from her long trip, wasn't she!"

"If you break that tablet, *I'll* break *you!*" said Josef, beside himself with rage.

"Oh? We'll see about that."

She swung the tablet over her head and threw it against the wall. It shattered with a sharp, almost metallic sound, leaving a rust-colored spot above the sofa. She turned toward him vindictively. For a moment she wondered where he had gone, then she stared at him in consternation, her hand over her mouth. He had fallen beside his desk and lay unconscious on the floor.

Saint O. put her finger to her lips. Quietly, Johanna sat down near Josef, who lay on his back, his long, bony hand hanging over the edge of the bed. He tried to raise his head.

"My little girl . . ." he murmured.

"I'm here," she said softly.

Saint O. smiled, patted the bed and walked out with a reassuring rustle of starched linen. Johanna took Josef's hand and kissed it.

"Stay, please stay," he pleaded, mistaking her intent.

"I'm not leaving."

"I don't want Martha to come here," he said, becoming agitated.

"No, she won't come, Josef."

"You should have told me what happened."

"You mustn't talk," she whispered.

He smiled faintly. A little later, when she thought he had fallen asleep, he raised his head again.

"And to think it's Easter today. . . . This morning, did you see the sun? . . ."

He drew a somersault in the air.

"You should sleep," she said. "You shouldn't talk so much."

His breathing became more regular. In the distance a clock struck eleven. Soon he really had fallen asleep. She waited a little longer, then quietly stood up and left the room. She made her way down the hall to the linen room, where she knew she would find Saint O.

"How serious is it?" she asked.

"He's had a classic heart attack," Saint O. replied. "What makes it worse is that he's had one before, and there were complications. That may happen again."

"So *that's* why he stayed here the first time! Did Martha know about it?"

"Of course."

Johanna sat down and put her head in her hands.

"This time it's my fault, Saint O. Martha hates me. I couldn't understand what she said to him, but there have been quarrels between them ever since I came. It's all my fault."

Saint O. stopped ironing.

"It was because you made him happy," she said. "That's what she couldn't accept."

"Do you think he'll . . . pull through?"

"This whole week is very important, especially the next three or four days. But I'm sure that knowing you're here will help him to get well."

The day before, it had been Saint O. who answered the phone when Martha called. Johanna had opened the door of her room just as Martha began her call for help. A few minutes later Milena and Saint O. came in the clinic's old ambulance and Johanna went downstairs. Josef had just regained consciousness. Stunned, Martha didn't even help to carry the stretcher.

"Saint O.," Johanna said, "is it true what Martha said about . . . about what the Germans did here—that they held children as prisoners at Terezin, and burned the village of . . . of . . ."

"Lidice," said Saint O. "Yes, it's true. It was part of the reprisals they took after Heydrich, the head of the Gestapo, was assassinated by patriots."

"My God!" Johanna exclaimed. "Then . . . then Martha has a right to hate me."

"You had nothing to do with those atrocities, Johanna. I've fought against the Germans and I've helped young people to hide from the Gestapo, but no one can tell me that German children and adolescents are responsible. Not even those poor boys who are being put in uniform nowadays."

"My mother didn't know anything either," Johanna said.

"When the war is over, I'm sure everyone in Germany will claim not to have known anything," Saint O. said bitterly. "But that's unacceptable."

"Then why are you taking care of my mother? Martha wouldn't have done it."

"Martha isn't a nun."

"Do you think Martha hates me mostly because I'm German, or mostly because she wants to have Professor Hutka all to herself?"

Saint O. had finished ironing. She looked at her pile of napkins with the satisfaction she always derived from the sight of freshly pressed linen.

"With an old lunatic like her, there's no telling," she said.

Leni was embroidering a doily. She paused with her needle in midair, seeming glad to see Johanna; then she resumed her work with the same stubborn determination she now put into everything she did.

"Let me see," Johanna said.

Leni willingly showed her. She had already embroidered two of the five birds in bright colors, like the colors in Martha's nephew's drawing.

"They're very pretty," Johanna said, a lump in her throat. "I can almost hear them singing."

"Milena is mean," Leni said suddenly.

Johanna frowned.

"No, she's not. She's been taking very good care of you. Everyone says you're making progress."

"Milena is mean," Leni repeated obstinately.

"If you don't stop saying that, I'll leave," Johanna told her impatiently. "Professor Hutka is sick, because of Martha— the woman who was in such a hurry to wipe away the footprints you left on her precious floor."

Leni nodded as if she remembered.

"Now *there's* someone who's mean," Johanna went on. "But not Milena!"

Leni took some bright yellow thread from her sewing kit and, her brow furrowed in great concentration, began embroidering the plumage of the third bird.

"Look what I brought you," Johanna said. From a paper bag she took the beautiful dark chocolate Easter egg that Josef had brought her. It was wrapped in a kind of golden mesh, with a marzipan fisherman on top.

"It looks as if the fisherman had caught the egg in his net," Leni remarked.

Johanna suddenly hugged her, and was almost pricked by her needle.

"Do you remember," she asked, "how we used to go to Dobels's, on Pragerstrasse, to buy our eggs, and how we used to decorate them in the kitchen?"

"Yes."

"And then what did you do?"

"I ate them with . . . Grete and you."

Johanna barely controlled her excitement. Leni had associated her with Grete.

"No," she said. "First you hid them in the garden. And always in the same places: above the window of the shed, at the foot of the Virginia creeper. . . ."

"At the foot of the Virginia creeper," Leni echoed.

Johanna nodded.

"Grete always found them," said Johanna.

"Poor girl."

For a few moments Leni stared into space as she used to do. Then she seemed to awaken from a dream; she took her needle and again leaned over her birds.

Johanna quietly sat down beside Josef's bed. He was still asleep, and his face seemed sickly and shriveled. For a long time she sat watching him sleep. The curtains weren't drawn, but dusk was gradually falling.

"Johanna?" she heard him ask in a breathy voice.

"Yes, Josef. I'm right here. I was here almost the whole time you were asleep."

"Turn on the light," he said weakly.

She turned it on and he blinked his eyes.

"Listen," he said. "There's something . . . I'd like to have . . . before night comes. It's at home."

"But Martha will be there," she protested.

He shook his head.

"On Sundays she always . . . goes to visit . . . her sister. But ask . . . Saint O. to go with you . . . anyway."

"All right. What is it?"

"In my desk drawer, beside . . . my article, you'll see an envelope marked . . . with the name of a hotel. . . . Bring it to me, before night . . . falls. . . . Go."

"I'll be right back."

When she reached the door she stopped.

"We didn't eat your egg," she said. "It's too beautiful."

He smiled faintly.

She went back to Saint O., who was still in the linen room.

"He asked me to bring him something from his desk at home," she said. "Please come with me. I'm afraid of Martha."

"Martha isn't there," Saint O. assured her. "She called to ask about him. She's spending the night at her sister's house. She's terribly upset. I think she's beginning to realize what she did."

"I'll go alone, then," Johanna said, relieved.

She passed the spot on the Narodni Obrany where Josef liked to stop on the way back from their walks because they could just see the house from there. "And now," he would say jokingly, "we're about to return to the joys of home life." Once she had replied, "You sound like a typical old bachelor," and he had laughed.

The house seemed empty. She unlocked the door and stepped inside.

"Martha!" she called out, just in case.

No answer. Relieved, she went into the living room. On the wall, like a spot of dried blood, there was still the mark where the clay tablet had broken. She opened the desk drawer. Josef's article was there, in its brown folder. She picked it up and held it, surprised that such a great discovery should weigh so little.

Curious, she opened it. Inside were about forty pages of typewritten text and columns of words with their corresponding signs. The title page read:

DEFINITIVE PROPOSALS
FOR DECIPHERING THE
MINOAN WRITING
KNOWN AS LINEAR B
BY
JOSEF HUTKA
Professor of Ancient Philology
at Carolinum University in Prague
DEDICATED TO:
Sir Arthur Evans, in memory of days at Knossos and
the Villa Ariadne, amid sunlight and fragrant flow-
ers, and

Dr. Rüdiger Seyfert, of Dresden University, for the
powerful current of friendship he created between
the Elbe and the Vltava to stimulate an old man in
his times of doubt.

At the bottom was a note in Josef's handwriting: "This
article is to be turned over to Carolinum University after my
death, so the Department will finally be convinced that my
research is sound."

Johanna put the folder back in the drawer. Beside it was the
envelope, unsealed, bearing the return address of the Pupp
Hotel in Carlsbad.

The full-length photograph showed her in a long, loose
dress. She had a longer face than Johanna, and she looked a
little older. But despite the poor quality of the faded, yellowed photograph, and the network of fine cracks that suggested that Josef had carried it for a long time, Johanna felt as
if she were looking at a twin sister. She remembered the way
Josef had looked at her in the station, with a mixture of
surprise, dismay and joy. She imagined him, so frail in his old
black overcoat, standing on the platform, incredulous, as his
life suddenly found its unity.

"She was killed when a stone pillar fell on her—one of the pillars you see in the background," said a toneless voice behind her.

Johanna spun around and opened her mouth for a cry that never came. Martha had been there when she came in, sitting motionless in the shadows in the midst of Josef's treasures. Trembling, Johanna slipped the photograph back into the envelope.

"She was fifteen," Martha went on. "I think he loved her very much. After the accident that killed her, he left the excavation." Her voice was detached, disembodied, blank. "He wants that picture, doesn't he?"

Johanna stepped toward her. She could now make out Martha's drawn, discomposed face.

"Yes," she said, "he wants it."

"How . . . how is he?" Martha asked, speaking very softly.

"He said he didn't want you to come to see him," Johanna replied.

Martha's shoulders sagged beneath her shawl. Johanna abruptly turned away and ran out of the room.

"Here," she said, handing him the envelope.

The room was lighted only by a night lamp. Josef took the envelope eagerly.

"I saw her," Johanna said.

"You're a curious little girl."

"Did she really look so much like me?"

He took her hand and a glimmer of amusement appeared in his eyes.

"Time flows in only one direction, Johanna. She didn't look like you: *you* look like *her*. Ah, yes. . . ."

He took the photograph out of the envelope, contemplated it and put it down carefully on the bedside table.

"She had a short life," he said. "I hope that you, at least, will have a long one."

"Saint O. told me you mustn't talk," she reminded him firmly.

The door opened and Milena came in.

"Now I've caught you!" she said with mock severity.

"I just slept for twelve hours, Milena, thanks to your drugs," Josef said, raising himself a little from his pillow. "It does me good to have Johanna here."

"All right," Milena said, bending down to straighten his covers, "but you know that the first few days are the most dangerous."

"Yes, and that's exactly why you mustn't do anything to upset me," he said sulkily.

Milena laughed. Then she drew Johanna aside.

"Don't stay any longer than five minutes," she whispered. "I'll see you at dinner."

After Milena left, Josef picked up the photograph again.

"She was fifteen, as I told you. She never reached her sixteenth birthday."

Frowning slightly, he seemed to be dreaming with his eyes open.

"Do you really think you should . . ." Johanna began.

"One morning . . ." he interrupted her. "If you only knew the mornings we had, those Oriental dawns. . . . I can still see the pink stone, the terrace, the glorious morning sunlight. We were making drawings of vaulted structures that we believed to be the hanging gardens of Semiramis. That morning we discovered a small bas-relief of a griffin, at the top of a pillar. She volunteered to climb the pillar with a bag slung over her shoulder, then sit on a projection near the top of it and make a drawing of the bas-relief. She was as agile as a cat, but when she was halfway up the pillar, I saw it move. For a moment I thought I was having a sunstroke. And then . . . The parts of the pillar must have been balanced precariously and I hadn't noticed, I hadn't realized. . . . The huge blocks came tumbling down. She didn't even scream."

"Please don't think about all that," Johanna begged him. "It will hurt you." Beads of sweat had broken out on his forehead.

He squeezed her hand to reassure her. They heard Saint O.

in the hall, pushing the squeaky cart with which she delivered the evening meal to her patients.

"How long was it after the ullu bird?" Johanna asked.

"About a year. And I'd had my year of happiness, just as I've had my month of happiness here, with you. Two beautiful periods, so many years apart. . . . It was worth waiting for, believe me."

He seemed out of breath.

"No more," she told him firmly. "Milena said five minutes. I'll turn off the light."

She kissed him on the forehead. He was still holding the photograph and his eyes were closed. She turned off the night lamp and left quietly.

Milena had given Johanna a room opening onto the garden. Johanna went there to unpack before going to dinner. When she joined Milena and Saint O., she had dark rings around her eyes. The three of them ate in silence.

"She was there," Johanna suddenly said to Saint O.

"What!" the nun exclaimed, her fork in midair. "Martha?"

"Yes. I think she'd been there a long time."

"She told me she was at her sister's house, and I believed her! What a fool I was not to go with you. You must have been frightened half to death!"

"I ran away when I found the envelope he wanted," said Johanna. "She didn't try to stop me."

"Did you tell Josef you'd seen her?" Milena asked.

"No, of course not."

"You're really a marvelous child," Milena said, smiling. "You're one of the few good things this war has brought me."

"I didn't tell him yesterday that Martha had slapped me," Johanna said. "She told him herself. She seemed furious because he'd drawn a bath for me, though I couldn't understand what she was saying. I'm sure she said terrible things to him in Czech."

"Try not to think about all that," Milena said. "I hope he'll be better in a few days."

"I can't forget what Martha said," Johanna went on, her head bent over her plate. When she raised it, her eyes were full of tears. "And Saint O. told me it was all true."

"I also told you that you had nothing to do with it, my little Johanna," Saint O. said.

"Yes, but all the grownups, my mother and father, Kerbratt, Rosi, all the others—why did they let it happen?"

"Don't think about that woman's insults," Milena said. "It was jealousy that made her talk that way. She would have been just as angry if you'd been a young Czech."

Johanna shook her head.

"No, then she couldn't have talked to me the way she did."

"I think Milena is right anyway," Saint O. said. "If you'd been Czech, she'd have thought of other vicious things to say."

Johanna looked doubtful. They finished their dinner, and Saint O. stood up.

"I'm going to have a look at my patient," she said.

After she left, Milena turned to Johanna.

"You may be seeing your mother more often now that you're here, so I want you to know that for some time now she's been taking refuge in a kind of childlike passivity. That's an improvement over how she was before, but I'd like to see her become more independent. Right now, she won't even try."

More than ever, it seemed that Leni would never find her way out of her interior labyrinth. Disheartened, Johanna began to cry.

"What's the matter?" Milena asked.

Johanna suddenly envisioned a crowd of faces like Martha's, contorted by hatred, shouting insults.

"Everything's falling apart, like that pillar," she sobbed. "What's going to happen to me?"

Milena affectionately put an arm over her shoulders. She didn't ask what pillar, and Johanna was grateful.

"With all the care and attention he's getting here, I'm sure Josef will recover," she assured her. "In a few weeks he'll be well again and you and your mother will go back to Germany.

In the meantime, you should feel completely at home here."

She gave Johanna a kindly smile. Johanna dried her tears and went to her room.

Early the next morning Josef took a turn for the worse. Saint O. came to wake Johanna.

"Hurry," she said. "He had a bad night. He's developed a pulmonary edema."

The gray light of dawn came in through the window. Johanna quickly got dressed and went to Josef's room. As soon as Milena saw Johanna she kissed her on the cheek and discreetly left, followed by Saint O.

Josef lay in the same position as when Johanna had left him the night before. The little photograph was on the bedside table. When he looked at her, he didn't seem to recognize her.

"It's me, Johanna," she said, wanting to make sure it was *her* that he saw.

His face relaxed into a faint smile.

"You don't have to tell me who you are," he said in a wheezy voice. "I'm not completely senile yet. The only trouble is that I can't breathe any more."

She put her hand in his. Sometimes he would grip it more tightly; he seemed to be suffocating, then he would seem to catch his breath again, and a little color would return to his cheeks.

"I'm afraid it may be . . . that damned left ventricle," he panted. "Like the last time . . . only worse. I can't . . . can't breathe."

Alarmed, she moved closer to him. "No, you're not going to leave me! You're staying with me!"

He smiled again, but this time his smile seemed more remote.

"You know very well . . . that you've made me . . . eternal," he whispered.

She put her finger to her lips. Just then he was shaken by a brief, hollow cough, and she wiped a bit of foam from his mouth with a towel. Then, afraid he was about to choke, she stood up to go and bring Milena, but he motioned her to stay.

"What about the Cretans?" she asked, trying to think of everything she still had to say to him. "What language did they speak?"

"They spoke Greek," he said, with a fleeting glow in his eyes. "Will you remember? Ariadne spoke Greek with . . . Theseus after saving him from the labyrinth. You're the . . . only one who knows. Don't forget."

"Am I really the only one?" she asked proudly.

"Yes."

Again he desperately tried to catch his breath, opening and closing his mouth like a fish out of water.

"My . . . article," he gasped. "In the . . . brown folder. Take it to . . . the Carolinum. Go . . . with Milena."

"I'll go with *you*," she said quietly.

He raised one eyebrow. His expression seemed to say that he didn't share her view of the matter, but wasn't bothered by their disagreement.

Then he lay quietly. From time to time a twitch of his hands showed Johanna that he wasn't asleep. Sometimes a little foam appeared on his lips again and she wiped it off. Milena came twice and left quietly.

When a little sunlight had just forced its way through the clouds, Saint O. came into the room to bring a clean towel. Just after she left, Josef moved his lips.

"And Leni," he whispered. "Leni. Milena told me .´. . that everything would be . . . all right. You'll go back to . . ."

"Yes," Johanna said. "When she's well again. And you too."

He shook his head.

"Tell Leni goodbye . . . for me. Say goodbye . . . to the wild woman. . . ."

"I will," Johanna said, her voice breaking.

He seemed to relax. She stood up to help him raise himself a little on his pillow, but he was too weak.

"Greek," he said.

She nodded to show that she had understood, that she knew. She gently put her fingers around his wrist, surprised to feel how thin it was. Almost without thinking, she took out her pen and lightly drew on his wrist the same word he had drawn on hers, the word brought by the bird. Then she took the photograph from the bedside table and slipped it between his fingers.

"For your passage," she said softly.

He hadn't opened his eyes again but she could still feel his rough breathing and she was certain that he knew what she had done. Then the time came when his breathing stopped. She stood up slowly and went to bring Milena.

TEN

wkward and red-faced, they burst into the vestibule as Johanna was on her way to the former linen room, where a small stove had been installed for cooking. They told her in German that they wanted to see the head of the clinic, and Johanna, frightened, ran down the hall and called Milena. Saint O. came out of the dispensary, where she had been busy with one of her endless inventories.

"Come, hurry," Johanna said breathlessly. "There are two German soldiers here who want to see Milena."

Saint O. paled.

"What! Are they SS men?"

"No. Where's Milena?"

"She went to get the newspapers. Did you talk to them?"

"No. I left them alone in the vestibule."

The two soldiers were talking quietly to each other when Saint O. came in. Apparently discomfited by the sight of a nun, they fell silent. The older man was about sixty and the younger could have been his son. They looked like peasants. Each had a thick neck emerging from an unfastened uniform jacket and a rifle slung over his shoulder. The younger one cleared his throat.

"The head of the clinic isn't here?" he asked in heavily accented Czech.

"No, she's gone out, but she'll be back soon," Saint O. replied in German. "What can I do for you?"

They looked at her mistrustfully.

"We want to see her, that's all," the younger one said, patting the stock of his rifle.

Saint O. motioned for Johanna to leave the room. Johanna went into the hall, leaving the door ajar so she could listen. She heard the older soldier rebuke his companion.

"Stop showing off," he ordered curtly. "All we want is some civilian clothes," he said to Saint O.

"But . . . The German army is still in control of the city, isn't it?" Saint O. said, seeming confused.

"When everything is all washed up, you come out better if you realize it before everyone else."

Saint O. looked out into the courtyard to see if Milena was coming.

"But how can I give you any civilian clothes?" she said finally. "Our last patients left on the fifteenth. All I have is some nurses' uniforms. . . ."

"Nurses' uniforms!" the younger soldier exploded. "Why not bathrobes, while you're at it? Stop lying to us, you fat fool!"

Saint O. stepped back, dumbfounded. "I . . . I can only give you what I have," she stammered.

The older soldier took the younger by the arm and whispered in his ear.

"Excuse him," he said contritely. "But I think you'd better try to give us what we want. I don't know if I can hold him back much longer."

"Ah, I understand!" Saint O. exclaimed. "You're deserters!"

"I wouldn't put it that way," the older one said. "We're going home a little sooner than the others, that's all."

"The Führer is the one who's deserted!" cried his companion, losing his calm again. "Isn't what he did yesterday a way of deserting?"

Just then Johanna, at her listening post in the hall, saw Milena come through the gate, carrying several newspapers.

"Are you wounded?" she asked the soldiers coolly as she entered the vestibule.

"They want civilian clothes and we don't have any," Saint O. said.

Milena put her newspapers down on the table. Their front pages were edged in black. The younger soldier looked at them and shook his head.

"I just can't believe it," he said.

The soldiers seemed less aggressive now, maybe because they felt that the newspapers had brought them all together in shared uncertainty about the immediate future.

"You have to find us some civilian clothes," the older one said urgently. "We'll leave you our guns. They may come in handy in the next few days."

"We must have old von Sparnberg's suits," Milena said, after thinking for a few moments. "He never came back for them. But they'll be much too big for you."

"Don't worry, we'll roll up the pants."

"Go and get them," Milena said to Saint O. "As for you two, come with me."

They followed her into the next room, where emergency cases were usually treated.

Johanna came into the vestibule to look at the newspapers. "Fighting to the end, the Führer has died in his command post at the Reich Chancellery," she read on the front page of the *Prager Tagblatt* beneath a photograph surrounded by a wide black band, showing Hitler in his uniform as supreme commander. And under the caption was a long obituary. There was an equally wide black band around an identical photograph on the front page of the Czech newspaper.

When Johanna saw the soldiers come out a short time later, it was hard for her to keep a straight face. They wore spats to hold up the bottoms of their trousers, but the old general's tweed jackets hung on them like tents. They fondled their silk polka-dot ties incredulously.

"In a general's clothes . . ." said the older one. "I'm glad we stopped by here!"

They tightened their belts another notch and opened the door. Milena shook her head as she watched them disappear. "I don't give them ten minutes before they get themselves hanged," she said.

"Did you hide their guns and their uniforms?" Milena asked.

"Yes, in the woodshed, under the wood," Saint O. replied. "It was the best place I could find."

"The wisteria is blooming," Leni said.

"Luckily I have you," Milena said affectionately, "to remind me that I have a garden."

The four of them were finishing their potato soup at the table that Johanna had set up in Milena's office.

"What were people saying," Saint O. asked, "about Hitler's death? Our visit from those two halfwits made me forget to ask."

"They were talking about the possible formation of a German-Czech state," Milena said, "that would take in part of Saxony, the Sudetenland and the Protectorate. I can't believe for a second that it would work."

"First of all," Saint O. said, "who would take charge of it? Schörner? Franck? You can imagine the fights."

"That's what I told Zlata, the pharmacist. I said she'd just have to get used to the fact that she won't get her German customers back any more than I'll get back my German patients. But she doesn't think the Germans are hated here as much as I do. She says people make a distinction between Germans who came after 1939 and those who came before. I don't believe it."

"They should be pruned, because they really have too many leaves," Leni said. "Next year the flowers may be smothered."

"Yes, Leni," Saint O. replied gently, "it's something that should have been done. But this year it's too late."

Johanna stood up to clear the table.

"We'll do it together," she said in her mother's ear.

She hummed to herself as she went to the linen room that
now served as a kitchen. Leni's condition was improving, on
the whole. Johanna felt confident that the hardest part was
over. And Hitler's death was bound to be a good thing. People
would finally wake up from a long nightmare and everything
would return to normal. For a moment she imagined living
with Leni in their house in Dresden, after it had been re-
paired.

When Johanna came back, Saint O., her ear to the radio,
was trying to catch a few scraps of the B.B.C. through the
jamming.

"Tomorrow will be a month since he died," Johanna said.
"You told me we'd go to the cemetery when it had been a
month."

"I'd rather not," Milena said. "The climate in the streets
may have changed since Hitler's death. We have to be careful, Johanna. Josef would never have let me expose you to
danger. The best thing we could do for him would be to find
that article he wrote."

"You still haven't heard anything from Martha?"

Milena shook her head.

"It's horrible," said Johanna. "A whole lifetime of
work. . . ."

"Sooner or later she's bound to send it back," Saint O. said.
"She knew there was no second copy."

"She took it precisely because it was the only copy," Milena said. "She still wants to get back at him, even after his
death."

"And maybe at me, too," said Johanna, "since my father
was one of the two people the article was dedicated to."

There had been about thirty people present at Josef's funeral. Johanna remembered looking to see if Martha was
hiding in the shadows, behind a pillar. A distinguished prelate
named Cibulka had spoken warmly of Josef, his personality,
his life, his work, and their friendship. "I saw him a few days
before his death and we talked for a long time," he said.

Johanna burst into tears at the thought of Josef chatting with
the prelate, holding his beautiful chocolate Easter egg, while
she waited for him in his house, bullied and terrified by the
woman who would soon kill him twice: first by causing his
heart attack, and then by stealing the only record of the
achievement to which he had devoted his life. They discovered the theft right after the funeral, and immediately notified
the police. Milena went to see Martha's sister, Jana, who
laughed in her face. Jana claimed she hadn't seen Martha
since long before Josef's death, and then unceremoniously
pushed Milena out the door.

"He always said he was fighting against everyone," Johanna
went on, "but without his article we can never prove he was
right, can we?"

"No, and that's exactly why its loss is so serious," said
Milena. "I'm sure it would have convinced his colleagues at
the university."

Johanna again thought of the pages she had held in her
hands. All the signs that he had interpreted. A language
gradually emerging from a baffling puzzle. His great discovery.

Milena had shown her the letter she received after notifying
the Carolinum of the theft:

> Thank you for informing me of the disappearance of Prof.
> Hutka's article on the deciphering of Minoan writing in Cretan
> inscriptions. We knew that he had been working on that prob-
> lem for years. Our sorrow is all the greater because we know
> nothing about the research he carried out after the publication
> of his first study in 1937. Something tells me, however, that
> the loss is not as serious as you think. You say that Prof. Hutka
> had concluded that the language recorded by Minoan writing
> was Greek, and had written his article to support that view.
> But it is a view that seems thoroughly implausible to most of
> us; we are inclined to believe, with Evans, that Minoan almost
> certainly has no resemblance to any known language. It there-
> fore seems rash, to say the least, to attribute to Greek civili-
> zation, already remarkably extended in time, the vast pre-
> Homeric antecedents envisaged by Prof. Hutka.

Though it was most likely in error, we nevertheless deplore the loss of such an important article, just as we mourn the death of our erudite and charming colleague Prof. Hutka.

Very truly yours,

Prof. Frantisek Handrasik

Johanna remembered the four or five men who had come to the funeral as a delegation from the university. She had probably been sitting near Professor Handrasik as she listened in tears to the prelate's heartfelt words about Josef. She grimaced with retrospective disgust.

In mid-April they had learned that the German Fourth Army had withdrawn into the Erzgebirge, cutting off the railroad between Freiberg and Prague, which made it temporarily impossible for Johanna and Leni to go back to Kerbratt's house. During the long April days when her walks in the garden with Leni were her only outdoor activity (Milena would no longer let her leave the clinic by herself), Johanna sometimes wondered if Franz still thought about her once in a while. Then she realized that she didn't care. *I must not have really loved him*, she thought.

"We could cut the dead branches now, you know," Leni said.

Johanna smiled. She had an oasis of happiness with Leni, in the garden, with the wisteria.

On May 3, Milena took one of her usual morning walks to "sniff the wind," as she put it. When she came back, she told Saint O. a piece of news that kept them both elated for the rest of the day: the American army had already reached Plzen and their arrival in Prague was only a matter of hours.

But that night there was no mention of the story on the radio. Milena told Saint O. it was probably one of many false rumors.

But another rumor was confirmed, unfortunately, when she called the central railroad station: since April 30, there had been no trains taking refugees out of the city.

Everything began changing on May 4. That morning there was constant talk in the streets about the exhaustion of Mar-

shal Schörner's troops and the anxiety of German civilians.
Yet the streets remained calm. A few German signs had been
defaced in front of the tower of the Charles Bridge, but that
was all. There were, however, more people in the streets than
usual. Newspapers were snatched up as soon as they appeared
on the stands. Milena could recognize the Germans in the
crowd by the anxiety on their faces, but she noticed no fric-
tion with the Czechs around them. *Maybe Josef and I were too
pessimistic*, she thought. *Maybe things won't go so badly after all.*

She decided to cross the river to get a better idea of the
situation. The first thing she saw on the other side reassured
her: in a café at the corner of Kaprova and Krizovnicka, German soldiers and Czech civilians were gathered around a radio
broadcasting a report on the formation of a Czech national
government. They seemed tense, but the very fact that they
were sitting together seemed a good omen.

Feeling more optimistic, Milena continued on her way.
The Karlova was crowded. Again she heard the rumor that the
Americans were about to enter the city. She also overheard
talk about SS violence in Carlsbad. Josef would have gone
there in a few days, she thought.

She was about to cross the river again when she saw that
three German soldiers, who were setting up a loudspeaker on
the embankment, were drawing a crowd. She became aware
of a distinct change in atmosphere. The soldiers seemed not
at all happy to be there, with the crowd around them growing
minute by minute as they clumsily laid out their cable.

Finally the loudspeaker crackled and a voice said in Czech
with a heavy German accent, "Go home! Go home! It is
forbidden to . . ." What followed was engulfed in an outburst
of jeering.

Milena left the crowd and crossed to the other side of the
river. As she walked toward Hradcany Castle, a broad view of
Prague, in all the freshness of morning, gradually unfolded
below her. From here, the city of a hundred steeples seemed
peaceful.

Almost as soon as she had opened the gate of the clinic,
Saint O. came out to tell her the latest news on the radio:
German troops were now confined to their barracks.

"The city is going to revolt," she said. "There's no doubt in my mind."

"But they say everything is calm. . . ."

"What they say doesn't mean anything."

Milena went inside while Saint O. watched her, frowning.

The next two mornings, Milena stayed in the clinic. Late in the morning of May 6 she sent Saint O. out to learn what was happening. The nun was perfect for such missions. With her broad headdress rising above her like a pair of outspread wings, she wandered easily through the crowd while everyone in front of her stepped aside. Nothing ever escaped her; she would gather an abundant harvest of true and false news, and then later, back at the clinic, she and Milena would try to separate the true from the false.

This time she came back sooner than expected, almost running, her face flushed.

"A division of Vlassov's army has come into the city," she said breathlessly. "I saw them. They were marching along the river and everyone was cheering."

"But they're pro-Nazi!" Milena exclaimed.

"I didn't understand the cheering either, at first. I thought people were throwing flowers to German soldiers! Then someone told me it was General Bunichenko's men and that he'd sided with the Czech resistance."

"To do that," Milena said, "they must really have felt they'd been taken in by the Nazis, just like the ones Leni had the bad luck to meet in the forest."

"I don't think the Germans can hold out much longer," Saint O. said, "if their soldiers are confined to their barracks and Vlassov has gone over to the Czechs."

"You're right," Milena agreed. "They'll probably surrender before the day is over."

"And that's not the only news," said Saint O. "Since yesterday Czech partisans have been hunting down Germans, and there's talk of summary executions. I don't know how much truth there is in that, but they *have* stripped German women in public, painted swastikas on them and shaved their heads. And you were right: they don't make any distinctions."

Milena nodded helplessly.

"What the Germans did at Lidice can't be undone," she said sorrowfully.

"How many German civilians did Josef say there were in Prague? Fifty thousand. . . . If you want my opinion, Milena, we're about to have another massacre, and because of Lidice and Terezin the same thing will be said about those fifty thousand as was said about the people of Dresden: that they only got what was coming to them."

"Maybe you're taking too dark a view of things," Milena said. "I thought *I* was pessimistic! Besides, you and I may not be able to affect what happens to other Germans, but at least we can save Johanna and Leni."

"We can't count on anyone but ourselves," Saint O. said bitterly. "To everyone else, we'll be traitors."

"Of course," Milena replied. "But we'll save them, you'll see."

Saint O. embraced her. Then she suddenly said, "Look, I told you. . . ."

Through the window they could see the Czech national flag and a flag bearing a St. Andrew's cross flying side by side above Hradcany Castle. Milena stared at them, scarcely able to believe her eyes, despite what Saint O. had told her. *We don't have a minute to lose*, she thought.

Johanna went down the stairs to the basement feeling that events had finally caught up with her. For the last few days the calm of the garden had seemed deceptive.

"A basement," Leni said placidly when she saw the little room where they were going to sleep. "I thought there wouldn't be any more basements, ever. . . ."

"It's just a precaution," Milena said. "Don't worry, it's not for shelter against bombs, it's just to keep you out of sight for a few days."

She kissed Leni on the cheek and went back up the stairs. As she closed the staircase door behind her, she wondered if

the hiding place was secure. It was only a small room next to
the main basement of the building, but it had a separate
entrance. The stairway that led down to the little room began
in the laundry and had a door indistinguishable from the
closet doors on either side.

For Johanna, the situation had become simple again: she
was alone with Leni in a basement. She had suffered so much
from her absence all through the night of the bombing. . . .

She took her hand and Leni gave her a taut smile. Leni
seemed above anxiety, as if she still kept herself at a distance
from the world, even though her eyes had lost their vacant
look.

She sat down calmly on one of the two cots that Milena and
Saint O. had brought, then looked up at the pipes overhead.
A short time later, there were three quick knocks on the door
and Milena came in.

"Listen, both of you," she said. "If there's any kind of
danger, I'll turn off the lights with the switch in the laundry.
And in that case, of course, you must keep absolutely quiet!"

"Would you like to play a game of checkers?" Leni proposed. "We'll have to pass the time. . . ."

"No, I'm going back up," Milena said. "I want to be ready
to block anyone who may come."

She left and Johanna set up the checkerboard. She and
Leni played in silence, then she deliberately made a foolish
mistake that cost her the game. Seeing Leni's half-smile, she
wondered if she knew she had let her win.

"Shall we play another game?"

"No," Leni said. "I'm going to do some embroidery."

"You'll hurt your eyes, in this dim light."

"It's bright enough."

She had long since finished the birds and was now working,
with exemplary patience, on a bouquet of different colored
anemones. Watching her, Johanna finally fell asleep.

At nine in the morning two days later, Milena came in with
two cups of ersatz coffee. She and Saint O. never went down
to the basement room at the same time: one of them always

stayed on the first floor to keep watch and listen to the radio.

Milena kissed Johanna on the cheek.

"It's happened, darling," she said. "Germany has surrendered."

After a moment of stunned silence, Johanna said, "You must be very happy!"

Milena nodded.

Leni was lying on her cot in her dressing gown. She sat up.

"Will we leave here soon?" she asked expectantly.

"We'll see what happens," Milena replied. "For now, there's nothing to do but wait."

Their fate was being decided a short distance away, overhead, Johanna thought. She remembered a quotation she had once heard, and now she understood it: "We are guilty and shall remain so. It will never end."

"Something new," said Saint O., in Milena's office.

They both looked out the window. Only one flag was flying now from the east tower of the Cathedral of St. Vitus. The flag with the St. Andrew's cross had been taken down.

"It doesn't surprise me," Saint O. said. "Bunichenko wants to side with the Americans now."

"And the general in command of the German forces in Prague—I forget his name. . . ."

"Toussaint. He gave the Czech National Council an offer to surrender in exchange for a guarantee that his troops and German civilians would be allowed to leave unharmed. They announced it early this morning."

"He seems to be the only one who cares about the German civilians," Milena remarked. "He . . ."

She was interrupted by a sound of rapid footsteps in the hall. She looked at Saint O. Two violent blows shook the door and then it was thrown open.

There were three men, young and armed. One of them, a little older than the other two, appeared to be in charge. He had a sheet of paper in his hand.

"Miroslav Pala, of the Vltava network," he introduced himself. "Are you Dr. Kucera?"

"Yes."

"We know you're hiding two German women," he said brusquely.

Milena stood erect behind her desk.

"That's not true," she replied.

Pala pressed his lips together. "I'm sorry, but we have their names," he said in a metallic voice. "Leni Seyfert, thirty-six, and her daughter Johanna, twelve."

"Yes, of course," Milena said brightly. "They were here till April 12 but then they left—like most of our patients, unfortunately. So many of them left that we had to close the clinic at the end of April." She turned to Saint O. "Do you have the register?"

"Yes, doctor," the nun answered, handing her the book.

Milena leafed through it.

"Here, gentlemen, you can see for yourselves."

All three of them leaned over the register. An entry dated April 12 indicated that Leni and Johanna had left the clinic.

"Are they still in Prague?" Pala asked.

"They went back to Dresden," Milena replied. "It's written here in the register. They had to hurry their departure because civilian train service between Prague and Dresden was discontinued when the German Fourth Army withdrew into the Erzgebirge."

"You seem sorry they're gone," he said sarcastically.

"Why shouldn't I be? We don't like to have our patients leave before they're completely cured."

Don't provoke him, Saint O. thought.

"And what were they treated for?" Pala asked.

"We treated the mother for problems resulting from shock."

"Shock?"

"She was in her house in Dresden when it was hit by a bomb."

"Too bad she survived!" one of the other men said.

"And look at this," said the third man, turning the pages of the register. "Nothing but Germans! If I had my way, we'd burn this place down, right now!"

"Let me remind you," Milena said sternly, turning toward

him, "that of the fifty thousand Germans living in Prague, more than half were here before 1939, and that thousands of German families have been in the city for several generations and consider themselves at home here. Those people have nothing to do with Franck and his henchmen."

Pala looked at the door without seeming to have heard her. "All right," he said.

"I'll show you out," she offered a little too quickly.

"You'll let us look around a little before we go, won't you?" he asked with a tight-lipped smile.

"I've already told you those two women aren't here!" she protested indignantly. "I'm not in the habit of falsifying my books!"

"No, of course not."

Pala and the others began throwing open doors, including the doors of closets, knocking down several piles of sheets and blankets. Milena anxiously watched them coming closer to the laundry. It was impossible for her to warn Johanna and Leni, but the three men were making so much noise that she hoped Johanna would hear them.

They went into the pharmacy and looked suspiciously at the big medicine closet. The youngest one tried to open it but it was locked.

"I'm sure I heard something," he said.

"Let me go back to my office and get the key," Milena said.

Ignoring her, he broke open the closet door with a violent kick. When he saw only medical supplies inside, he angrily unrolled one of the bandages.

"We didn't endure the Gestapo for five years so that you could use their methods," she said coldly.

He glared at her. For a moment they defied each other in silence. Then he slapped her.

The two others stood still, surprised. Milena hadn't uttered a sound. She stood unsteadily, holding her cheek, with her back to the closet.

Saint O. slowly walked around the table in the middle of the room and came toward the young man, who seemed fascinated by the inexorable approach of her majestic head-

dress. Suddenly, with surprising agility, she leapt forward and
seized him by the collar.

"You dirty little last-minute terrorist!" she said, shaking
him as if he were a rag doll. "Do you know how many men I
hid and took care of here, men who fought in the resistance
but didn't have to show their courage by hitting a defenseless
woman? Do you know?"

Pala, the oldest of the three, interrupted.

"Forget it, Karel," he said sharply.

" 'Forget it' won't do!" Saint O. said. "He's going to apologize to Dr. Kucera!"

"That's enough!" Pala shouted.

He went out into the hall and into the next room, which
was the laundry.

"More closets!" he exclaimed. "How many are there altogether?"

"Quite a few," Milena answered calmly. "We have room
for forty patients, so we need a lot of storage space."

He looked at the row of doors. Milena was relieved to see
that Saint O. had discreetly pushed the switch that turned off
the light in the basement room.

"What's in this one?" he asked.

"Linen," Milena said, keeping her hand on her cheek.

He opened the closet door, saw piles of sheets, shrugged
and rejoined his companions in the hall.

"I want to know that man's name," Milena said to Pala,
pointing to her attacker, who looked at her sullenly. "I know
his first name, but I want to know his last name too, so I can
lodge a complaint. We sheltered members of your organization all through the war, as many witnesses will testify."

Followed by the two others, Pala headed toward the door.
He seemed embarrassed.

"What's his name?" Milena insisted.

"I'm not going to tell you," he said. "We haven't slept for
a week, so it's understandable that we're a little edgy."

"There's something else I want to know," Milena said.
"Since your information was so precise, you must have received an anonymous letter. Am I right?"

"It wasn't all that anonymous," he said mockingly.

Thinking of Josef's article, Milena wondered if she should try to trace the letter. But if the men were leaving, she didn't want to delay them.

At the door, Pala nodded curtly, then he and his companions went down the steps. But the one who had slapped Milena came back.

"Listen to me," he said, without raising his voice. "Pala has his reasons for leaving. If I'd had my way, we'd have gone over your whole building with a fine-toothed comb. I'm warning you: I *know* those two women are here. They'll get what's coming to them. So will you. I'll be back, and I won't be alone."

He turned away and ran down the steps. The others were waiting for him at the gate.

"If they come back," Milena said to Saint O., "they'll find them, and if they find them, they'll kill them."

In the vestibule, Saint O. sat down. Her face was as white as her headdress.

"We have to get them out," she said.

"Where would we send them? Don't be ridiculous."

"But if those men come back in half an hour . . ."

"Now that I think about it," Milena said, trying not to panic, "it seems to me that if they came back they wouldn't find them any more than they did the first time. We could always steer them into other parts of the building."

"We could put Johanna and Leni in Josef's house," said Saint O. "We have a key."

Milena stared at her in amazement.

"Josef's house? When all this is Martha's doing? Have you lost your mind?"

"Are you sure? . . ."

"They knew their names and even their ages! Isn't that enough? And maybe she watches the clinic to see who goes in and out. She has a key to Josef's house too, and she knows every nook and cranny of it! No, it's out of the question."

Milena paced the vestibule, glancing uneasily at the gate. Suddenly she turned to Saint O.

"Go down and tell Johanna and Leni that everything's all

right. Say it was just a routine visit from the new administration. For now, I'm sure they're safer here than anywhere else."

Milena stood looking out at the courtyard. The silence was punctuated by distant gunfire.

She went out to the garage. Inside it, next to an old ambulance, was the little Skoda that Josef had asked her to keep for him. She got into the ambulance and, with difficulty, started it. It hadn't been driven since they had brought Josef to the clinic. Just as she was backing out of the garage, Saint O. came up, breathing heavily.

"Where are you going?"

"I'll be back in half an hour," she said. "While I'm gone, find a Czech flag, or make one on your sewing machine if you have to, and put it up in front of the building as quickly as you can."

Saint O. looked at her in dismay. There was more gunfire in the distance, coming from the bridges.

"Please come back soon," Saint O. said. "It will be better for both of us to be here if . . ."

Milena nodded and slowly drove out of the courtyard. The streets on the left bank of the river were deserted. There were tanks on the New Bridge. She turned back, drove north and crossed the river on the Cech Bridge.

After the bridge she drove along the river till she was able to get a closer look at the tanks. They were German tanks; they had been stopped so that they blocked the bridge, and then abandoned. On the Kaprova, all the signs in German had been covered with black paint, some of it still wet.

Just before Starometske Square she stopped, locked the ambulance and continued on foot, pushing her way through the crowd. The old city hall had been set on fire the night before in the course of street fighting, and the crowd there was particularly dense. The bystanders were jeering at some naked women pushing wheelbarrows full of rubble.

She tried to go back to the ambulance, but moving in that

direction had become impossible. Each time she heard more shooting she wondered if the shots had been fired at soldiers or at civilians. But the crowd seemed unconcerned, as if gunfire had already become part of everyday life.

Unable to go back the way she had come, she decided to make a detour past the old Jewish cemetery. Near the Kinsky Palace, a group of German civilians were surrounded by a turbulent, howling crowd setting fire to smashed furniture that lay in the street. Five or six German families were trapped by the mob.

Finally, by going along the river, Milena succeeded in getting back to the ambulance. Once inside, she sat clutching the steering wheel. What she and Saint O. had feared was happening.

Suddenly a man stuck his face in the window.

"Is it true that there's been some real slaughter in the hospitals?" he asked eagerly, pointing to the red cross painted on the ambulance. "I heard that people have been going into them, taking those bastards out into the courtyard and spraying them a little."

He mimicked the firing of a submachine gun, sweeping his arms back and forth.

"You're . . . you're . . ." Milena began, but her disgust made her speechless.

"You mean it's not true?" he asked, disappointed.

She started the engine and made a U-turn to go back toward the river. *The hospitals . . . Saint O., alone . . . Am I losing my mind?* She turned right but had to stop to let a motorized division pass. She recognized the emblem of Vlassov's army. Apathetic-looking soldiers were packed into the back of the trucks, their rifles upright beside them. There was none of the enthusiasm among the people watching that Saint O. had described two days earlier, only passive hostility and indifference.

A jeep stopped beside Milena's ambulance and an officer called out, "The Americans?"

"What about them?" Milena asked, puzzled.

"Have you seen them?"

"No."

The officer seemed disheartened and the jeep started off abruptly. Milena heard more shooting in the distance. Suddenly she imagined she could hear the cries of people dying in the courtyards of all the hospitals in Prague.

Saint O. had been waiting in the vestibule. She was alarmed as soon as she saw how pale Milena was.

"They'll be back," Milena said. "There have been massacres in the hospitals. They'll come back, with Martha, and they'll search the building from top to bottom."

She threw herself into Saint O.'s arms, sobbing.

"Josef was so . . . so afraid of what might happen," she said. "Johanna and Leni won't escape. No one will. . . ."

She fell silent. Finally she wiped away her tears.

"I'm glad Johanna and Leni didn't see me like that!" she said.

Saint O. smiled, hoping to calm her.

"Some will get out of the city safely," she said. "I heard on the radio that one last German convoy will be formed at seven o'clock tomorrow morning, at the central station. Civilian vehicles will be protected by tanks as far as Plzen."

Milena shrugged.

"I saw some of those tanks. They were abandoned on a bridge, not trying to prevent massacres. . . . Seven o'clock, did you say? At the central station?"

"That's what they said on the radio," Saint O. replied wearily.

She looked at Milena, who was deep in thought.

"But . . ." she began. Then her voice rose: "I didn't tell you about that convoy for any special reason. It doesn't concern you! You're not thinking of joining it, are you?"

Milena began to pace.

"Listen," she said. "A little while ago I got the idea of hiding Johanna and Leni in the ambulance and taking them out of Prague. I was mainly worried about partisans stopping me on the road and searching the ambulance, and now you've told me that a protected convoy will leave tomorrow morning! It's like a gift from heaven!"

Saint O. was dumbfounded.

"I'm determined to save them," Milena went on. "I won't let Martha turn them in. I'll leave the convoy as soon as we're outside the city, and find a farm where we can wait a few days till things settle down."

"What a fool I am!" cried Saint O., clapping her hand to her forehead. "Why did I have to tell you about that convoy? You're forgetting the clinic, Milena! If I'm here alone, it will be wrecked! With all the German patients we've had. . . . There won't be anything I can do!"

"You'll intimidate them," Milena said. "Make sure you're wearing your headdress. And swear up and down that Johanna and Leni left on the date I wrote in the register. When they ask where I am, tell them I'm out working in support of the Czech National Council."

Saint O. smiled in spite of herself at the reference to her headdress. Without it, she knew she looked tired and vulnerable.

"If Martha comes," she said, "I'll . . . I'll spit on her."

At dawn, Milena went to wake Johanna and Leni. She had decided not to tell Johanna the night before because she didn't want her to spend the night worrying.

As soon as the light went on, Johanna sat up on her cot, startled.

"Don't be afraid," Milena said calmly. "A convoy is leaving the city at seven o'clock this morning and I want us to join it. Saint O. and I are afraid of street fighting in the next few days. I'll take you in the ambulance and we'll try to find a farm where we can stay till things get better."

Johanna got dressed in the glare of the bare bulb. Beside her, Leni did the same, while Milena sat on a cot and watched them. *What a relief it will be to escape from this little room, and to stay on a farm!* Johanna thought.

Saint O. came down with breakfast, then went back up to keep a lookout.

"My anemones," Leni said despondently. "I haven't finished them."

"You'll come back to them in a few days," Milena told her gently.

She had already parked the ambulance in front of the clinic. She had put all her reserves of gasoline, and part of her food reserves, under the stretcher.

The three of them slowly came down the steps, each carrying a bag. It was cold. Saint O. followed with a box of medicine and a first-aid kit that could be used, if necessary, to justify the red crosses on the doors.

When everything had been piled up in the back of the ambulance, Saint O. embraced them, one after another. Her face was ashen.

"Don't forget to water my flowers," Leni reminded her.

Johanna and Leni got into the rear of the ambulance while Milena sat behind the wheel. Milena and Johanna waved to Saint O., who responded with a quavering smile that was more like a grimace. Her eyes were moist. Milena started the engine and drove out of the courtyard.

"Lie down as if you were sick," she told Johanna and Leni. "And from now on, no talking. I'll answer all questions, in Czech or German, depending on the situation."

The city was deep in mist and still asleep, which made it seem unreal after the turmoil and fighting of the day before. Here and there a Czech flag gave a touch of color to the pale façades of buildings. As they passed the Letna Esplanade, Milena could see that the tanks had left the New Bridge. Near the Powder Tower she had to slow down: the street was clogged with cars. Many Czechs had gathered on the sidewalks to watch the convoy form. Up ahead, Milena could see several tanks in the square in front of the station.

She managed to make slow progress. Czechs and Germans alike seemed surprised to see the ambulance, but no one questioned her. Suddenly a space opened in front of her and she found herself driving behind a truck full of glum, silent German soldiers. Soon they reached the square. Beside the tanks were several official Horscht cars packed with military and civilian personnel. She thought she recognized Franck, the German "protector" of her country, whose face was so familiar from the pages of the now-defunct *Prager Tagblatt*. She managed to slip in behind the Horschts. Their drivers greeted her with friendly gestures, evidently glad to see that an ambulance would be following them so closely.

Beneath the gray sky, there was an atmosphere of heavy, dazed resignation. Then suddenly, perhaps because of some incident that Milena hadn't seen, the crowd on the sidewalks began shouting.

"They won't do anything to us, will they?" Leni asked anxiously, raising herself on one elbow.

"Lie down, and stay that way," Milena ordered. "Don't worry, we're protected by the tanks."

A forest of clenched fists rose above the crowd. As if this was the signal that the tanks had been waiting for, there was a roar of starting engines and the convoy slowly got under way. The tanks were followed by the official cars, with Milena's ambulance behind them. In the rearview mirror she saw a motley assortment of vehicles maneuvering to find places in the convoy, while the crowd began to surround those that were still unable to move. The noise of the tanks drowned out the taunts and insults, but the grimaces and upraised fists made the sentiments of the crowd clear. Some onlookers followed the convoy on foot, shoving their way past those who stood and watched. They pounded on the outside of the ambulance. Milena was afraid that a paving stone might shatter one of the windows at any moment.

She had to stay in low gear, but they were moving steadily forward. *House by house, we'll eventually get out of this damned city*, she thought. Then, near the main post office, the tanks stopped abruptly.

Milena frowned. Fifty yards in front of the convoy, beside the trees of the Vaclavske Namesti, there was an unruly-looking crowd. *We're still a long way from Plzen*, she thought. *At least there's been no shooting.*

But the convoy still didn't move on. Johanna was tempted to get out, walk to the nearest tank and ask its driver why they were stopped. Then she realized what was happening: the Jindrisska was filled with the last motorized units of the Bu-

nichenko division, leaving Prague. Each truck carried a flag
with a St. Andrew's cross. They too were heading for Plzen.
"That's the Bunichenko division," Milena said. "It looks
as if they've decided to go over to the Americans."

The procession of trucks seemed endless. The onlookers
gathered at the intersection didn't seem to know whether to
cheer, as they had when Bunichenko's men entered the city,
or curse the minor part they had played in fighting the Germans, whose uniform they still wore. But then came a cavalry
squadron of four troops, moving along at a brisk trot, banners
flying in the wind. Perhaps, in their minds, the spectators saw
a legendary Russian army, an army of fierce Cossacks gallop-
ing wildly across the steppes. In any case, their ambivalence
vanished. The crowd was electrified. Everyone cheered.

As soon as Leni saw them, her face froze with fear. She sat
up on the stretcher and uttered a long, agonizing cry. Before
Johanna could stop her, she opened the rear door of the
ambulance, jumped out and ran toward the cavalrymen, curs-
ing. After a moment of shock, Milena jumped out and ran
after her.

"Stay there!" she called back to Johanna.

Leni quickly reached the first tank.

"Leni!" Milena cried, feeling the menacing presence of the
crowd around her. "Leni! *Those aren't the same ones!*"

Leni crossed the intersection diagonally, rushed at the lieutenant riding at the head of the last cavalry troop and tried to
pull him off his horse. The horse shied and the officer drew
his pistol. People quickly drew back and Milena, jostled from
all sides, couldn't see Leni any more. The cavalrymen kept
their formation. The lieutenant, having brought his horse
back to a trot, looked behind him with a bewildered expression on his face. There was so much noise that Milena might
not have heard a shot if there had been one.

She desperately tried to elbow her way through the crowd.
Now that the cavalrymen had passed, people filled the streets
in front of the tanks. This would at least keep the convoy
from leaving, but there was still no time to lose: she had to
find Leni quickly.

She finally reached the spot where Leni had attacked the

lieutenant. People milled around, still not understanding very well what had happened. But there was blood on the pavement and Leni was being carried away, her blond hair hanging down over the shoulders of one of the men carrying her.

"They'll cut off her hair!" a woman cried hysterically as she passed.

With a final push, Milena caught up with her and touched one of her dangling arms.

"Get away!" ordered one of the bearers.

But that was enough. Milena had seen a bloodstain spreading over the front of Leni's dress, under her gaping coat. And her face . . . Her eyes were wide, with the astonished expression of a young girl.

For a long second after she had seen Leni jump out of the ambulance and Milena run after her, Johanna was paralyzed. Then she too jumped out and began running. Leni had already disappeared. To her right, Johanna heard screams. She ran toward them, along the edge of the crowd. Twenty or thirty yards ahead, she saw Leni make a dash for a cavalry officer. His horse shied so violently that he was nearly thrown from the saddle. Then he took out his pistol.

"No!" she screamed, and just then Leni disappeared in the crowd.

Maybe the officer drew his pistol only to frighten her, Johanna thought desperately. When he rode past, he was already putting it back in its holster. Then she caught a glimpse of Leni being carried away, but the crowd was so dense she couldn't move. She had to brace herself to keep from being pushed back.

"Let me through," she said, "Mutti . . ."

Her German set off angry cries around her.

"So you're that bitch's daughter!" a woman exclaimed in German. "She's dead, and good riddance!"

Johanna saw an ordinary woman with two eyes, a nose, a mouth—a mouth to say *that*. *Oh, Mutti*, she thought, *if I could just hold your hand!*

"Mutti!" she screamed.

A surge in the crowd nearly made her fall. She heard the sound of tank engines starting. *I'll lie next to you and they won't pull me away.* She was lost in a dark forest of raised arms and fists. Leni had disappeared. The tanks began moving forward. Suddenly she saw Milena wandering along the sidewalk a few steps away.

"Milena!"

The young woman stopped and looked around. There were tears in her eyes.

"Johanna," she said, her voice quavering, "I've been looking for you. I went back to the ambulance. You were gone."

"Where's my mother?"

Milena shook her head.

"I don't know. They took her away. Johanna . . ." She took her by the hand. "Come with me. We'll try to catch up with the convoy. Maybe there's still time. . . ."

Johanna pulled her hand away.

"She has to come with us!"

"I saw her," Milena said. "Before they took her away. I was even able to touch her."

"But *I* wasn't," Johanna cried. "Where is she? Tell me! I want to kiss her." She burst out sobbing. "I want to kiss her."

She was pushed from behind and felt Milena grab her to keep her from falling. Near them several German families trying to leave had been surrounded by people jeering and overturning their carts of belongings.

"Come," Milena said weakly. "Now we have to try to save *your* life."

"But I didn't get to say goodbye," Johanna said tearfully. "Even Josef wanted to tell her goodbye."

Milena was on the verge of collapse. She closed her eyes, afraid she might be about to faint.

"Come, Johanna, please come."

Some of the tanks began shooting into the air in an effort to scatter the crowd, but this only encouraged the mob taunting the German families. Women were screaming, but whether they were tormentors or the tormented, Johanna couldn't tell.

A man in front of her was thrown against her and his elbow struck her in the chest. She fell to her knees, gasping for breath, while the crowd swirled around her. When she got to her feet again, Milena was nowhere in sight.

"Milena!"

There was shooting on the other side of the river.

"The Russians are coming!" someone shouted. "They're at Hradcany Castle!"

The crowd cheered.

Milena, where are you? Johanna came to the place where the ambulance had been, but it was gone. She walked on, dazed, in a crowd suddenly less dense. This time there would be no Grosse Garten in which she could take refuge, but this time she wasn't alone either: all the people, living and dead, who had helped, protected and loved her in the course of her long wanderings—Hella, Kerbratt, Franz, Annette, Rosi, Josef, Milena, Saint O.—were there around her. But someone was missing, the one she needed most. *You won't finish embroidering your anemones, Mutti. The crowd kept me away. I wish they had trampled me to death, so I could have gone with you.*

She came to a bench under some trees and sat down, exhausted. She still heard gunfire from the direction of Hradcany Castle, but here she felt surrounded by such calm that she was able to think clearly. She recalled the little Parthian horseman and the Saint Hubert that her mother had tried to destroy. The cavalry had stirred up the only real desire Leni had left: her will to attack her attackers. How much she must have suffered that night! Johanna remembered: five black dots on a snowy plain. So they had come back to devastate everything inside Leni one last time. *She would never have become the way she was before*, Johanna thought. *And now she has what she wanted: she's with Grete again, with the smell of wisteria in her hair.*

Johanna was surprised that her eyes were dry. Her greatest sorrow was that there had been no way to foresee what was going to happen. She and Leni hadn't been able to prepare for it even by exchanging glances or squeezing hands.

A ray of sunlight pierced the gray sky. She stood up, walked for a time and then turned right, into a little street where there were houses like those in her neighborhood in Dresden. She looked for a door that would suit her, chose an attractive, freshly painted one and rang the bell. There was a sound of footsteps and an old lady opened the door. They looked at each other. The old lady's white hair was pinned back in a bun and she had a kindly face.

"*Bitte, sprechen Sie Deutsch?*" Johanna asked, inwardly congratulating herself on having made a good choice.

"Yes, of course," the old lady replied in German. She looked up and down the street. "Is anyone after you?"

"No."

"Come in quickly, anyway."

She stepped aside and Johanna went in. The living room, with its knickknacks and porcelain stove, reminded her of Frau Gildemeister's.

"It's very foolish of you to be walking around in the streets today," the old lady scolded her. "Do your parents know where you are? I'll call them right now."

"They know," Johanna said quickly. "Don't worry. I just wanted to ask you for some paper and an envelope. I have to write a letter."

The old lady looked at her curiously, then left the room and came back with a pad of paper and an envelope.

"Why don't you stay here, at least overnight?" she asked. "Things will have calmed down by tomorrow."

"No, thank you," Johanna replied. "I'm staying with a Czech lady. She'd worry if I didn't come back tonight."

"I see," said the old lady. She pointed out a table and a chair. "Sit down there, if you want to write now."

She went into the next room and Johanna heard her turn on the radio. The lamp on the table had a pink silk shade. She looked at it a few moments, thinking, before she began to write.

Dear Franz,
   This letter probably won't get to you, but I have to write it anyway, and I've come into a stranger's house to do it.

I hope you're in Herr Kerbratt's house now. Sitting here, I imagine you in your little room. There's a lamp here like the one on the table next to your bed. I hope you'll learn to walk again easily. I'm sure you will, in fact.

I can't help wondering if we'll ever be able to get married. It might have been wonderful but we really didn't meet each other at a good time.

I want you to tell Herr Kerbratt about a discovery that Professor Hutka made. The article he wrote about it has disappeared but I don't want his discovery to be lost. It's that the Cretans, 3500 years ago, spoke Greek. You won't forget, will you? Herr Kerbratt will have to tell some scientists, and he must be sure to say that Professor Hutka discovered it. He died a few weeks ago. My mother is dead too. It happened just a little while ago. That's something else I want you to tell Herr Kerbratt, but try to do it gently. You can say she's gone to be with Grete.

I wonder how this is all going to end.

Love and kisses,
Johanna

She folded the letter, slipped it into the envelope and wrote the address. She had forgotten Franz's last name. No matter; his first name, with Kerbratt's name and address, would be enough.

When her hostess came back, she was already standing up with the letter in her hand. The old lady looked worried.

"You can't leave now," she said. "I'll call the Czech lady you're staying with. I just heard horrible things on the radio. The Russians are here, and people are taking revenge on German civilians. There have been atrocities. It's no surprise that people want revenge, after all that's been done. No," she insisted, "I won't let you leave. Please . . . What's your name?"

"Johanna."

"Please, Johanna. Stay with me. I'll make a cake for you, I have flour."

Johanna shook her head.

"No, thank you," she said gently, moving toward the door.

The old lady shrugged helplessly, sighed and looked at the envelope Johanna was holding.

"And I don't even have a stamp to give you for your letter," she said.

"It doesn't matter." Johanna curtsied and awkwardly held out her hand. "Goodbye, and thank you again."

"Keep away from the Vaclavske Namesti, the riverfront and the Karlova quarter," the old lady pleaded. "Please, Johanna, will you promise me that?"

Johanna promised; then, still holding the letter, she left. The sun was shining now. She didn't hear the door close behind her. *She must be watching me walk away*, she thought.

She went back the way she had come, saw a mailbox and dropped her letter into it. Sounds of gunfire, in single shots or short bursts, came steadily from the direction of the river. The crowd grew denser. She passed circles that had evidently formed around people she couldn't see. As she made her way along the Vaclavske Namesti toward the statue, she kept thinking she was going to see Martha, her face contorted by hatred, somewhere in that shouting, bloodthirsty mob.

Meanwhile something strange was happening: she felt lighter with every step she took. And from that strange state arose an equally strange thought: if Ishtar had been *really* light, as Johanna felt herself becoming, would the pillar still have fallen?

There was a volley of shots from very close to her. A group of men wearing caps and armbands ran past, gripping the stocks of their submachine guns. To the right, near the place where the shots had been fired, the crowd opened to make way for the men wearing armbands and the shouts grew louder. Johanna saw a group of terrified women huddled beside an overturned truck. All their hair had been cut off and they had been beaten. Two men took one of them by the arms and dragged her through the frenzied crowd. A bystander turned to Johanna and she heard the word "Reich." She nodded as if she had understood.

The men with armbands were dragging the woman to a lamppost. People began to move away from the truck and form a new circle. Johanna darted through the crowd. Before the men could stop her, she reached the woman and said in German, "Give me your hand."

The woman looked at her as if trying to understand why she was there. She seemed about forty. Her face was bruised and the scissors that had cut off her hair had made a long gash in her forehead.

"Go away!" she said in German after a moment. "You're crazy! Get out of here, hurry! Don't you know what they're doing?"

"Give me your hand," Johanna repeated stubbornly.

She took it. It was damp from fear. She squeezed it, wanting to communicate the joy that had suddenly begun to well up in her. She looked at the faces of the crowd, but didn't see them. There was a long burst of submachine-gun fire nearby, followed by a great silence. The woman trembled, then tried again to make Johanna leave.

"I told you to go away! I was in an organization controlled by the German government. *Now* do you understand? They're going to kill me!"

"I'm holding your hand in place of the one I wanted to hold but couldn't," Johanna said.

The woman looked bewildered. *I can't tell her how happy I am*, Johanna thought.

They were now surrounded. The partisan leader shouted something in Czech that Johanna understood because Josef always said the same thing when they finished waiting in line for food coupons: "Now it's *our* turn." The woman began trembling again.

It seemed to Johanna that the onlookers had all fallen silent, because their shouts didn't concern her anymore. She squeezed the woman's hand harder and raised it, with their fingers intertwined, toward the sun. It was as if she had been reunited with Leni and, hand in hand, they were entering eternity together.

*   *   *

Kerbratt and Franz were told that the letter reached them only because it had no stamp. In the course of its journey, it became covered with postage-due notices that saved it from destruction and helped it to make its way through the curtain of hatred.

After twelve days it arrived at Kerbratt's house late in the afternoon while he stood on the little road, watching mist envelop the distant city of Dresden.

ABOUT THE AUTHOR

Henri Coulonges was born in Deauville, France, in 1936, and now lives in Paris. *Farewell, Dresden* is his second novel, for which he won the Grand Prize of the Academie Français. A best-seller in Europe, it has been translated into a dozen languages.

11- 6/25/94
12- 5/03/05